HIS MOTHER'S SON

Marianne had no doubt that the Dowager Lady Lat-teridge had been the ardent instrument of her downfall. This social lioness had sunk her teeth into the story of Marianne's night of folly and ripped her good name to shreds.

Marianne thought she was now safe in York, where no one knew of the scandal that London society had savored.

But Marianne had forgotten one thing. The dowa-ger had a son. A son as handsome as he was high-born and as irresistible to women as he was fond of them.

That son had a mansion in York—a stone's throw and a heart's beat from Marianne's refuge. And now the Earl of Latteridge had arrived for a stay in which he might do far more than his mother to ruin Marianne . . . since making love was far more po-tent than merely telling lies. . . .

THE LADY
NEXT DOOR

by

Laura Mathews

A SIGNET BOOK

SIGNET
Published by the Penguin Group
Penguin Books USA Inc., 375 Hudson Street,
New York, New York 10014, U.S.A.
Penguin Books Ltd, 27 Wrights Lane,
London W8 5TZ, England
Penguin Books Australia Ltd, Ringwood,
Victoria, Australia
Penguin Books Canada Ltd, 10 Alcorn Avenue,
Toronto, Ontario, Canada M4V 3B2
Penguin Books (N.Z.) Ltd, 182–190 Wairau Road,
Auckland 10, New Zealand

Penguin Books Ltd, Registered Offices:
Harmondsworth, Middlesex, England

Published by Signet,
an imprint of New American Library,
a division of Penguin Books USA Inc.
Originally published as *The Lady Next Door*
by Elizabeth Neff Walker.

First Signet Printing, September, 1993
10 9 8 7 6 5 4 3 2 1

 Printed in the United States of America

1

Fortunately there was no one in the kitchen at the time. The scullery maid had swept the ashes from the bread oven, deposited the loaves within, and hurried off to the larder to set out the eggs for Mrs. Crouch's planned custard. Mrs. Crouch herself had left for the fishmonger's some time previously, so the room was still, save for the sizzling sound of the roasting pork fat dripping into the pan, and the dull mechanical thump of the turn-spit. Near the fire hung the great kettle on an idleback, and suspended from the kitchen rafters were a large ham, the bread car, bunches of herbs, and several cheeses.

In her hurry to insert the loaves, Molly had set Mr. Geddes's breakfast tray on the hearth and subsequently forgotten it. There had not been a moment's peace the whole of the morning, what with Mr. Oldham scheduled to move into his lodgings that day, and she had failed to notice the strange sack which Mr. Geddes had absentmindedly left beside the empty mug. It took no more than one stray spark landing on it to cause the ensuing explosion.

The windows onto the kitchen garden were blown out and brass and copper pans hurtled about the room. Acrid smoke overwhelmed the normal pleasant aromas of baking bread and hanging cheeses, and the scullery maid, fearful of yet further damage, huddled behind the stone basin until she heard her name called.

"Molly! Are you all right? What happened?"

Timidly the maid presented herself at the doorway into

the kitchen, surveying the damage with a wary eye. "I don't
know, ma'am. I just put the loaves in the oven and went
into the larder for a moment when—BOOM!—the whole
place seemed to shake and there was breaking glass and
clattering pans. I didn't do nothing different than usual."

"You suffered no harm?" asked the young woman, her
natural alarm beginning to abate somewhat.

"No ma'am. Naught but the fright. Think you it will happen again?"

Her employer cast a puzzled glance about the shambles
of the kitchen. The pork loin rested greasily on the stone
floor in a spreading pool of water from the kettle. The
bread oven seemed to have suffered no harm, but the hearth
itself had chipped and cracked in numerous places, and the
remains of the breakfast tray were almost unrecognizable.
A faint glimmer of understanding lightened Miss Findlay's
face. "Mr. Geddes's tray?"

"Yes, ma'am. Beth brought it down and gave it to me,
but I had to put the bread in. I meant to tidy it away soon as
I set the eggs out for Mrs. Crouch."

"Of course. Molly, will you run up and beg Mr. Geddes
to spare me a moment of his time—here in the kitchen?"

But it was unnecessary to do so. Even as Miss Findlay
made the request, the door from the hall had pushed precip-
itately open and a young man entered, his wig askew and
his brocaded waistcoat yet unbuttoned. "My pouch of gunpowder," he mumbled unhappily. "Left it on the tray. Is
anyone hurt?"

"Luckily, no, Mr. Geddes, but only by the grace of God."

"I'm frightfully sorry, Miss Findlay. I've been experi-
menting with dipping waxed string in the very smallest
amounts, you see. Catches flame ever so much more
quickly that way."

"I dare say," she replied dryly, and might have had a
great deal more to say on the subject had not the door
opened once again to admit a short, elderly lady who
peered nearsightedly into the wrecked room. "Don't alarm

yourself, Aunt Effie! There has been an accident, but no one has suffered any harm, if we may discount poor Molly's nerves, which I am not at all sure we can. Will you take her into the parlor and pour her a glass of wine?"

"Oh, no, ma'am," the girl protested stoutly. "Long as I know it won't happen again, I'll just start to clear the mess before Mrs. Crouch gets back."

Miss Findlay said only, "I am sure Mr. Geddes will wish to compensate you for your unnerving experience, Molly," before she took hold of her aunt's arm and gently ushered her out the door.

Left behind, the young man frantically dug in his pockets, one after the other, until he at length extracted a crown which he pressed in the astonished girl's hand. "Very sorry, miss. Won't happen again, I promise you. Careless of me. Usually I keep it quite away from any flame. The pouch, that is." He backed uncertainly toward the door and made her a formal bow before disappearing from sight. Once on the other side of the green baize door, he wiped his forehead with a spotless handkerchief which he proceeded to tuck distractedly up the sleeve of his shirt. He listened for the sound of voices, and discerned that Miss Findlay and Miss Effington were in their drawing room at the front of the house. His hesitant tap was promptly answered and he apologetically presented himself in the sparsely furnished room.

"I realize our arrangement was that I could lodge here so long as I caused no damage with my experiments, Miss Findlay. The thing is, if you consider the matter in a certain light, I didn't actually cause any damage with my *experiments*. I left a pouch of gunpowder on my tray—which I never meant to!—and only by the most unlucky chance was it not found before it—ah—exploded. I shall pay for all the damages!" He regarded her beseechingly. "It's so terribly difficult for me to find a place where I can work. Won't you let me stay?"

"Gunpowder?" Miss Effington asked sharply, turning to

her niece. "Marianne, I cannot believe it at all safe to have gunpowder about the house."

Mr. Geddes found and applied his handkerchief. "If I were to promise not to further my experiments with gunpowder, would you permit me to stay? There are any number of other things I'm working on, none of which is the least bit dangerous."

His earnest countenance, so at odds with his untidy appearance, caused Miss Findlay to reconsider the verdict she had mentally established. "I won't be able to keep any of the servants if you put another scare such as this in them, Mr. Geddes. True, it was not entirely your fault, but I shudder to think what the consequences might have been. If Molly had been in the kitchen . . ."

"I know." The young man's face paled. "Never would I have forgiven myself if I had caused anyone harm. If you say I may stay, I promise not to keep even the least bit of gunpowder about, nor anything else that could prove injurious."

"Very well, Mr. Geddes," Miss Findlay sighed. "Since dinner is bound to be late, I would request that you go around to Mr. Hobart yourself and ask him to come to reglaze the windows. I have a new lodger arriving and I cannot myself leave just now."

A grateful smile broke the gloom of his youthful countenance and he pumped her hand with enthusiasm. "Thank you, ma'am. Your faith in me is not misplaced! I'll bring Mr. Hobart, and I'll fix the clockwork for the turnspit, too, as soon as I return."

"The turnspit is quite ingenious, Mr. Geddes. My cook is rapidly spreading its fame, and I don't doubt you will one day have a whole slew of houses desiring them."

"I have my eye on a little workshop off Blossom Street where they could be made."

"I don't suppose it has living quarters," she said wistfully.

"No." He laughed as he released her hand. "You will give me a list of the damages?"

"Certainly." She watched ruefully as he left, his wig still askew and his waistcoat unbuttoned, but obviously unaware of his condition, as she heard the front door thump home behind him. "I'd best give Molly a hand in the kitchen, Aunt Effie, if you are settled now. Mr. Oldham said he would arrive around noon with his belongings. I've sent Beth out for a bootjack for his room. Can I get you anything?"

"No, my dear. It was extremely kindhearted of you to allow Mr. Geddes to stay, Marianne, but I think it most unwise."

"Oh, he'll be more careful in the future, I think. He's a pleasant, serious young man, if a bit absentminded. I feel rather aged when he calls me 'ma'am,' though."

Miss Effington surveyed the glorious auburn hair, the lively hazel eyes, the delicately molded features, and the trim figure her niece presented, and said with a snort, "For six and twenty you do very well, Marianne. Don't let me keep you. If you will just hand me my spectacles, I'll have this finished by the time Mr. Oldham arrives."

Because she was too vain to wear her spectacles when anyone but her niece was nearby, Miss Effington was forever misplacing them, and such a request as she now made, rather than a simple chore, was often the labor of a profound search. Marianne had taken to noting where her aunt most frequently deposited these invaluable items, and when that failed on any given occasion, she produced the alternate pair she had long since found it expedient to keep in her own bedchamber. It was not necessary on the present occasion to resort to the spare, as she found the spectacles negligently resting in a potted palm near the drawing room door where her aunt had relegated them in her hurry to the kitchen. "I won't be but a short while, Aunt Effie. If there is too much to do, I'll send around to Mrs. Whixley to see if she can spare Sadie for an hour or so."

Indulgently deciding that of course of all days, Mr. Geddes would have to leave his gunpowder on his tray when they were expecting Mr. Oldham, a very proper gentleman who maintained a respectable practice in York as an attorney. Only recently had Marianne completed the restoration of the other half of the first floor where he would lodge in the four rooms which were directly opposite to, and the exact match of, those occupied by Mr. Geddes. Sitting room, dressing room, bedroom, and dining saloon were more than adequate accommodation, Mr. Oldham had assured her, as he carefully inspected the old furniture (newly refinished), the floral coverlet (embroidered by Aunt Effie), the new sash windows (to replace those which rattled and let in an intolerable amount of cold wind), and the fireplaces (freshly swept and checked for draw). If he noticed the wainscoting was scarred in several places, or that the rug was somewhat worn, he did not say so. Nor had he objected to the handsome price Marianne unblushingly asked for the rooms. If one had to be a landlady, one might as well do it properly.

Marianne had almost reached the door to the kitchen, when there was an imperative summons from the front of the house. No respectful tap on the brass knocker, this, but a determined, angry drumming, much as though the visitor intended to work his way through the hapless oak portal. All the servants were busy on various errands in preparation for the new lodger's arrival, and Marianne herself retraced her footsteps with some annoyance at the persistent pounding. It would not be Mr. Oldham; he was far too genteel to engage in such sport.

Without the least hesitation, Marianne drew open the door to find before her a man of perhaps her own age, his brow furrowed with extreme displeasure, and his lips pressed tightly together. The hand which wielded the door knocker so vigorously, also sported a variety of rings just visible for the elegant fall of lace at his wrists. He wore a red velvet coat which flared out over matching breeches, and his waistcoat sparkled in the sunlight with its gold embroidery. Rows of gold buttons danced before her eyes, on the length of the coat, the cuffs, and waistcoat, on the knee breeches, and echoed in the gold buckles on his shoes, and in the gold fob he wore. That he came directly from the hands of his *friseur* was evident in the tight curl of his powdered wig and in the heated flush of his cheeks from the hot curling irons. Though Marianne had never before met him face-to-face, she knew precisely who he was.

"In what way may I help you, Sir Reginald?" she asked pleasantly.

"I wish to speak with the owner of this house—immediately," he rapped out impatiently.

"You are."

With sharp eyes he surveyed disparagingly from the top of her flaming hair to the satin shoes, unfortunately spattered with grease, which poked out from under her simple gown with its embroidered muslin apron. "Do you realize, madam, that an explosion in your house has blown out full half a dozen windows in mine?"

"Did it? I'm so sorry. I shall, of course, have the damage repaired. Mr. Hobart, the glazier, has been sent for. If you wish, I will have him attend to you first."

Her apologetic smile and casual acceptance of the situation merely exasperated him. "Perhaps you fail to realize that Barrett House is but newly constructed. I have only this week taken residence. It is no small matter to have my windows blown out from under me!"

"I could hardly have failed to notice your new house a-building, sir," Marianne replied dryly. "For no less than six months there has been a continual racket of men at their work—hammering, sawing, cursing—and no little damage caused to my own house and garden in the process. I shall have your windows taken care of directly. Now, if you will excuse me . . ."

"What assurance have I that such a disaster will not take place again?" he asked with insulting condescension.

"I should think it highly unlikely, sir. A pouch of gun-powder was accidentally left on a breakfast tray, and caught a spark from the fire." When his contemptuous expression did not soften, Marianne suggested sweetly, "You might, of course, sheath your house in gold buttons, which would doubtless render it impervious to gunpowder explosion. Good-day, sir."

Sir Reginald Barrett was not accustomed to anyone, let alone a woman with greasy shoes, making mockery of him. Having decided to give her a proper set-down, but not being quick-witted, he found he had not the time to settle on an appropriate one, as he saw, to his astonishment, that she was closing the door in his face. "I shall send my man of business with a list of damages!"

The door continued to swing shut as Marianne said, "To-morrow, if you would. We are inordinately pressed today."

Sir Reginald was left staring at the freshly painted door, and not at all in a happy frame of mind. He had no little be-lief in his own consequence, and he found it irritating in the extreme, to be so brusquely treated by a mere slip of a woman. When he had first contemplated building his new house in Micklegate, it had been his intention to purchase and tear down the two derelict properties which stood side by side there, for a grandiose scheme. To have been thwarted in that aim, to have to contain the proposed pro-ject to one lot, had rankled him through the long months of planning and construction, and now this! The morning's damage had spurred him to confront her with his wrath, and instead of cowering before him, she had laughed at his but-tons, for God's sake! He conferred one last, glowering look on his neighbor's house and turned on his red-heeled shoes to stalk the short distance to his own front door.

At precisely twelve of the clock, Mr. Oldham was shown into the ladies' drawing room where Marianne and her aunt, the one in clean garb now and the other minus her spectacles, were discussing the absurdities of neighbors.

Mr. Hobart, the glazier, had arrived and been sent to Barrett House, and Mr. Geddes advised of the extra expense which was likely to fall to him, a matter which he accepted cheerfully before springing up the stairs to delve into the mysteries of clockworks and turnspits.

Obviously, Mr. Oldham regarded this as something of an occasion, for he was dressed impeccably, wore a newly curled wig, and carried with him a book of poetry which he presented to Miss Findlay, solemnly intoning, "I thought you and your aunt would enjoy these verses of Thomas Gray. They say he will be poet-laureate one day."

"How kind of you, Mr. Oldham. I had no idea you were interested in poetry." Marianne accepted the book, mentally noted that she already owned the volume, and passed it along to her aunt who held it close to her nose to read the title. As Miss Effington was more likely than not to comment quite frankly on what a shame it was that it had not been a different work of the author's, it was just as well that Mr. Oldham found it convenient to take the opportunity to expand on his philosophy of education.

"I am interested in any number of learned pursuits, Miss Findlay. One's horizons should not be limited by what one imbibes at a university by any means. Nor yet again should one be circumscribed by one's profession. You would hardly credit the number of attorneys I personally number of my acquaintance, who take no interest in anything but the law. A thousand pities! There is a whole field of arts and sciences ignored for lack of industry in seeking them out. And I do not mean the occasional attendance at the theater! Poetry, painting, sculpture! And the sciences. Why, I have seen all manner of collections of minerals, insects, fish, birds, and animals—including the remains of a dodo! That is not to mention such oddities as a woman's breeches from Abyssinia, a purse made of toad skin, figures and stories carved on a plum stone, and a great many others." He proceeded to enlighten them on the interesting phenomena he had witnessed at a museum in London, and on his advanced knowledge of agriculture and manufacturing.

When an opportunity arose for Marianne to interrupt him, she deemed it wisest to do so before her aunt exploded with indignation. "I think you will be pleased to know, Mr. Oldham, that the gentleman who has the lodgings across from yours, Mr. Geddes, is an inventor. Perhaps one day when you have the time, he will show you the ingenious turnspit he has constructed."

"An inventor! I should consider myself honored to know such a man. My friend Mr. Midford will be green with envy. He is already beside himself that I have taken lodgings between the homes of an earl and a baronet, I have no need to tell you. Why, his lodgings are in The Stonebow and not the least distinctive."

"Shall I have Beth show you to your rooms? You must wish to see to the dispersal of your belongings," Marianne suggested hopefully.

"Why, yes, I suppose I should. My man is best when closely supervised, and I am not at all sure I shall keep him." Marianne was guiding him to the door even as he spoke, but he could not be denied his last words. "Appearances count for a great deal in my profession, you know, and one can not afford a careless or indifferent servant. Not that I care a great deal what the world says of me, so long as I am acknowledged a sober, solid professional. Confidence, Miss Findlay. An attorney must inspire confidence in his clients."

"I'm sure you do, Mr. Oldham." His grave thanks for her approbation were declared as he exited, and she leaned against the door thankfully when she heard his tread on the stairs. "Aunt Effie . . ."

"For God's sake, Marianne, whatever were you thinking of to take such a pompous long-tongue into the house? Did you ever hear such drivel? Why, when I was a girl, Mr. Addison did a marvelous satire on such 'virtuosos.' He detailed the will of Shadwell's Sir Nicholas Gimcrack and we laughed over it for days. A box of butterflies, a female skeleton, and a dried cockatrice to his wife; his receipt for preserving dead caterpillars, and three crocodile eggs to his daughters. He cut his son out of the will for having spoken disrespectfully of his little sister, whom he kept by him in spirits of wine." Miss Effington laughed reminiscently, but her face soon darkened. "We shall never rid ourselves of his company. I give you fair warning, he will be forever dropping in—just to tell us of the dragonfly which landed on his brief, or inviting us to lectures on petrified things."

Marianne absently picked up her aunt's spectacles and crossed the room to hand them to her. "He was the only one who would pay what I was asking, Aunt Effie. And now you can see why. I can just hear him telling his friend Mr. Midford, 'You will find my lodgings in the house between that of the Earl of Latteridge and Sir Reginald Barrett, my dear fellow. Quite a convenient and exclusive location.' No wonder he didn't remark on the worn carpet and the bruised wainscoting, with such attractions right by. But you mustn't think he will pester us, my dear, for he keeps regular office hours and I am determined to ward off any attempt at familiarity."

Adjusting the spectacles firmly on her long nose, Miss Effington grunted. "It's as plain as paper he's interested in you, my girl, and I doubt he's one to take a hint, so be on your guard."

"Interested in me?" Marianne chuckled delightedly. "He may be interested in my *house*, Aunt Effie, but you may be sure he would find me sorely lacking in the more sober virtues a man of his position must look for in a wife."

"Humph. He could just as easily decide that the house is more important in the long run."

2

After Sir Reginald's visit in the morning, it had occurred to Marianne that her other neighbor's property, too, might have been damaged, but she could not see from the gardens any broken windows or signs of disruption. Nonetheless, she had penned a note to Mr. Vernham, the earl's secretary, whom she had met on several occasions, inquiring into the matter. Now, when she sorely needed to relax with a dish of tea, Roberts came to inform her that Mr. Vernham had called.

"Show him in, Roberts, if you will, and have Beth bring tea for us all, and some biscuits if Mrs. Crouch has any fresh." She smiled gratefully. "And thank you for all your efforts, Roberts. I fear it has been a hectic morning."

"Everything's right and tight now, ma'am." He permitted himself the ghost of a smile before exiting, to return almost immediately with the caller.

Mr. Vernham, dressed soberly in an olive green kerseymere coat and black knee breeches, approached to take Marianne's hand. "I'm delighted to see you again, Miss Findlay. And you, Miss Effington. I trust you are well?"

This last, directed to the older woman, who was carelessly stuffing her spectacles in her work basket, brought a sharp retort. "I would be a great deal better if Mr. Geddes had not taken it into his head to destroy the kitchen. Have you come to claim damages on the earl's behalf?"

"I wouldn't dare," he murmured under her piercing gaze.

"Rest assured we have suffered no ill from the explosion, save only that it woke his lordship much earlier than he had intended to rise."

Marianne's eyes sparkled with merriment. "A great pity, especially since his lordship had a late night, or so I would infer from the roisterous comings and goings until all hours."

"Just so. Harry Derwent is with us at present and we are expecting the earl's mother and sister in a week or two. The mourning period for the late earl is over now, and we will probably be in residence for several months."

A faint shadow passed over Marianne's face, and she exchanged a glance with her aunt which Mr. Vernham could by no means interpret, but she merely smiled and said, "The house has been empty very nearly the entire time since we came here. I'm sure it will be pleasant to see it occupied. I pray you will convey our apologies to his lordship and his household for the disturbance."

"Certainly. If I may be of any assistance . . ."

"You are very kind, Mr. Vernham, but I believe matters are in hand. We did have an irate visit from the baronet, which is perfectly understandable, as any number of his windows were blown out. Hardly an acceptable circumstance, when the house is but newly finished."

"Yes, a shame. Sir Reginald is not known for his placidity of temper, and I hear he wished to buy your property for the lot."

Marianne grimaced. "Perhaps I should have sold it to him, but we had begun making the improvements and he offered no more than for the Moore house, which was in a shocking state of decay. If he had agreed to compensate for the added investment . . . But of course he would not, since he only wished to tear it down. It's a pity he didn't have his man of business approach me when we first came, before I had done anything. Heaven knows I would as soon have had a house elsewhere."

Again the mysterious exchange of glances occurred between aunt and niece, vastly piquing Mr. Vernham's curiosity. "You've never met Lord Latteridge, have you?" he asked conversationally.

"No, he's not been at his townhouse but for a day or two the whole year we've been here. At least I've seldom seen much activity there."

"He's spent most of the time since his father's death at Ackton Towers setting things to rights. The old earl lived largely in Italy due to his health, and my lord was often there or in France. We've spent little time in England these last ten years."

It was on the tip of his tongue to ask if Miss Findlay knew any of the other members of the Derwent family, but she seemed to sense his curiosity and, during the refreshments, pressed him for details of his travels, showing not the least interest in the earl, but only in his own impressions of the continent. When he took his leave, Marianne abstractedly retrieved her aunt's spectacles from the work basket, a rare frown on her forehead. "We're bound to see her."

"Don't let it fret you, my dear. She's done her worst, and we've known, since before we came here, that it was well nigh inevitable. What's a snub, after all? Consider the source!"

"You're right, of course." Marianne picked up her tambour frame, but her eyes were still troubled. "You don't think Lady Susan and Freddy will come here, do you?"

"Why should they? They're probably in Hampshire or in town. I can't see any reason for them to traipse off to Yorkshire at this time of year. If the weather turns bad, the roads will be impassable, and Mrs. Whixley swears it is bound to be a blustery autumn."

Marianne carefully set a stitch before replying. "I hope you're right, Aunt Effie."

The Earl of Latteridge surveyed his younger brother with amused eyes as he grimaced over the contents of a glass set before him. "Drink it down, Harry. It tastes foul but it will clear your head. You cannot expect to down three bottles of claret, and as many pints of strong beer, and feel at your best in the morning."

"You never seem any the worse for wear," the young man grumbled. "How you can face a plate of eggs and sirloin for breakfast, I shall never comprehend." With an unsteady hand he lifted the detestable brew and, wrinkling his nose and screwing his eyes shut, he consumed it in two lengthy drafts. "Wretched stuff! Where the devil did you come across it?"

"Turkey. You'll find it's more efficacious than rhubarb. What now, William?" the earl asked lazily, as he glanced up at the breakfast room door where his secretary had entered wearing a rueful smile.

"Sir Reginald has called and declares he must see you immediately."

"Does he?" The earl lifted a quizzical brow. "A matter of great urgency, no doubt. Perhaps he has lost one of his patches."

"He has several on, but I suppose it is possible."

Harry snorted. "Damned jackanapes. You should have seen the buckles on his shoes last night, Press. Gold rings with diamonds studded all over them. Harper watched all evening to see if any of them came loose."

"I'm surprised Harper didn't just pluck a few of them off," the earl remarked dryly.

Harry flushed. "He ain't *that* bad, Press."

"You reassure me." Languidly the earl rose from his seat, casting a regretful eye on the remains of his breakfast. "Since I've not called to welcome him to the neighborhood, I suppose I must sustain this interview. Where have you put him, William?"

"The gold drawing room, sir."

In the drawing room there were any number of excellent paintings and pieces of sculpture to attract a visitor's eyes, but Lord Latteridge found his guest studying his own reflection in a gilded glass. Not that he primped or rearranged any detail; Sir Reginald seemed entirely enthralled by the vision before his eyes. Instead of a greeting, he commented, "It rather magnifies, don't it? I should get a few of those."

"My dear sir, if your mission is to investigate mirrors, you had much better have spoken with my secretary. I haven't the slightest idea where they may be had."

"I didn't come about glasses," Sir Reginald replied shortly, as he followed the earl's lead in seating himself. "It's that damned woman next door, Miss Findlay. Do you know there was an explosion in her kitchen which broke half a dozen windows in my new house?"

"How unfortunate."

The earl's patent lack of sympathy, in fact his total lack of interest, drove Sir Reginald to more strident tones. "She was not the least concerned with causing me any inconvenience! She said she would send a glazier and told me to run along because she was busy."

"Such magnificent disregard of your consequence is inexcusable. Have you considered having her drawn and quartered?"

"This is no joking matter, Latteridge! When I asked her what assurance she could give me that my house would not be subjected to future explosions, she told me I should sheath it with gold buttons!"

A lazy survey of his guest's apparel (no less distinguished than it had been on his visit to Miss Findlay the previous day) inspired a certain approval of his unknown neighbor in Lord Latteridge. "My secretary informs me that the blast was caused by gunpowder accidentally left near the kitchen fire. I doubt such a freak circumstance could happen again, Sir Reginald."

"But did you know," his visitor asked spitefully, "that Miss Findlay takes lodgers?"

His host remained unmoved by such a dire revelation, taking the opportunity to glance at his watch. "You don't say."

"I *do* say. When I had my man of business deliver a list of damages to her, she had one of her lodgers down to see the reckoning."

"Ah, I understand. He wouldn't pay. You probably padded the sum too much."

"That's not the point! The fellow raised no objection; it was his gunpowder, foolishly left on a breakfast tray, for God's sake. What *is* important is that my man of business cleverly ascertained that there are *two* lodgers there. Now I ask you, is that to be tolerated? This is Micklegate, a perfectly respectable street; nay, a great street. The Bathursts, the Courchiers, the Garforths, and the St. Quintons all have houses or are planning them here. What would they say to be living side by side with Miss Findlay and her lodgers? It is not to be tolerated. I have decided to get up a petition."

"A subscription, you mean," the earl suggested blandly. "When you attempt to raise money to help someone in financial difficulties, it is called a subscription."

"I don't intend to raise money for the woman!" Sir Reginald yelped. "That is the last thing on earth I would consider. I want her drummed out of the neighborhood. Clearly it is illegal to keep lodgers in a residential district."

"I doubt it. Let's have William in and ask his opinion." Despite his companion's protest, Latteridge rang the bell which rested on the marble mantelpiece and considered his secretary gravely when he entered. "Ah, William, we have a question to put to you. Do you think it would be legal for someone to let lodgings in this street?"

William Vernham was an excellent secretary: intelligent, efficient, and diplomatic. He also had a good understanding of his employer, and did not doubt for a moment the situation which was being considered. The earl's hooded eyes might have given a lesser man no indication of his wishes on this occasion, but William had no misgivings. "No, sir, I should think it perfectly legal. There is, however, an attorney lodging with Miss Findlay and I would be happy to get his opinion if you wish."

Ignoring the profanity which escaped his guest, the earl said, "I think that won't be necessary, William. That will be all."

Sir Reginald's chagrin took a nasty turn. "She's probably involved with one of her lodgers."

"I once," mused the earl, "heard a man do public penance for defaming the character of a woman. A most unnerving experience, I would think."

"So you are content to let matters rest as they are?"

"I find nothing distressing about our neighbor letting lodgings, Sir Reginald. I should think she had a great deal more to complain of in us than we do in her. Ever since he came, Harry has had rowdy friends in and out of here most of the night. And for the last half year or so, your house has been a-building with a consequent disturbance of the peace of this charming little street." At the other's scowl he relented slightly. "A fine building you have there. Designed by Carr, I take it?"

"Yes, he's making quite a name for himself. Of course the exterior is dignified rather than showy, and I have a mind to call in someone who will decorate the interior a little more to my taste, but it's a handsome place, ain't it?"

"Indeed, and likely to be a great deal more convenient than this pile. Are there any races scheduled for the Knavesmire this afternoon?"

Having successfully diverted his caller from further animadversions on the lodging-keeper, the earl patiently waited out the length of Sir Reginald's astute observations on the various matches and watched him depart with unconcealed relief. When William Vernham returned from seeing the visitor out, he presented himself in the library where he found Latteridge contemplating a paperweight. The earl lifted humorous gray eyes. "It wasn't a patch after all, William, but his offended dignity. Our neighbor laughed at his gold buttons. What's she like, Miss . . .?"

"Findlay. A handsome woman, perhaps in her mid-twenties, and obviously gently born in spite of her present circumstances. I've met her only a few times when I've been in York on business for you. She lives there with a maiden aunt and two lodgers, one of whom is but recently moved in. The house was a shambles when she inherited it and she is little by little restoring it to its former glory. Miss Effington, her aunt, has a sharp tongue, but I find I like the old lady. Apparently Sir Reginald tried to buy the house from Miss Findlay, to tear down with the other one, but she wouldn't sell because he refused to compensate her for the renovations she had already made. Not that she blames him, but I don't think she could afford to see the money wasted. I doubt he offered her very much."

"He wouldn't. Findlay. It's not an unusual name. Does she come from Yorkshire?"

William considered the question for a moment before replying. "I couldn't say. She never makes any mention of her past except . . ."

His hesitation awakened the earl's flagging interest. "Some mystery, William?"

"I'm not sure," the young man admitted. "She seemed . . . distressed that you were in residence. Or it may have been when I said your mother and sister were coming to stay here."

"And you didn't pursue the matter?" the earl asked, surprised.

"I tried. She said she had never met you, but then she turned the discussion."

"I see. Did you mention that Harry was here?"

"Yes."

"Perhaps that would explain it. The boy appears to have been up to the devil of a lot of mischief while we were abroad. Has he ever come here with you?"

"Never. He may have come on his own."

"I'll speak with him. Not now, though. His head is about as clear as cotton wool this morning. Was I that ramshackle at his age, William?"

His secretary grinned. "Worse, my lord."

* * *

Marianne pulled the faded draperies across the window saying gently, "I have sent for Dr. Thorne, Aunt Effie."

"There is not the least need," her aunt retorted as she plucked agitatedly at the bedclothes. "It's the merest fever and you know I have a great detestation of being coddled." She glowered on her niece whose cool hand rested for a moment against her forehead. "You know I have promised Mrs. Whixley to visit her this afternoon."

"I'll have a note sent around, Aunt Effie. You mustn't stir from bed until Dr. Thorne has come. You wouldn't want to have the Whixleys all down with a fever, now would you?"

Miss Effington sniffed at the possibility that she could communicate her illness to her friend, but she was, in fact, too feverish to rise from her bed despite her protests. "It's all Roberts's fault for letting us run out of rhubarb."

"Then you must blame me, my dear, for I kept him too busy preparing for Mr. Oldham's arrival to remind him about the rhubarb. Rest now and I'll show Dr. Thorne in to you when he comes."

"How you can place any faith in that young man is incomprehensible, Marianne. Do you know he told me I would do well to eat less and not drink more than a glass or two of port a day? Mr. Garrowby in London—now there was a doctor!—said I would build my blood by drinking no less than a pint a day."

"Dr. Thorne believes overindulgence causes all manner of evils, especially gout. You wouldn't want to have your legs all wrapped up, would you?"

Although the thought horrified her, Aunt Effie stoutly mumbled, "Little he knows. Is there no older man in this town who's qualified?"

"Mrs. Whixley recommended him, if you will but recall, and I am inclined to think him very capable. There's the door now. Aunt Effie, do try to be civil." Marianne plumped the pillows and tucked in a wisp of her aunt's luxuriant white hair before slipping through the door into the hallway where Dr. Thorne was being relieved of his cloak and bicorne hat.

The doctor did look absurdly young, as though he should be attending declamations, rather than calling on patients. His own black hair was tied back with a black ribbon, and his round face was totally devoid of the solemnity one might have expected a doctor to gain through years of attending hopeless cases and viewing gruesome sights. Nor did he dress in the sober fashion one thought of in regard to the medical profession. The burgundy coat was trimmed with silver lace, and the ruffles of his shirt peeked out in front and at his wrists, so that he might have been any one of the fashionable gentlemen about town who frequented the coffeehouses and the assembly rooms. He beamed a smile on Marianne as he retrieved his black bag from the floor.

"What's this I hear of your aunt being in queer stirrups, Miss Findlay? I wouldn't have expected her to tolerate being ill."

"She doesn't tolerate it very well, Dr. Thorne," Marianne returned mournfully. "I hope you will make allowances for her. She's had a fever since last evening, but she made sure it would go away through dosing herself with brimstone, cream of tartar, and treacle. If anything, she's worse this morning."

"I'm not surprised! Let's have a look at her."

Despite Miss Effington's fierce scowl, Dr. Thorne smilingly approached and took her pulse as he matter-of-factly informed her, "I have half the Whixleys down with the influenza, ma'am. Have you been there recently? I should not be at all surprised if you suffer from the same. Have you been able to take any food?"

While Miss Effington grudgingly answered his questions, her niece withdrew to the window, and watched as the doctor examined his impatient patient. He was unfailingly polite despite Aunt Effie's uncooperativeness, and once or twice hazarded a rueful glance at Marianne. Eventually he pressed the old woman's hand and said, "Sleep as much as you can, Miss Effington, and don't take any purgatives or other home brews without my concurrence. You're going to feel downright awful for several days, and don't assume that any lessening of your fever is a sign that you may rise from your bed! I'll be back to see you tomorrow."

"By tomorrow I shall be hale and hearty again," Aunt Effie snapped, but there was no real conviction in her querulous voice, and she allowed Marianne to tuck the bedclothes about her chin without demur.

Her niece took Dr. Thorne into the drawing room and offered him a dish of tea, which he gladly accepted. He sank rather wearily into the lone chair.

"Does she have the influenza, Dr. Thorne?"

"Yes, I should say so, but I don't like the sound of her chest, Miss Findlay. I very much fear she has developed an inflammation of the lungs as well." He studied her intently to see if she understood the gravity of his pronouncement. "Even in older folks it is not always fatal, you understand, but there is a definite risk. She *must* keep to her bed and stay as quiet as possible. Feed her custards and rice water if she can take them, and don't let her physick herself. You're in for a rough time," he said sympathetically.

Marianne nodded. "And the Whixleys?"

"Mrs. Ida, Miss Kate, and Master John all have the influenza, too, but I apprehend no danger there. Mrs. James is likely to wear herself out caring for them but she's taking on some additional help for the time being. There seems to be a case of influenza in every tenth house."

"Poor Dr. Thorne. You must be run off your feet."

"Just take care you don't come down with it yourself, young lady. And the easiest way to do that is to ruin your own health nursing your aunt and fretting." The maid Beth brought in refreshments, and Dr. Thorne gladly accepted a cup of tea. "I'll send around a draught for Miss Effington with instructions on its administration. If her condition worsens, you mustn't hesitate to send for me."

"Thank you, Doctor." With an effort, Marianne thrust aside her worry and set herself to entertain Dr. Thorne for the few minutes he allowed himself to stay with her. The lines of tiredness which she had been unable to perceive in the dim light of the hall were clearly etched on his face, though the blue eyes retained their vitality, and he laughed readily at her description of her encounter with Sir Reginald.

"I don't see," he said as he departed, "how your aunt can fail to recover with such a tonic as yourself here, Miss Findlay."

3

After spending the early afternoon at the races and Hilyard's bookshop at The Sign of the Bible, the earl had a modestly late dinner at four, and repaired to Sunton's Coffeehouse in Coney Street for all the latest news, which largely consisted of the unending discussion of Byng and Minorca, the queen of Hungary, and a little gossip about the Countess of Pomfret. Since his younger brother had not the least interest in politics or social scandal, Latteridge was more than a little amused when Harry entered Sunton's on the arm of his friend Harper, and proceeded to give ear to the incessant babble about him, with only a careless nod at his brother. Harry's attempt to appear knowledgeable about my Lord Granville's speech with the Austrian Minister Coloredo was quite enough to charm the earl for the rest of the day, but he had recalled his intent to question the lad about their neighbor and beckoned to him, a summons which Harry reluctantly obeyed.

"I trust your head is feeling better," Latteridge drawled.

"Much. That Turkish stuff was just the ticket. I say, Press, you don't mind if I bring a few of the fellows around again this evening, do you? Everyone's pretty rolled-up til quarter day."

"Do just as you please. I won't be in this evening."

"Oh. Well, that's fine, then, isn't it?" Harry gave a nervous tap with his cane. "Was there something you wanted to see me about, Press?"

"Ah, yes. Do you have any acquaintance with our next-door neighbor?"

"The Major? For God's sake, Press, we've known him since we were in leading strings."

"Other side, Harry. A Miss Findlay."

Harry's brow furrowed with an effort of thought. "Can't say as I've ever seen her. What does she look like?"

"I haven't the slightest idea. William says she's handsome."

"I'd remember if I'd seen her, then, so I haven't. Only been in town this last week, you know. Why are you interested?"

"Nothing important. The name isn't familiar to you?"

"I knew an Arthur Findlay at school, but he's ugly as sin, so I doubt they'd be related. Though you never know, do you? Look at Cassie Windbrook—a veritable beauty, with the proverbial beast for a brother. On the other hand, Geoffrey Summers is as fine as fivepence and his sister Julia is as plain as toast. At least she was the last time I saw her. That must be five years ago—come October—so she may have changed. It must be rather hard for her with no looks and no dowry to speak of, but James Balforth used to hang around her like a lost puppy, so perhaps she'll not wither on the vine. Do you know who I heard has become an ape leader?"

"Harry, why don't you rejoin your friends? I have an appointment and I would hate to keep you from enjoying yourself." The earl stifled a yawn and rose to lay a kindly hand on his brother's shoulder. "Harry, if you are going to play cards with your friend Harper, do keep a clear head."

"He don't cheat, Press," Harry said stubbornly.

"I'm sure he doesn't, but with all his companions thoroughly disguised, there's hardly any need to, is there? Try it this once as an experiment."

"I'd probably lose my shirt, and I wouldn't have any fun."

Latteridge sighed and pulled out his gold watch to check

the time. "Never mind. I didn't believe Father when I was your age, either. Enjoy yourself, Harry; Mother and Louisa come to town in a few weeks."

As the earl strolled from the coffeehouse, his graceful figure and elegant dress distinguished even in such gentle company, Harry shrugged and rejoined his companions. He was not entirely sure that his brother was not right about Harper, and he had already written several notes to his friend which would make a considerable dent in his next allowance, were he not to make a recovery. But on each new occasion, instead of the looked-for run of luck, he merely sunk deeper into debt; never enough at any one time to cause alarm, but the total was beginning to feel vastly uncomfortable. Just this once, he thought glumly, he might see if Press's strategy would work. After all, the earl seldom rose from the tables a loser.

Sunton's Coffeehouse was not Harry's natural milieu, but he and Harper had come there with a specific goal in mind, viz., to see if they might meet Mr. Hall, and induce him to join them for the evening. Not that this was their ultimate goal. It was rumored that Mr. Hall at his family seat, Skelton Castle (adorned with turrets, buttressed terraces, and a stagnant moat) occasionally played host to a group named the Demoniacs, whose revels imitated, if in a rather mild way, the doings of the monks of Medmenham Abbey. Harry had the greatest curiosity as to their activities, and Harper had urged the very sound logic that if they were to meet him and entertain him, Mr. Hall might be pleased to include them among his roistering parsons and squires for a week or so. Certainly, it could do no harm to give the scheme a chance, particularly as the earl did not intend to be at home that evening.

Although he had not left word that he would be in to supper (and obviously his brother would have informed his staff that he would *not* be), Harry had no qualms in inviting his cronies home to take their mutton with him. The house in Micklegate, geared up as it now was with the owner in residence, was bound to provide sufficient sustenance for half a dozen young men whose dinners had been makeshift, but whose general inclination was for the punch bowl in any case. And indeed, Mr. Hall appeared perfectly satisfied with the roasted pigeons and peas, the cold ham, and the eggs in their shells. Because it had taken some time for this repast to be prepared for so many, the men had settled down with their cards and claret, and by the time they had worked their way through the gooseberry pie, they were feeling unusually merry.

Afterwards, Harry could not recall who it was who had suggested that he could douse the candles in the candelabra with the boiled eggs, but a serious contest, complete with scorecard, ensued. No one seemed to mind much that the eggs smashed against the wall, whether or not they came anywhere near the flames. And when the eggs were exhausted, the contestants looked around for other objects which might serve the same purpose.

Harry was not so far gone that he would allow them to pitch the knives and forks, the candlesticks, or salt cellars, but Mr. Harper hit on the idea of pitching coins at them, and for well over an hour the game continued, accompanied, as might be expected, by whoops of delight and groans of disgust. The only advantage to such a pastime, Harry decided in a rather muddled way, was that it was good sport and kept them from settling back to the cards, and he had dipped far too deep to even contemplate holding a hand, let alone playing it. When his companions tired of their sport, they drank and sang glees until most of them vanished under the table. Harry felt sure, however, as he allowed himself, somewhere around dawn, to be led off to his room, that Mr. Hall *had* suggested something about Harper and himself joining the house party at Skelton Castle later in the month.

For Marianne it had been the longest night of her life, bar one, and she watched the light grow in her aunt's bedchamber with relief. Aunt Effie had spent a frighteningly restless night owing to her room being across the party wall from the dining saloon in the earl's house. Even the sturdy old walls were not proof against the sounds of intoxicated revelry, and Marianne was at a loss to explain the continual thumps against the wall which her aunt, not usually superstitious, had interpreted, in her fever, as the insistent spirits attempting to reach her, and claim her for the next world. Not until dawn had she finally fallen into a real sleep; Marianne, too, allowed herself to doze in the armchair drawn up to her aunt's bedside. The maid Beth peeped around the door when there was no answer to her knock and judiciously decided not to disturb her resting mistress.

But when Dr. Thorne came late in the morning, he was admitted to his patient's room without hesitation. Awaking to find him taking her aunt's pulse, Marianne hastily got to her feet, smoothing down the wrinkled gown as best she could. "Forgive me, Dr. Thorne. How is she?"

"No better," he said grimly. "I had hoped the draught would be more useful. Did she have a bad night?"

"Yes. There was a great deal of noise from next door and she couldn't get off to sleep."

"Shall I stop there and speak with Lord Latteridge? Miss Effington *must* have quiet in her condition."

"I'll ask Mr. Vernham over and explain the situation to him." Marianne lifted a helpless hand. "After the explosion . . ."

The doctor rose from listening to Aunt Effie's chest, a slight smile on his lips. "I would say her lungs are no worse than yesterday, and she has the proper fighting spirit, God knows. I could recommend a woman to sit with her in the nights if you wish."

"Not just yet, Dr. Thorne. I would prefer to be here if she calls for me." Marianne brushed a stray strand of auburn hair back from her forehead. "Can I offer you some coffee or tea?"

"Thank you, no. I have a full schedule today. You'll want

to know that all the Whixleys are going on well now." He closed his black bag and made a gallant bow. "When we have all our patients back on their feet, I hope you will accompany me on a stroll by the river. You'll need the fresh air and I love to watch the sloops and barges. Someday I intend to have a sailing boat of my own. They can't track you down on the river."

She met his grin with a warm smile of her own, and failed to notice that her aunt had awakened and was watching them curiously. "I'll hold you to your offer, Dr. Thorne. The promenade is a favorite of mine—watching the river through the grove of trees, seeing it disappear in the meadow grounds one day and under the bridge the other . . . Don't let me keep you; I know you're more than pressed today."

If Aunt Effie had any thoughts on this interchange, she kept them to herself. Her throat was parched, her eyes burned, and her chest hurt, so she had little energy to consider anything but her own health. As Marianne watched the door close after the doctor, Aunt Effie shifted in her bed and said in a hoarse voice, "I want a glass of port."

"Do you, love?" Marianne asked sympathetically. "I'll get you something to drink."

When she had urged her aunt to drink the unpalatable rice water, she allowed her a sip of port to wash it down. The old woman then lay back exhausted, her face pale but for two bright spots on her cheeks. Marianne regarded the closed eyes sadly and asked, "Shall I read to you, Aunt Effie?"

"No, thank you, dear. I think I shall sleep now."

Marianne waited until her breathing became regular, and then went to her writing desk and drew forth a sheet of plain parchment. The ready-sharpened quills stood at hand, and she quickly addressed a simple request to Mr. Vernham before shaking the sand over the sheet. Hopefully she would have time to change before he called.

But Roberts returned to inform her that Mr. Vernham

would be out of York until the next day. Marianne had not considered that possibility, and she was for some time unable to decide whether to write to the Earl of Latteridge himself, but her aunt's pale face eventually decided her. It would not do to ask him to call, of course, so she attempted, in the most delicate of phrases, to express her concern for her aunt's health and the debilitating effect of the previous night's tumult. She had a strong desire to underline the "humble and obedient servant" phrase, but forced herself to fold the note and ring once again for Roberts.

As she waited for a reply, or lack of one, she rested her head in her hand, and thought how ironic it was that she should have to apply to a Derwent for a favor. Marianne did not think herself overly endowed with the kind of pride which foolishly rose to support one's self-conceit. If one had sufficient self-respect, that sort of pride was mere vanity. Yet even Marianne could not quite envision herself penning such a request to the Dowager Lady Latteridge, and it was only slightly less uncomfortable to do so to her son, albeit unknown to Marianne. Ah well, she thought with the return of her penchant for seeing the ludicrous, if his lordship took offense, she could always don sackcloth and ashes and beg his pardon on her knees. One should grant the nobility their due deference.

Nonetheless, she bade Roberts enter with some misgivings.

"Apparently both his lordship and Mr. Vernham have gone to Pontefract, and will not return until tomorrow afternoon," he informed her as he returned the note. "I thought you would not wish me to leave this."

"Quite right, Roberts. Thank you." When he had left her, she set the note aside with some relief. Surely if the earl was away from home, they could expect a peaceful night and tomorrow . . . well, tomorrow she would perhaps contact Mr. Vernham.

Harry's head ached abominably when he awoke early in the afternoon, and as soon as he had hauled himself out of bed, he noticed with trepidation the sheet in his brother's handwriting on the dressing table: *Harry, was it necessary to destroy the dining saloon? I have taken William with me to Pontefract on business. We will return tomorrow afternoon. L.* Harry replaced the note with a sinking feeling as he recalled their activities of the previous night. Whether Press's comment was an over or understatement, he would not be able to determine until he had seen the room, but it was characteristic of his brother to make no further comment.

When Harry's man had shaved him and powdered his hair, assisted him into a red silk coat with enormous cuffs, and secured his cravat, Harry made his painful way to the ground floor where a footman immediately leaped forward to open the door of the breakfast parlor. Unable to face the thought of so much as a slice of toast, Harry shook his head, causing it to spin regrettably, and approached the dining saloon. Within, he found all in tidiness, except for the wall against which they had pitched at the candles. Here, there were the stains of spattered eggs, grease drippings from the candles, and smoky and scorched spots where candles had rested burning against the wall. On the huge mahogany table were piled a vast array of coins, no one having thought, in the intoxication of the moment, to retrieve his money.

Indicating the coins with a feeble gesture, Harry said, "Distribute it among the servants who waited on us last night and cleaned up this morning. Did everyone go home last night, or are some of them still in the house?"

"They were all seen home, sir," the footman answered, his face impassive.

"I'm grateful. Bring me something for my head, will you, Davis?"

"Certainly, sir."

Harry slumped into a chair, neglecting even to spread the skirts of his coat, and stared miserably at the once-fine wallpaper. The damage had not been confined to a small area, as two sets of candles had eventually served as targets for so many eager participants. Luckily, the carpet did not extend to the walls, and only the oak floor had received its share of debris, which had already been cleared away. But look at it how you would, the room would have to be repapered, probably in its entirety, since it was old enough not to find a likely match. And the Dowager due in a few weeks . . .

Instead of the footman, the butler entered with a glass of the wicked Turkish brew on a silver tray and set it silently on the table. Harry accepted it reluctantly, but the man did not withdraw as he had expected. With a groan he asked, "What is it, Woods?"

"After the earl and Mr. Vernham left, a note was brought around for Mr. Vernham, and when the footman was informed that he would not be here today, he went away and returned a short while later with a note for Lord Latteridge. I, of course, had to disappoint him again and he took the second note away, too."

"So you feel that it may be a matter of moment? Who were the notes from?"

"It was Miss Findlay's footman."

Harry knew he had recently heard the name, but his fuzzy brain would not function properly. "Who is Miss Findlay?"

"The lady who lives next door, sir."

"Oh, yes, Miss Findlay." Harry set down his empty glass carefully and rubbed a hand over his brow, attempting to at least look as though he were considering the matter with some gravity. He could think of nothing but how wretchedly his head hurt. "What would you suggest, Woods?"

"If you will excuse my presumption, sir, I believe I would call on her to inquire if I might be of service."

"An excellent idea. You do that."

For a moment the butler looked puzzled, then he said patiently, "What I meant, sir, was that *you* should call on her to see if you might be of service."

"Me!" yelped poor Harry. "What service could I be to her? I can't even see straight this morning."

Replacing the empty glass on the tray, the butler murmured, "I believe that is what the earl would do if he were here," before he silently exited.

Although Harry rather doubted that his brother would actually so bestir himself, there was the strange coincidence that only yesterday Press had mentioned the woman. And if he behaved civilly over this matter, the earl might well forgive him for the mess in the dining saloon, or at least not take him to task for it. Perhaps not even deduct the expense from his allowance. Yes, definitely it behooved him to see if aught was amiss next door. Having made the decision, still Harry did not move. He was in no condition to see anyone just now, and he knew from the previous day's experience that if he merely sat still long enough, the wretched brew would have some effect, and he might face the prospect with some degree of gallantry, rather than desperate resignation.

4

Mr. Oldham considered Miss Effington's illness a propitious opportunity to work his way into Miss Findlay's good graces. What could be better than to sympathize with her in her distress? Consequently, he left his office in Little Stonegate in charge of his chief clerk at dinnertime, but instead of adjourning to the ordinary where he usually took a meal, he walked purposefully to the market where he purchased a basketful of fresh fruit and a bouquet of flowers. He then summoned a sedan chair, as he was not of an athletic inclination, and directed the chairman to deposit him half a block from Miss Findlay's house (because he did not like to have anyone *think* him lazy). After all, he retained the outward appearance of vigor which he had had a dozen years previously, never allowing himself to run to the stoutness of some of his acquaintances, notably Mr. Midford.

Long had it been Mr. Oldham's policy to speak with enthusiasm if his clients introduced the subjects of hunting or riding. One must, of course, appear to share the prevailing appetite for such strenuous activities. But in fact, Mr. Oldham had never hunted in his life, and had not been on a horse for better than five years. He was quite content to hire a carriage when the need arose, and as his substance increased, he intended to purchase a house and keep a carriage of his own, as befitted a man of his eminence. As he was set down, he contemplated the intriguing notion that it might not be necessary to *purchase* a house at all.

Before Roberts let him into the house, he stared at it

raptly for several minutes, determining that a portico would
make the entrance a great deal more elegant. And it seemed
entirely feasible to him, as the houses on either side were a
story higher, that his might have an additional floor added
as well, perhaps making it just a slight bit taller than either
the Earl of Latteridge's or Sir Reginald Barrett's. Not that
he would have anything gaudy done to the facade; he was a
man who abhorred vulgarity. (And besides, there was very
little one could do with a brick facade in any case.)

"I wish to see Miss Findlay," he informed the footman as
he stepped into the hall.

Roberts took his hat and greatcoat with some difficulty,
since Mr. Oldham was reluctant to part with the basket of
fruit or the flowers during this operation. "If you will wait
here, Mr. Oldham, I'll see if she's free."

"I'm sure she will wish to spare a moment as I've
brought her aunt something to cheer her up, and I've come
all the way here from my office to do so."

To the stolid Roberts it seemed a stupid thing to have
done, when the man would have returned home in a few
hours in any case, and might have spared himself the extra
journey, and the extra expense. Roberts was well-aware that
the new lodger took a chair each evening, and in the morning as often as he could find one. And Miss had her hands
full with her aunt so sick; she didn't need to waste time
with the prosy attorney. Nevertheless, Roberts informed
Miss Findlay of her visitor and perfectly concurred with her
exasperated sigh.

"Show him into the drawing room. I'll be with him in a
moment."

Marianne set the little brass bell where her aunt could
easily reach it if she awoke, and straightened the mobcap
which hid a good deal of her auburn tresses. Trust Mr. Oldham to take her away from important matters to listen to his
pompous platitudes. When she had met him in the hallway
the previous evening he had mumbled such phrases as "the
burdens laid on the downtrodden," "the true strength of

Christian fortitude," and "the hallowed sanctity of persever-
ence," none of which had made the least sense, but he had
seemed inordinately proud of his easy rhetoric.

On entering the room, she found him eyeing the furniture
speculatively, his arms still full of the flowers and fruit.
"Won't you sit down, Mr. Oldham?"

"Ah, my dear lady, I didn't hear you come in. I've
brought a few little things for your esteemed aunt. I hope
she does rather better today."

"Much the same as yesterday, Mr. Oldham, but she is
sleeping now. How kind of you to think of her." Marianne
set the basket of fruit on a scarred side table which she had
intended to restore this week, and placed the flowers in a
small urn saying, "I'll give them some water later. You really shouldn't have made a special trip here, Mr. Oldham; I
realize what a busy man you are."

"Not too busy to inquire after your aunt, and see that you
are not dissipating your strength. Your aunt would not wish
you to overtire yourself. 'They also serve who only stand
and wait.' Milton, you know."

Marianne knew it very well, and wondered what it had to
say to the present circumstance. As always when someone
called, she seated herself on the stained spot of the sofa.
Probably she should offer her visitor refreshment, but she
had no intention of doing so; it would only encourage him
to stay. "Have you read a great deal of Milton, Mr. Oldham?"

"More than most, I dare say. I am a firm believer in our
own English classics. The Romans and Greeks are all very
well, but for my money give me Sir Thomas More, Sir
Philip Sidney, William Shakespeare, John Milton, John
Dryden, and a dozen others. I have long held the opinion
that the most intelligent men are those who are able to recognize the works of genius of their own time. To be able to
sift through the welter of brochures, articles, books, and
poems and come up with the golden egg, so to speak. A
book may prove of temporary interest, or for a moment be-

guile the reader, but will it stand the Test of Time?" He paused dramatically to emphasize his point, wagging an admonitory finger. "Will anyone a hundred years from today read the works of Henry Fielding or James Thomson? I think not. But those of Thomas Gray and Robert Blair—ah, there is the work of intellect, of mental and artistic genius. Of course, Blair is dead now, but I promise you I recognized his worth even when I was at university."

Marianne was struck dumb by his theory, and Mr. Oldham preened himself on the impression he had made. This was, perhaps, as good a time as any to further his prospects, so he suddenly dropped his pedantic air, hurriedly shifted from his chair to the sofa beside her, and grasped her hand with a most sympathetic and kindly air. "Forgive me for being the tutor when you are in distress, my dear. Your interest alone could have prompted me to digress at such a time, when your aunt lies so deplorably ill but a few feet from us. I want you to know that if anything happens to her—God forbid!—you may count on my support. I will stand your friend through the vale of sorrow to the shores of composure . . . and further. Has she a will? I would be happy to draw one up for her—gratis."

"You are too kind, Mr. Oldham," Marianne replied smoothly, withdrawing her hand from his moist clasp. "Aunt Effie already has a will, and I'm persuaded matters will not come to that extreme."

There was a tap at the door and as Marianne bade Roberts enter, Mr. Oldham abruptly started to his feet. The footman announced in suitably impressive tones, "Harold Derwent has called, madam. Shall I show him in?"

While Mr. Oldham's eyes widened incredulously, those of his hostess narrowed in perplexity. "I . . . Yes, certainly, Roberts."

The young man who entered, although he looked a little pale, was a striking figure, possessed of the usual Derwent height and the characteristic gray eyes, high cheekbones, and an astonishingly determined chin. His powdered hair, however, instead of inveighing him with the dignity he strove for, served only to bring a twinkle to Marianne's eyes, and she exclaimed unthinkingly, "My God, how you've grown!"

"Miss Findlay? Have we met before?" he asked, confusion written plain on his countenance. "Forgive my poor memory."

"There is no call for you to remember. You were but a boy in those days and never properly introduced." She extended her hand to him. "I knew Lady Susan many years ago."

"You don't say!" he replied cheerfully, convinced now that the interview could not go too badly amiss. "Made me an uncle three times over, has sister Susan, and brats they are, every one of them. Well, perhaps not the youngest. Little Carrie was just beginning to walk when last I saw her, but she has the most devilish smile!"

"Has she?" Marianne remembered the presence of a third person, and turned to her lodger. "May I present Mr. Oldham, an attorney who has rooms on the first floor? He has been so good as to come and inquire after my aunt's health."

"An honor!" Mr. Oldham declared with a low bow. Harry's polite, "Servant, sir," positively made him glow, but never did the attorney lose sight of the fact that there were but three places to sit in the room, and he had every intention of claiming the seat on the sofa with Miss Findlay.

Marianne had other ideas. "Won't you sit here by me?" she said to Derwent. "Are you at school?"

"Lord, no!" Harry shuddered. "Came down in the spring and I hope never to see the halls of academia again. Deuced dull material they want you to stuff your head full of and I ain't inclined for the books."

If Mr. Oldham took exception to this view, he gave no sign. Instead he offered ingratiatingly, "No doubt you are a man of action—more interested in the field than the library."

"Right ho! Press, my brother, you know, gave me a hunter who can lead the field with his eyes closed. Never saw such heart in an animal. There may be faster, but there are none gamer." His eye fell on the basket of fruit and he was reminded that he had had no breakfast. Politeness forbade him to ask, but Marianne saw the direction of his gaze and the longing look he bestowed. Not so far removed after all from the boy who had nipped into the drawing room to steal tarts.

"Help yourself. Aunt Effie is not well enough just yet to enjoy them."

Mr. Oldham did not know whether to be chagrined that his gift was useless to the sick aunt, or proud that Derwent should seem to appreciate it so. First the young man crunched his way through an apple, and then through a bunch of grapes. Mr. Oldham took the liberty of dominating the ensuing conversation—since the fellow's mouth was full, a dissertation on York's desirable location with regard to its being as well-furnished with provisions of every kind, and cheap!—as any city in England. "Defoe said so in his writings, you know. And it is as true now as it was then. The river so navigable, and so near the sea. Craft of eighty tons can come up to the very city."

"Fancy that!" Harry mumbled between the grapes and a juicy peach, but he regarded Mr. Oldham with less respect for his erudition than astonishment at his long-windedness.

"I imagine Mr. Oldham must needs return to his office," Marianne suggested, rising. "You have been exceedingly thoughtful to come, but I must not hold you back from your business."

Forced to take the hint, Mr. Oldham stood, pulled out his watch and remarked the time. Distracted by how late it was, he murmured, "I'll never be there on time, and you may be sure there won't be a chair to be had!"

"How vexing," Marianne sympathized. "It was perhaps

imprudent of you to let your generosity so overcome your responsibilities. I pray you won't do so on another occasion."

When she had seen him out, her eyes met Harry's and they shared a mischievous grin. "I should think he would more likely make someone take to their bed than rise from it," he laughed.

"Especially Aunt Effie," she agreed. "Would you excuse me for a moment while I check on her? I won't be a minute."

Marianne did not bother to go into the hall, but through the door which led directly into her aunt's bedchamber, which had originally been the breakfast room of the house. Curious, Harry followed her to the door and watched as she bent over the pale old lady, brushed back the damp hair from her forehead, and rubbed her temples with lavender water. The patient did not awaken but her hands moved restlessly about the coverlet, her breathing labored. Marianne placed a kiss on her forehead and whispered words of comfort before straightening to see her visitor at the doorway.

"Should I go?" he asked softly.

"No, I can't do anything more just now." She joined him at the doorway, looked back unhappily for just a moment, and drew the door behind her. "I suppose you came because of all the notes I sent this morning."

"Woods thought perhaps you needed some assistance. Do you?" he asked bluntly.

"My aunt is dangerously ill and needs her rest. Last night . . ."

"Oh, Lord. It's entirely my fault, Miss Findlay. I had some friends home with me and we drank too much. Got to pitching coins at the candles." He groaned. "And I thought ruining the wallpaper was the worst of it."

"Aunt Effie's room must be directly opposite where you were. I could perhaps move her into my room, but . . ."

"Please don't! I promise it won't happen again." He drew

a distracted hand through his hair, causing the powder to cloud about his head.

"You have every right to do just as you please in your own home, but I would count it a great favor if, while she is sick . . ."

"Not another word! If I had known . . . Well, I know now, and you may be sure your aunt won't be disturbed by me again. And I'll tell Press—my brother. Not that he would cause any disturbance even if he didn't know, you understand. He's not given to unruly pastimes. I won't keep you. May I come tomorrow to enquire how your aunt goes on? Is there anything I can have sent over?" His eye was caught by the sadly depleted basket of fruit, and he silently determined to rectify his rude assault on it, whether or not the sick lady was able to partake of it.

"I have imposed quite enough on your good nature," Marianne protested. "Thank you for being so obliging."

If she had meant to dismiss him, or to give him the opportunity to dissociate himself from her and her household, Harry was oblivious to the intimation. He had, for whatever reason—her offering him the fruit, or sharing his view of Mr. Oldham, or his sympathizing in her aunt's illness—taken a liking to her, which was not unusual for Harry. "My pleasure, Miss Findlay. Until tomorrow, then. I hope your aunt will rest easier."

With a cheery wave he was gone, leaving Marianne to marvel at his ready compliance with her wishes. But then, she should hardly wonder at that. Save the Dowager Lady Latteridge, every member of the family whom she had met was possessed of the most amiable temperament and the most obliging of manners. Lady Susan had not been the author of her downfall; even at the time Marianne had read in her eyes the painful necessity of complying with her mother's strictures. True, it had surprised Marianne that no communication had been forthcoming later, but it was hardly to be wondered at in the circumstances. An episode fraught with disaster for Marianne could only have proved an embarrassment to Lady Susan, and one which she might well have thought her friend Marianne could never forgive her. The little brass bell rang, and Marianne hastened to her aunt.

Mr. Geddes, whose inventive genius ran toward the practical rather than the esoteric, was returning to Micklegate with his most recent device when he encountered a friend who carelessly asked, "Well, Arthur, and what have you been up to?"

Long since had the explosion been erased from Mr. Geddes's mind in the enthusiasm he had developed for his convenient new walking stick. Mr. Longworth was not the least surprised to have the inventor demonstrate the cleverly concealed sword, flask, snuff box, quizzing glass, and watch worked into the one slightly long stick, but Harry Derwent, descending from the stoop of Miss Findlay's house, was amazed, and drew closer to watch the demonstration. In the amber nob was concealed the liquid, below which in turn slid out a snuff box filled with Martinique, a miniature timepiece, the bit of magnifying glass, and then a snap catch could be released to draw off the lower end of the stick to reveal a narrow-bladed sword, whose usefulness might have proved doubtful, considering the oddities in its grip, but which nonetheless would serve as a perfectly good deterrent, according to Mr. Geddes.

"I say, would you mind my having a look at it?" Harry asked as Mr. Longworth, not as intrigued as he, excused himself with many protestations of a pressing engagement.

Since Mr. Geddes had not the least objection, Harry exposed once again each of the hidden accessories and tested the blade with a practiced thumb. "Where can I get one of these? Oh, pardon me, sir, I've not introduced myself. Harold Derwent, your servent."

The inventor did not recognize the name but cordially offered his own and proceeded to explain, "I didn't buy it; I made it. Seems to me that if one can have a sword in a stick, one can have any number of other useful gadgets. Saves remembering to push a bunch of little bits of things in your pockets." He frowned over the stick for a moment. "I wish I could find a way to keep a handkerchief in it."

Harry could sympathize with such a view, but he was too engrossed in what he saw as the one drawback to reply. "The glass wouldn't be of much use where it is, you know. You'd have to hold the stick at a very awkward angle to look at people through it."

"Look at people?" Mr. Geddes asked. "I had in mind to use it for studying small print in shops, don't you know. Prices of things and such." He watched thoughtfully as Harry demonstrated the odd angle required to view an approaching milkmaid, her pails empty and jangling on the yoke. "What I'd have to do is put it on a swivel."

"Could you do that? Could you make me one?"

Nothing pleased Mr. Geddes more than someone appreciating one of his devices, but he said warningly, "It would be dear. The supplies for this one cost me almost three guineas. I'd have to charge, say, four."

"Five," Harry said with cheerful determination. "But could I have it soon?"

"Well, if you want this one, I could put a swivel on it for you now. I'm bound to have one in my rooms but you'd best come along and see if that makes it look ungainly."

So Harry found himself reentering the house in Micklegate, though there was no sight of Miss Findlay, and climbing to the rooms on the first floor where the inventor used his dining parlor as a workshop. Untidy boxes of wheels, cogs, screws, and miscellany were scattered over every table and chair in the room, but Mr. Geddes swept aside the strange leather tent on one chair to offer his guest a seat. While he worked, Harry curiously surveyed the various half-finished experiments on which Mr. Geddes was currently working. One in particular drew his attention. "That looks like a turnspit."

Mr. Geddes glanced up from his work and proudly eyed

the contraption. "It is. I've devised a way to run it with clockwork. That eliminates a skipjack or a dog, since it only has to be wound up. The most difficult problem is in finding the right spring for a particular size jack. They've let me experiment downstairs and I believe I've found the right one, but Miss Findlay insisted I enclose it in a metal case so as to prevent any accidents if it's wound too tightly. Would you like to see it operate?"

Which was how it came about that Mr. Geddes at length accompanied Harry (and his new walking stick) to the earl's house and inspected the turnspit there with an eye to installing one of his inventions in the kitchens there. Harry was absolutely positive that his brother would approve, and more, he would entirely overlook the fiasco in the dining saloon in light of such a brilliant advance in the culinary department. Such is the faith of youth.

5

Lord Latteridge and his secretary reached Pontefract early in the afternoon, and took rooms at the Red Lion, where his lordship was well-known and expected. There was a private parlor ready for them, with a meal consisting of pea soup, a saddle of roasted mutton, stewed beef, goose giblets, and a second course of chicken, a roasted hare, collared eel, and a variety of pastry and creams. When the cloth was removed, Latteridge stretched out his long legs and disposed his lanky frame more comfortably in the ribband-back chair, nodded dismissal to the servant who had set out a bottle of the inn's finest claret, and closed his eyes. William poured out two glasses and set one within reach of his employer, and awaited some pronouncement of moment. His lordship did not disappoint him.

"I am thinking of marrying, William."

"Are you, sir? I had no idea."

"Nor had I, until I received a letter from my mother the other day. She is determined that, as our mourning period is over, I must look about me for a bride and settle down at Ackton Towers."

William raised an eyebrow unbelievingly. "I am all astonishment at your complacent acceptance of her decree, sir. Has she chosen someone for you?"

"Therein lies the rub," Latteridge replied, his hand reaching languidly for the glass of claret. "I am informed that she intends to bring Everingham's oldest daughter with her to

York when she comes. As a companion for Louisa, of course."

"Of course."

"Have you ever met Sophia Everingham?"

"I don't believe I've had the honor."

Something very like a snort emanated from his lordship. "She is a great favorite of my mother's, and very like her."

William took a healthy sip, and carefully placed his glass exactly four inches from the edge of the table. "I see."

"Yes, I thought you would. It occurs to me that my mother is likely to persist in bringing eligible young ladies to my notice until I marry, and I am forced to observe that her choices are not likely to agree with my own requirements. Not that I think myself particularly demanding, you understand. A lady of good breeding, gentle manners, a fair understanding, reasonable beauty of face and person, but above all, a solid character. In short, an amiable, unaffected woman whose conversation is sensible, and whose deportment is acceptable."

"I dare say you'll have no trouble at all finding such a lady," William replied with a grin.

Latteridge opened lazy eyes and asked with mild surprise, "Do you think I ask too much?"

"Not at all. In your position you should have included her being of one of the first families and fortunes of the realm, and possessed of more than ordinary beauty. But I would remind you that you have, over the years, met an inordinate number of foreign and domestic ladies, and yet apparently never found anyone acceptable as a wife."

"I wouldn't say that, precisely," the earl rejoined. "I simply was not *looking* for a wife then." He pursed his lips thoughtfully. "There was Miss Hotchkiss."

"Married to Lord Wilberfoss."

"Well, Maria Wandesley."

"Ran off with the family coachman, I believe."

"Did she? How extraordinary. I admit I admired her

spirit. In Rome, what was her name? Charlotte Martin? No, Marshfield."

"She was already married," William said dampingly.

"Was she? Ah, yes, the irascible member of Parliament from . . . Well, it was years ago, and he's probably gone off in an apoplectic fit. Still, if I didn't remember she was married, she may not be *quite* the right sort of woman." There was a lurking twinkle in his eyes, and William bit back the acerbic retort he had intended to make. "My dear William, the point is that there are any number of suitable ladies, some of whom, in all likelihood, would prefer marriage to the single state. Look at my sisters, if you will. Susan is the picture of conjugal bliss, and Louisa is intent on contracting an alliance as soon as may be. Of course, that could be so that she may leave home; I do not overlook that possibility."

Very few people rubbed along with any ease in the Dowager Lady Latteridge's company, and certainly her youngest offspring did not number of their company. The enforced inactivity of the year's mourning had caused tempers to rise, even in such a phlegmatic family as that of the Derwents. Lady Latteridge had condemned any proposal of diversion as disrespectful of the dead, though her attitude toward her husband while living (and though she rarely saw him), had been anything but a model of domestic accord. It was her wont, on receiving the occasional missive from him, to throw up her hands in a characteristic gesture (Lady Latteridge was French) and cry, "*Imbecile!* Does he think I cannot manage without his advice? If he is so convinced of my *inutilité*, why does he not return to direct his own estate and family?"

The questions were rhetorical, as it was entirely owing to Lady Latteridge herself that the previous earl had found it necessary to leave England. But he was not a man to be pitied, as he had found his exile enjoyable in the extreme, and over the years had, through his services abroad, worked his way back into the good graces of his government. Perhaps it would be more precise to say that through his *son's* services, the previous earl had been latterly clasped to his Majesty's bosom, but that is mere nit-picking. The results were the same: The third Earl of Latteridge, having departed under a cloud of disgrace, had returned in triumph to his native land, bearing his eldest son home in his train, to settle once more at Ackton Towers, where he promptly succumbed, not to his wife's acid tongue, as was rumored, but to the English weather, developing a chest complaint within weeks and dying, full of fond memories of his travels, within the month.

William Vernham had found it no simple matter to settle in the same house with Lady Latteridge, for she tended to look on him much as she did any other servant, and was given to sending him on errands more properly bestowed on the footmen. When Latteridge had come on him one day in the hall, the countess's work basket in his hand, he said nothing to his secretary, but subsequently the Dowager had developed a frosty attitude toward him which was no better than her previous condescension. Certainly William felt only sympathy with Lady Louisa's firm resolve to establish a life of her own, away from the Dowager's ruling hand. Harry, too, was feeling the stifling weight of his mother's overbearing personality, and had gladly escaped with his older brother to York. Only the earl himself remained seemingly oblivious to his mother's autocratic sway, imperturbably going his own way whether it accorded with her sense of propriety or not. He had, three times during the year of mourning, slipped off to London with never a word to her. When she had expostulated each time on his return, he had smiled lazily and said, "I had matters to attend to, Mother. Pray excuse me; I should like to change."

Eyeing the earl's calm countenance now, William had a sudden inspiration, produced, perhaps, by the faintest of twitches to the lips betraying a secret amusement in his employer. Cautiously, he voiced an inner certainty. "If you marry, your mother will probably move to the dower house."

The earl sighed. "Perhaps even to the estate in Dorset. I would make it very comfortable for her there, and she has often complained of the Yorkshire weather."

"I dare say the change in climate would do her a world of good, sir."

"Yes, she's been . . . out of sorts since my father died. Her companion—Madame Lefevre, is it?—would doubtless welcome the change of scene, too. I think Harry and Louisa are a strain on her nerves."

William lifted his glass to hide the grin which refused to be squelched. "Apparently there are any number of advantages to your lordship's marrying."

"I believe there are." The earl sipped the last of his claret, set the glass on the table and rose. "Shall we go? I have a mind to call on several of the neighborhood families after our business is finished with Hardwick."

Few sounds penetrated to the sick room in the black hours of the night, but neither aunt nor niece slept, the one struggling for breath, and the other gently wiping the damp forehead. One candle burned on the bedside table and by its light, Miss Effington studied Marianne's watchful countenance. She spoke in a voice hardly louder than a whisper. "What will you do if I die?"

"You aren't going to die, Aunt Effie."

"You can't possibly know that," the old woman said fretfully, her fingers reaching out to clamp onto Marianne's wrist. "What will you do?"

"Honestly, Aunt Effie, I haven't given the matter any thought."

"You should, my girl. You can't stay here unchaperoned. For all you think yourself so advanced in years, your character would be in shreds if you lived here with two lodgers."

"I wouldn't do that." Understanding that her aunt was

tormented by the thought of leaving her abandoned, Marianne said calmly, "I would find a companion, I suppose, until I could sell the house. Then I would move somewhere—to a village, perhaps, where I would keep chickens and a cow and maybe a few pigs. With my spare money I would invest in Mr. Geddes's inventions."

"This is not a jesting matter! Marianne, you should marry."

"My love," she laughed, "how can you say so? Have you not convinced me that a woman's true freedom lies in the single state?"

Much to her surprise, a tear escaped the old lady's eye and glinted in the candlelight as it slid unheeded down the pale cheek. "You are clever enough to know I spoke so only because of your situation, Marianne. Here in York you needn't pay the least heed to the London gossip."

"With Lady Latteridge expected any time?"

"Lady Latteridge can influence only the quality." The words hung in the air as though written there in burning letters, and Miss Effington shivered despite the fire on the hearth, and the blankets piled about her. "Do you set much store in position? The finest man I ever knew was a gentleman-farmer. Look about you. The doctor, the inventor, the attorney—all minor gentry. What counts is not the orders they can pin on their coats, but the goodness in their hearts. Not that I would have you marry Mr. Oldham. Promise me you won't marry *him*!"

"I promise," Marianne said firmly, pressing her aunt's frantic hand.

"Of course not. You have a great deal of sense, my dear, and you know it would be disastrous to ally yourself with such a prosy fool." She struggled for breath and Marianne laid a finger on her lips.

"Don't talk anymore now, love."

"I must. I want to tell you something important. Tomorrow may be too late."

"It won't be. You'll feel better in the morning."

"Perhaps, perhaps not." The old lady moistened her lips and said very slowly, "I loved that gentleman-farmer, Marianne. But we were quality, as you are, and he was beneath my station. My parents forbade the banns, shuffled me off to France, lavished me with exquisite clothes and jewelry, always, always drumming into my mind the gulf between us. A whole parade of elegant young men was brought forth, in the hopes that one of them would catch my eye, and daily my parents pointed out the differences between their polished behavior and the simple rustic manners of my gentleman-farmer. And it was true. John never in his life could have bowed so gracefully, or conversed so politely, or held a teacup with such poise. My mother would say, with a sad smile, 'Poor Mr. Deighton would be so uncomfortable at a London rout, wouldn't he?' And I realized that he would. I was pretty as a girl, you know, and much attention was paid to me when we went to London for the season. My head was turned, and all those little refinements came to seem so vastly important. Can you understand what I'm saying, Marianne?"

"I think so."

"We returned to the country in the summer and there was John, just as rustic and honest and straight-forward as he had always been, and I told him . . ." The pale face turned aside on the pillow as though only to the darkness opposite could Aunt Effie confess her shame. "I told him we were not suited, that I would never be able to marry him, that he was not to wait until I came of age. At the time I thought I had uncovered a major flaw in him, one that I could not live with. Only later did I come to understand that the flaws were superficial, and infinitely small compared with the ones I found in my suitors. My lord Hercules cheated when racing his horses, my lord Ulysses had gambled away the whole of his family's fortune, Sir Achilles seldom endured a sober moment, the Honorable Mr. Nestor was anything but honorable. In addition," she declared, the strength returning momentarily to her voice, "they all quite deserted me when Papa lost most of his money in the South Sea scheme."

"And what of Mr. Deighton?"

"He had married poor Lavinia Trapper. She was orphaned when her parents were killed in a coaching accident, and it was found that her father was deeply in debt. Do I credit John with too much humanity in thinking he married her out of kindness? Or is it only that I cannot believe he could have loved someone other than me? What a foolish old woman I've become."

"Hush, love. You are nothing of the sort. Can you sleep now?"

Aunt Effie shook her head fretfully. "I haven't told you what I meant to. I'm rambling on about my stupid affairs. The point is this, Marianne: There are good men among the gentry. They may not have the polish or refinement of a viscount, but for all that, they are honorable, generous-hearted men. If the quality is closed to you, that does not mean you cannot marry. I would rather have married my dear John, for all his muddy boots, than have remained a spinster all my life. No, that is not strong enough. I would rather have married him than any man I ever met, and I should have but for a false pride instilled in me. But it was *my* fault, too ready to believe my own consequence. How many ladies pace out their lives alone because a *proper* match is never made for them? One in ten, one in five, one in three? When I think that I could have sat beside the hearth with him every night for the last thirty years . . ." There was a quiet satisfaction to her voice as she said simply, "I have loved him all this time. I could never seem to love anyone else."

"You are fortunate indeed to have loved such a man, Aunt Effie. If I find so worthy a fellow, you may be sure it will not deter me that he is not from the *ton*. Sleep now, my love. You need your rest and we can talk more tomorrow."

"I only spoke of him so that you would understand. Tomorrow I will not wish to share my memories." She cast a pleading look on her niece.

Marianne nodded. "We won't speak of him again."

Of the five calls the earl and his secretary made in the evening and the following morning, none could be considered a success, so far as Lord Latteridge was concerned. At Lord Haxby's he was introduced to two comely maidens who seemed so appallingly young that he afterwards queried his secretary as to whether they were yet out of the schoolroom.

"I wonder if they've ever been in one," was the amused reply. "Miss Agatha seemed to believe that the earth was flat, and Miss Amelia thought Walpole was still the king's first secretary. But I believe there is a school of thought, in addressing marriage matters, wherein the gentleman should take to wife a woman whom he can mold to his own design. The tabula rasa principle, we might call it."

"I do not subscribe to such a theory," the earl grumbled.

Miss Condicote, on their next visit, presented a different problem altogether. If not precisely a bluestocking, and only from large-mindedness would one refrain from the epithet, she was at the very least a scholarly woman, dogmatic beyond her years and beyond reason, holding views on every possible subject, and often on the most scant knowledge. Her learning ran to the classics, and if a contemporary situation could conceivably be compared, or even if it could not, she managed to do so. Latteridge politely excused himself after she had drawn a parallel between Byng's disaster at Minorca and Ajax's at Troy.

My Lord Winscombe lived beyond Castleford, and though his medieval manor was somewhat out of the way, the earl remembered hearing the daughter's name mentioned by his sister. He had no recollection of the context until he had sat with the family for half an hour. Then very clearly he recalled Louisa's remarks: "Sarah is a flirt. I have seen her cast sheep's eyes at the parson and the blacksmith, and lift her skirts above the ankles when her brother brought home his friends. Mama would have an hysterical fit if I fluttered my fan the way she does."

The fan Sarah used on this occasion had ivory sticks and gossamerlike lace insets. Latteridge had seen fans worked with consummate skill by ladies of every European country, but he had never seen the like of Sarah's artistry, not even by the most accomplished courtesans of the day. Fascinated, he watched as she drew the partially extended fan across the milky white expanse of her bosom, largely revealed in her low-cut gown. The sensuousness of the gesture was only heightened by the luminous blue eyes which rested adoringly on her beholder. With a longing sigh she proceeded to manipulate the accessory in such a way that each stroke brushed lightly against the taut fabric across her bosom. Some scientific observation concerning the concurrent heating and cooling of an object distracted Latteridge's mind so that he entirely missed Lady Winscombe's sage counsel on the pruning of fruit trees.

When he was once more seated in the phaeton, the ribbons in his hands, he murmured, "Dear God!" to which the staunch William replied, "Just so, my lord."

6

At this point, the earl would as lief have discontinued his endeavors for the day had he not, in his usual courteous manner, sent word ahead that he would call on Mr. Tremaine and Sir Joseph Horton. Despite years spent out of England, the earl had some acquaintance with most of the county families, and knew which possessed daughters of marriageable age. He found that his knowledge was rather out-of-date, however, in the case of the Tremaines, since all four of their daughters were apparently now married and the only one to encourage his attention was Mrs. Tremaine herself, who, looking to the future (her husband being seventy-five to her youthful fifty-eight) thought to provide herself with a splendid match in the event of Mr. Tremaine's timely death.

"One could tire very quickly of this pursuit," the earl remarked as he stepped once more into his carriage, having successfully disengaged his hand from the hopeful widow-to-be. "I have the most lowering feeling that the Hortons are abstainers from intoxicating beverages. Shall we stop at an inn on the way?"

"We would likely be unable to avoid dining with them if we arrive after two, sir."

"Then by all means let us press on."

When the requisite time had been spent with the Hortons, Miss Clare Horton had not as yet presented herself, being above stairs dressing for the weighty occasion. As it turned out, her toilette was well worth the effort, and she floated into the great drawing room much as a goddess might, trailed by the poor cousin who lived with the Hortons in a rather servile capacity. The cousin's cheeks were aflame from the abuse Miss Horton had heaped upon her during the delicate operation of dressing for his lordship's presence, and the earl found that the family considered the girl of so little notice that they did not even bother to introduce her. Annoyed with such vulgar behavior, he performed the service for himself and his secretary, grimly pleased at the baronet's discomposure.

Miss Horton was oblivious to the entire proceeding. Standing where the light caught her profile and silver-blonde hair to her best advantage, she smiled on the assembled party and said graciously, "Lord Latteridge must stay to dine. I have had no opportunity to speak with him yet."

The earl avoided his secretary's speaking eyes and declared his willingness to comply with the lady's command. The expedition had degenerated to such depths that he may have had in mind to amuse himself, or his purpose might have been to gain an acquaintance with the silent cousin, but if it was the latter, he was doomed to failure. Sir Joseph placed the girl beside William and proceeded to ignore both of them, while encouraging his only child to demonstrate her accomplishments in the art of conversation.

"You will find, Lord Latteridge," she announced, "that the county families have deteriorated during your long absence from Yorkshire. You must accept my condolences on your father's death, of course. It is the greatest pity that you both should have spent lengthy periods on the continent, as your presence here might have added a very necessary tone to the county. I must tell you that the manners one sees displayed in York are anything but pleasing. That is lemonade, my lord. We are of the opinion that intoxicating beverages are at the root of the demoralization of our society."

"An interesting theory." The earl pushed his glass far enough away that he would not mechanically reach for and imbibe of it since, although he had no violent objection to the beverage itself, it did not accompany the boiled tench, roast beef, and broiled blade bone of veal to perfection. "Have you considered serving coffee or tea with meals?"

A pained expression contorted Miss Horton's lovely countenance. "Coffee and tea are ruinous to the body. Although they are not intoxicating, one's health is as surely destroyed by partaking of them as of spiritous liquors. One's body is a temple, my lord, and must not be abused."

"You must have a difficult time keeping servants."

"I beg your pardon?"

"On principle I suppose you would not make a beer allowance, nor one for tea. Our servants at Ackton Towers would be sorely put out under such hardships." Finding himself automatically reaching for his glass, the earl let his hand fall motionless to the table.

Miss Horton looked perplexed; she had not the slightest interest in servants and had no idea whether those at Cromwell were allowed beer or not. Rather than turn to her father or mother for enlightenment, she said, "We are removing to our town house in York next week. I trust you and your family will be in Micklegate for the season."

"Mother and Louisa come in a week or so; Harry and I are already installed."

A complacent smile did nothing to warm her glacial beauty. "Then we shall meet at the assemblies."

If the earl was surprised that Miss Horton would partake of such a frivolous pastime as an assembly, he said nothing to indicate it. "Louisa is particularly looking forward to some entertainment. She was to have come out last year, but my father's death of course prevented that. I fear it has seemed a long year for her, and doubtless I shall escort her to the rooms for the first assembly after they arrive."

"Children," declared Miss Horton, who was all of twenty years of age, "are all too impatient to fling themselves into the gaieties of society. I myself find within me reservoirs of peace and devotion which sustain me quite happily at home and abroad. Few ladies are so fortunate. They must look to the world for their amusement and diversion—balls, card parties, and plays, are the food on which they nourish themselves. A diet of trivialities, my lord, can only develop a weak mind and a slovenly character. Just so have the county families deteriorated, along with their intemperance, of course. You would do well to speak severely with your sister before she is beyond hope."

Much to Miss Horton's astonishment, the earl laughed. "Poor Louisa is unlikely to be swayed by a few harmless entertainments, Miss Horton. She has the steadiest, most easygoing character of any young woman I've met; a delightful sense of humor allied with no common amount of understanding."

Miss Horton was offended. Not only had he laughed at her, but implicitly compared her unfavorably with his sister. She said stiffly, "Levity is not a characteristic I much admire, Lord Latteridge. I fear it shows a want of judicious consideration of the serious nature of life itself."

"Do you think so? I have always viewed laughter as the most treasured gift bestowed on man, to lighten his burdens and heighten his joys." As though to validate his argument, in the pause which followed, a soft chuckle was the only sound in the room. All eyes turned to observe the cousin, Miss Sandburn, her face animated with pleasure at William's droll observations. The two were oblivious alike to the censure of the Hortons or the earl's approval; left to their own devices, they were finding pleasure in one another's company. Which was a great deal more than Latteridge could say for himself. He was surprised by a grating sound from Miss Horton's direction, and turned in alarm to see if she was choking. But, no! Her face was strained into a configuration of merriment, and she was valiantly attempting to laugh, unfamiliar as such an effort was.

"My lord, you have a ready wit," she pronounced, as though quoting from a century-old script. "I shall look forward to renewing my acquaintance with Lady Louisa if she is grown as clever as you say. Seldom do I find someone who shares my tastes. Mark my words, we will become bosom friends."

A fine array of peaches, nectarines, plums, and pears was set out on the table, enabling Latteridge to question Lady Horton on whether they came from their own orchards. Although Miss Horton intervened to answer the question, the subject was changed and did not return to Lady Louisa. As soon as he was able without positive rudeness, the earl begged to excuse himself and his secretary.

Once they had left the well-named Cromwell in the distance, Latteridge said, "I did not mean to drag you away from Miss Sandburn, William, but another ten minutes in that house was not to be borne. Forgive me for ignoring you at table; I fear I had little choice."

"The Hortons are not to be your in-laws, then?" William asked impudently, his eyes dancing with mirth.

"The Hortons will be lucky if they ever become *anyone's* in-laws. I'm glad you were able to draw Miss Sandburn out. No doubt she has a wretched life there."

"She's an appealing young woman. You would do well to get to know her better."

"Ah, but, William, you have stolen a march on me and after my unfortunate inability to include her in the conversation, she would have every right to look on me most unfavorably." The earl regarded his secretary speculatively. "Have you a mind to pursue the acquaintance?"

William met his eyes with perfect candor. "I believe I do. I trust you have no objection."

"None. You may find some difficulty in seeing her, however. They will probably bring her to York with them, but I would hazard a guess they treat her as an unpaid servant, and would be astonished to see someone pay attention to her. If I can be of service . . . short of involving myself with that family," Latteridge hastened to add, "let me know."

William sighed. "And here I'd thought to simply accompany you on all your calls to Miss Horton. A sad letdown."

"Hogwash! And one other thing, William. If you hear

that that woman has come to call on my sister, I am not at home. Louisa may decide for herself, of course, but I imagine one visit should answer that purpose. Now then, did you think Hardwick's proposal for the drainage was excessive?"

By noon Aunt Effie was breathing a little easier and Dr. Thorne was greatly encouraged by her progress. "The compound peony water seems to have brought some relief. I'll send you another bolus of powdered Peruvian bark to administer this evening." He noted Marianne's drawn face and shook his head disapprovingly. "You're not getting enough rest, Miss Findlay. Have the maid sit with her and get yourself to bed."

"I will, I promise you, as soon as she falls asleep again. Do you think she's out of danger now?"

"I'm optimistic."

"Just like a doctor," Marianne complained, rubbing a weary eye. "Never a straight answer."

Dr. Thorne laughed. "That's because we know so little, and the human body is so complex. Remind me to tell you one day of the astonishing things I saw with Mr. Kelly's microscope when I studied in London. I've sent an order to Benjamin Marten for one of my own. Through the microscope I have seen the circulation of globules of blood in a frog's toe web. Imagine! And not a thing could I see with my naked eye. Mr. Kelly holds that disease comes from without and is not an excess or lack of one of the vital humors. A fascinating theory, but one for which he can give little substantiation. Still . . ." The doctor grinned. "Here I am running on when what you need is sleep, Miss Findlay. I'll come again tomorrow."

Valiantly attempting to stifle a yawn, Marianne offered her hand. "I should like to hear more about the microscope sometime, doctor, when Aunt Effie is better." She watched him out and turned to speak with her aunt, but Miss Effington, unable to overhear their discourse, had succumbed to sleep once more. The maid Beth was called to sit with her and Marianne, as promised, wearily laid down on her bed and immediately fell asleep.

When Harry Derwent called, he was informed that Miss Findlay was unavailable, but that Miss Effington was improving. He was about to leave his card and depart when a commotion arose from the sickroom and, assuming a turn for the worse had occurred, he impulsively followed Roberts, who hastened in that direction. Instead of the expiring old lady he had expected, Harry found the invalid sitting up in bed commanding, "Well, find them! How am I supposed to read without my spectacles? I had them only a few days ago. Look on the table in the drawing room."

Miss Effington at this point noticed Derwent at the door of her room and asked sharply, "Who are you? What are you doing in my bedroom? Where's my niece?"

In a persuasively mild voice Roberts tried to reassure her. "Miss Findlay is resting, ma'am, and this is Harold Derwent from next door come to inquire as to your health."

"I don't know him. Why should he care about my health?"

Harry stepped forward to explain. "I met Miss Findlay yesterday. That is, apparently we had met before, years ago, but I didn't recall."

"A Derwent, are you?" Aunt Effie asked suspiciously, and gave a snort. "And you don't remember my niece? How convenient for you."

At a loss to understand, but thinking the old lady's wits were wandering from her illness, Harry was conciliating. "Apparently Miss Findlay knew my sister Susan."

Aunt Effie sniffed. "Little good it did her. But I will say nothing against Lady Susan. A charming, well-behaved girl she was, there's no denying it, and the question of filial obedience is a mare's nest. *I* certainly am no one to cast aspersions on it. Though in both cases it proved infelicitous, as a rule I respect the theory. Abuses of parental authority abound, God knows, but overall one *should* be able to look to the wisdom of elders."

Now thoroughly lost, poor Harry murmured, "Yes, ma'am." Miss Effington was eyeing him as though she expected a great deal more, and he was mercifully saved by the return of Beth, who shook her head and proclaimed her inability to find the spectacles.

"Then you shall read to me from *Sir Charles Grandison*," the old lady declared.

Beth flushed. "I don't read at all well, Miss Effington."

To prevent another crisis, Harry interposed. "I would be delighted to read for you, ma'am."

"I won't ask any favors of a Derwent," Aunt Effie said stubbornly. "My niece will read to me."

"Miss Findlay is resting just now, and I dare say needs some sleep after her long attendance upon you." Harry strode to the bedside table, picked up the book which rested there and purposefully drew a chair up to the bed. Before Miss Effington could utter another word he asked, "Are you only starting it? Good. I much prefer reading from the beginning."

Beth and Roberts shared a glance and slipped from the room as Harry's voice poured forth the adventures of Sir Charles Grandison and his companions. By the time Marianne arrived, his throat was beginning to tire, but he refused to pause, lest the old lady start a new tirade. He had failed to notice that she was fast asleep, and only raised his head when Marianne's gurgle of laughter caught his attention. Sheepishly setting aside the book, Harry rose and made his bow. "We couldn't find her spectacles," he explained as he followed Marianne into the drawing room.

"I have both pairs in my bedroom. How very thoughtful of you to read to my aunt. I fear we are putting you to a great deal of trouble, and we never meant to. Will you stay for some tea and cakes?"

"With pleasure. My throat is parched."

"Would you prefer wine? We have a fine claret from Mr. Bottoms."

"If you'll join me."

Over the cakes, Harry confessed, "I thought your aunt was a bit dotty for a moment there, Miss Findlay, but she seemed all right when I read the book. Perhaps the illness makes her mind wander."

Marianne studied his frankly puzzled face and asked with trepidation, "What did she say?"

"Oh, a lot of jumbled nonsense about filial obedience and parental authority. I thought for a moment it had something to do with my sister Susan, but then it seemed she was talking about her own past. She's not . . .?"

Marianne laughed. "No, she's not the least unstable. Crusty, yes, but crazy, no. She liked Lady Susan."

"So I gathered, but for some reason she seems to have no affection for the Derwents. She was very put out when she learned who I was." His gray eyes regarded her with unbounded curiosity, but he was too well-mannered to ask any questions.

"I think it's silly to hold grudges, don't you?" Marianne asked calmly. "I mean, how many biographies have you read where Mr. So-and-So after a period of time no longer spoke to Mr. Such-and-Such? Feuds look so ridiculous from a distance. I think if there is one vice from which I would most like to be spared, it is pettiness."

Harry regarded her with exasperation. "Spare *me* from obscurity, Miss Findlay. I haven't the slightest idea what you're talking about. Did your aunt have a quarrel with someone in my family?"

"Not a quarrel, exactly. A misunderstanding. And it was not my aunt but myself. Your mother . . . Well, something happened, and your mother no longer wished me to be your sister's friend. My aunt resents that. I suppose I do, too, but I shouldn't. It was a very long time ago, and best forgotten. But I must tell you that your mother would not approve of your calling on me."

His face spread in a wide grin. "Shall I tell you a secret, Miss Findlay? No one in my family pays the least heed to Mother's whims. If you were to read *her* biography, you

would find that there is not a soul living with whom she has
not quarreled, sooner or later. Usually sooner. Keeping a
staff at Ackton Towers is a chore of herculean proportions.
Her companion, Madame Lefevre, for years hasn't spoken
to her more than was strictly necessary. I'm not at all sure
why she stays; perhaps for the opportunity to needle
Mother when she can—she's very good at that. So you see,
you are in excellent company and mustn't give another
thought to the matter."

Consoling as this information might be, it had little bearing on Marianne's case, but she had no intention of telling
Derwent so. "You relieve me, sir, and Aunt Effie will be delighted! She had a cousin once, a Miss Snapply, whose
neighbors had her declared a common scold, and it quite
made my aunt's day when she received a letter informing
her."

Harry found the conversation turned to Mr. Geddes and
his inventions with hardly a pause, but he had the uneasy
feeling that he had not set Miss Findlay's mind at rest. Although he was not given to deep thought, he left her house
so perplexed over the mystery that he failed to notice his
brother, until the earl, stepping down from his carriage,
said, "I thought you were not acquainted with Miss Findlay,
Harry."

Startled from his revery, Harry protested, "I wasn't! That
is, I didn't know I was, though she told me she had seen me
years ago when I was a child. She knows Susan, Press."

"Does she? You will have to tell me all about it, Harry,
but not, I think, in the street. Let me rid myself of my dust
first, will you? I'll meet you in the library."

7

If most of the rooms in the earl's house in Micklegate reflected the Dowager's taste, the library was a notable exception. The previous earl had made of this one room a sanctuary, and it had been a fast rule, albeit known only to himself and his countess, that, not only was she not to have anything to do with its decor, she was never to set foot in it. Consequently, the room abounded with leather chairs, an eclectic collection of books, several pipe racks, prints of questionable artistic merit, and bronzes of the third earl's favorite horses. During his long sojourn on the continent, the earl's only real regret was being divorced from the library in Micklegate. No room at Ackton Towers had ever acquired quite the same patina; only here was the illusion of independence, of peace, of harmony.

The present earl stood in the doorway, surveying his father's private domain with a measure of understanding. The Dowager had not been an easy woman to live with . . . and time had not mellowed her disposition. And yet, Latteridge clearly recalled the night in Venice when his father, deep in his cups, had confessed to his having loved his bride. "The problem," his father had said mournfully, "was that she did not love me. Her family forced her into the match. She didn't want to marry an English milord, she didn't want to live in England, and she has spent her entire energies attempting to prove that her immature judgments were correct. Lord knows I am as fond of Paris as ever she was, but each time I took her there, she made life unbearable on our return, so that I eventually refused to take her any more. Her haughty disdain of our aristocracy only made the *haut ton* swarm round her, believing that if she was even more high in the instep than they, she was someone to be courted."

His father had laughed reminiscently. "She publicly scorned their attempts to draw her down to their level, as she put it, but privately I think she found the efforts gratifying to her vanity. It's unlikely she would have had so much attention in her native land." With bleary eyes the third earl had studied his son sadly. "She has become a bitter woman, Pressington. Take my advice. Don't marry a woman against her will. The weaker sex—ha! I have seldom seen a *man* so tenacious in holding to his prejudices, so single-minded in pursuing his goals. Strange, but I still have an affection for her, and sometimes, in spite of everything, I believe she has inadvertently developed a fondness for me. I must be devilishly drunk, Pressington. Get me to bed."

The library was flooded with light from the courtyard beyond, and though impeccably clean, had the feel of a room shut up for years. Harry seemed incongruous, slumped back in a leather chair, his forehead puckered in thought, and his hand absently toying with his new walking stick. The earl strode to the doors opening onto the courtyard, and flung them open to admit the late afternoon breeze into the still room. Choosing a chair near Harry's, he elegantly disposed himself in it, his long legs stretched out, and his hands lying unmoving on the arm rests. "Well, Harry, much as I dislike disturbing your meditations, I must admit I am all curiosity to hear how you happened to have become acquainted—or should I say reacquainted?—with our neighbor."

"Yesterday Miss Findlay sent a note to William, but of course he wasn't here, and then she sent one to you, but you were gone, too. Woods mentioned the matter to me and I thought I should perhaps see if there was some problem. Actually, I rather did it to please you," Harry confessed.

"I am duly impressed, I promise you."

"Yes, well, it turns out her aunt is very sick and our gathering—my gathering—of the previous night had disturbed the old lady's sleep. Not that Miss Findlay was complaining! She's a trump, Press. Didn't want to ask a favor of us, but the old aunt was in a pretty bad way. She's better today." Harry flushed. "I read to her for a while."

Lord Latteridge regarded his younger brother with something akin to incredulity. "You have, perhaps, taken a fancy to the old lady?"

"She's a regular tartar! But Miss Findlay was resting and the maid said she didn't read very well, so . . . What else could I do?" Harry fingered the walking stick uncomfortably, but this brought inspiration. "And I've bought the most astonishing invention for the kitchens, Press! One of the lodgers at Miss Findlay's is an inventor. Look at this stick! Have you ever seen the like of it?" Proudly he demonstrated the many handy devices contained in the one elongated item, explaining the correction made to the quizzing glass as he proceeded. "I can order one for you if you like. Five guineas! Mr. Geddes asked four, but Lord, I'm no nip-cheese. It's as plain as the nose on your face that it's worth a great deal more. There can't be another gentleman in York with one half so clever."

"No, I should think not."

"And the turnspit. Just wait till you see it, Press! You wind it up like a clock, and it turns for hours on its own! Mr. Geddes will have it ready in a few days, but I can take you next door to see the one they have there, if you like."

Latteridge did not appear as pleased as Harry had thought he would. "What about the boy?"

"What boy?"

"The one who is hired by Lady Day as a skipjack. What are we to do with him?"

Harry gave the matter serious consideration, rubbing the head of the walking stick as though for wisdom. "I have it! He can be Louisa's page!"

"What in hell is Louisa to do with a page?"

"He can run errands for her and accompany her when she goes out shopping—carry her packages and such. She'd love it, Press. Suit him out in a livery and Mother wouldn't have the slightest objection, I dare say. It would give Louisa consequence, don't you see?"

"Hardly Louisa's most fervent desire," Latteridge retorted.

"No, but it *is* my mother's, and Louisa would probably prefer a page to a footman forever tagging along after her."

"Harry, sometimes you amaze me with your perspicacity. I am all admiration."

Confused, Harry asked, "Does that mean you're pleased or cross?"

"Pleased, my dear brother. The plan will suit very well."

"And shall I take you to see the turnspit?"

"No, I think not. Miss Findlay cannot wish people tromping through her house when her aunt is sick. I shall have to contain my curiosity until your Mr. Geddes brings ours."

Harry met his brother's laughing eyes. "I really am sorry about the dining saloon. Will you deduct the expense of redoing it from my allowance?"

"After you have rendered us such a signal service as providing a self-propelling turnspit? I wouldn't dream of it. Though Mother will be annoyed, I should dearly love to see the room done over."

"That reminds me, Press." Harry's forehead puckered once again and his eyes narrowed with thought. "There is some misunderstanding between Miss Findlay and Mother. I told her—Miss Findlay—that Mama quarrels with everyone and she shouldn't take it to heart if Mother snubbed her or something, but somehow I don't think that was all there was to it. She said Mother wouldn't approve of my calling on her. Oh, yes, and that Mother hadn't wanted her to be Susan's friend anymore. Apparently she and Susan *were* friends, because Miss Findlay had met me when I was a boy, and that could only have been in London, don't you think? If she had lived near Ackton Towers I'm sure I would remember her. She's quite striking-looking."

"So it was Mother, and not you," the earl mused. "William also felt there was something amiss. Could you not find out more about the problem, Harry?"

"Well, the old lady, the aunt, rambled on about filial obedience and parental authority, and it must have had something to do with Susan, because she said Susan was charming and well-behaved. Susan! Just goes to show you how observant old people are. And then Miss Findlay talked about biographies and feuds and her aunt resenting Mother's treatment of her, Miss Findlay I mean. I couldn't make head or tail of it, Press, but I don't think she wanted to talk about it further."

"How old is Miss Findlay?"

"For God's sake, Press, I couldn't ask her that! She's not young. Susan's age, perhaps, or a little younger."

"A veritable ancient," Latteridge laughed. "Did you have some fruit or soup sent over for the aunt?"

"Damn! I forgot. I ate most of the fruit Mr. Oldham brought her."

"You restore my faith in you, Harry. It's customary to send something to a neighbor when there's sickness in the house. I'll have William attend to it. Do you expect to visit Miss Findlay again?"

"Of course I do. You don't think I'd worry about Mother not approving, do you?" Harry was indignant.

"Miss Findlay's aunt is her chaperone. While she's ill, the young lady is in an awkward position with regard to male visitors."

"For God's sake, Press, there are two men *living* in the house!"

"True," the earl said thoughtfully. "I merely offer you a word of caution, Harry, for Miss Findlay's sake."

"I doubt she cares a fig for such stuff." Harry rose and made for the door, stopping only to say, "She's not some helpless miss, Press. If you knew her, you'd understand."

When his brother had left the room, Latteridge sat for
some time contemplating the ormolu clock on the mantelpiece, then shrugged off his thoughts and sat down at his
desk to compose a letter to his sister Susan. His curiosity,
more than the fact that such a missive was long overdue,
prompted him; much better to have the facts from his sister
than the fiction from his mother.

Miss Effington became more irascible as she grew
stronger. Several times Marianne left the room for a short
while, only to return and find her aunt attempting to walk
about the room with a walking stick cajoled from Mr. Geddes. Both lodgers made it a point to inquire after the old
lady; Mr. Geddes because he was concerned, and Mr. Oldham because he thought Miss Findlay would expect it of
him. Mr. Oldham had no desire to see the old lady in person, for she had an alarming way of speaking her mind
when he was kindly instructing her on some medical super-
stition put to rout by modern science. Once she had sput-
tered, "Balderdash! Where is the difference between
putting a roasted onion in your ear for the earache, and a
doctor dosing you with snail tea for chest complaints?
Rhubarb, Mr. Oldham. Rhubarb and ass's milk are the only
proven medicines. You may take all your possets and
panadas and elixirs and dump them into the river."

When her aunt had been feeling better for some days,
Marianne agreed to accompany Dr. Thorne on the promised
promenade along the river. Her tabby sack gown, the only
suitable dress she had for the occasion, had been recently
refurbished with a triple fall of lace at the elbows, and a
new handkerchief secured by the breast knot. Over this she
donned a blue swansdown cape with charming hood that
framed her face, and allowed the auburn ringlets to appear
unhampered. Although the sun was bright, there was a
brisk wind blowing, and Marianne breathed deeply of the
late summer fragrance, smiling at her companion. "I can't
tell you how delightful it is to be out-of-doors again! Most

days we used to walk at least to Micklegate Bar, if not a great deal farther. We have some dahlias and asters in the garden, but I love seeing the phlox and gladiolus as we walk along, and smelling the nicotiana in the evenings." She paused and then asked, "Are most of your patients better now?"

"On the mend, every one of them, but I have a few new cases—gout mostly. Town is beginning to fill up for the season. Once the entertaining is under way in earnest, I have any number of calls for sprained ankles, fatigue and overindulgence. And there's the occasional actor hit by a well-directed orange from the pits," he told her cheerfully.

They passed the Barber-Surgeon's Guild Hall on the Ouse Bridge and turned onto the promenade on the river banks. The high wind whipped the water into caps, and the sloops and barges tossed about like cockleshells. More protection for the boats was available once past the center arch of the bridge ahead, but several small crafts struggled upstream with difficulty. As Marianne and Dr. Thorne watched, a sudden gust of wind rose from a new quarter, causing Marianne to draw the hood more closely about her head. When a rope snapped on an unwieldy timber barge closest to shore, the boom swung violently about, knocking two sailors into the water. The one remaining sailor was unable to come to their assistance, as the boom whipped about crazily, the sail ripping and the boat drifting toward shore.

Although the two sailors were not far from the bank, one had suffered an injury when the boom struck him, and the other thrashed violently in the water calling for help, apparently unable to swim. A scattering of well-dressed gentlefolk, fewer than usual perhaps because of the high wind, watched fascinated as the sailors struggled; only Marianne and Dr. Thorne moved forward to offer assistance. After handing Marianne his coat, the doctor waded into the water waist deep and called encouragement to the closest sailor, but the second man was being carried downstream by the choppy, strong current of the river. Even as Marianne turned toward the gaping spectators for help, she saw a gentleman emerge from the grove of trees, take in the situation at a glance, and hasten toward them. For a brief moment she thought it was Derwent, but she was soon disabused of the notion, for the man was older, taller, and more elegantly efficient in his stride.

With only a pause to rid himself of his boots and coat, he dove into the river and swam toward the hapless sailor drifting downstream. Marianne turned her attention to Dr. Thorne, who was trying to get the first sailor onto the bank, though his leg was obviously useless and probably broken. She held out her hands and caught his, while the doctor boosted him up onto safe ground. There was a murmur from the watching audience, but whether of relief or disappointment Marianne did not choose to consider. When he was comfortably settled on the grass, Dr. Thorne bent over him to see to the wounded leg, and Marianne again turned her attention to the other sailor. To her relief, she saw that the gentleman had him clasped firmly and was swimming with powerful strokes toward the shore. As they came within reach of the bank, she offered a hand to the dazed sailor, saying, "Now don't pull me in. That won't do either of us the least good. You're quite safe now." She paid no heed to the fact that each dripping man only served to further soak her cloak, but handed first the sailor and then the gentleman out of the water, calmly smiling encouragement and thanks in turn.

Dr. Thorne was no less bedraggled than the sailors or the gentleman, but he surveyed her own condition with admiration. Although undoubtedly wet and cold, she still looked lovely, with her wind-tossed hair, her shining hazel eyes, and glowing cheeks. "Poor dear. I'll have to take the sailor home to set the leg. Shall I see you back first?"

"Certainly not! I'm perfectly capable of making my own way. Thank you, Dr. Thorne." She forced herself to turn to the gentleman whose sparkling white knee breeches were muddy, and whose velvet coat would soon be wet through from the sopping brocaded waistcoat. His resemblance to Harry Derwent and to Lady Susan was unmistakable. Though not positive, Marianne had the distinct impression that he had to be the Earl of Latteridge. There was, of course, the off-chance that he was related to them in some other way, but the very fact that he was in York made that possibility remote. "And thank *you*, sir. I feared no one else would have the humanity to help."

Latteridge was seated on the bank trying to force his wet-stockinged feet into elegant boots. "I enjoy a good swim now and then," he said ruefully. Rising to stand over her he asked, "May I see you home, ma'am?" When she hesitated, he raised a comic brow. "Unless, of course, you object to being seen with a gentleman in such a disgraceful condition."

"Pray don't delay for me. It is but a step to my home."

"Then I shall suffer no inconvenience in attending you," he drawled, "and I am sure the good doctor would appreciate my rendering you such a service after you have provided him with a new patient."

Dr. Thorne, meant to overhear this remark, regarded Marianne cheerfully. "Go with him, my dear. It will make my mind easier."

Marianne had no choice but to accept the earl's offered escort; any other course would be churlish. Pulling the hood back up over her flaming curls she smiled and said, "Very well. Good day, Dr. Thorne. I shall remember that if I wish an exciting morning's excursion, I have only to accompany you."

Already occupied in directing the removal of the wounded sailor, Dr. Thorne protested somewhat absently, "I might say the same! Run along now and change into some dry clothes before you catch your death. I'd hate to answer to your aunt for *that*!"

Hardly a loverlike parting, Latteridge decided with surprising satisfaction. Unlike Marianne, he had no idea who she was, but he had every intention of finding out. "It's not then a habit with you? Rescuing people?" he asked as he guided her along the promenade.

Marianne laughed. "My first occasion, I promise you, and I could just as well have done without the excitement. How could so many people stand by and not do anything?"

The question was rhetorical and the earl made no attempt to answer it, since it was unanswerable. "Do you live in York, Miss . . .?"

"Yes, though we haven't been here long. It's quite a lovely city, isn't it? And excellent theaters, beautiful assembly rooms, shops of every description, the horse races. And with few of the distressing elements of London. Things are less hurried here."

Latteridge noted with surprise that she was headed for the Ouse Bridge. Still he did not suspect; his only thought was that she could not possibly live far from his house in Micklegate. "Dr. Thorne seems a competent young man. Has he practiced here long?"

"Several years, I believe. He went to Oxford, then trained as a surgeon at St. George's Hospital in London. But I believe he holds his Doctor of Medicine degree from the University of Aberdeen. He's fascinated by microscopes."

"Is he?" The earl was fascinated by the smile that played between her lips and eyes.

"Yes, he says he's seen the circulation of globules of blood in a frog's toe web."

"Has he? How extraordinary! And he thought you would be interested to hear of it?"

Her eyes danced. "Of course I was. Everyone should have an enthusiasm, don't you think?"

"Undoubtedly. Do you have an enthusiasm, Miss . . .?"

It was more difficult this time to ignore the query but Marianne managed to do so. "I confess that I am especially interested in *other people's* enthusiasms. Have you seen Miss Morrett's tapestries? My aunt is so agog with how clever they are, that she will wear her spectacles in public to study them. And Mr. Geddes is currently intrigued by the possibilities for further innovations to candlesnuffers. Did you know a fellow in London has patented one with a device to prevent the previously snuffed stuff from falling out when you go to snuff the next candle?"

The earl caught the unmistakable gleam in her eyes and protested, "What you mean is that you are amused by other people's enthusiasms."

"Not at all. I find them wholly endearing."

A thought had occurred to Latteridge and he asked, "The Mr. Geddes who invents walking sticks with embedded accessories and self-propelling turnspits?"

Their rapid pace had brought them to Marianne's door and she offered an apologetic smile. "Yes, that Mr. Geddes."

"Miss Findlay?" There was a note of incredulity in his voice, though his ever-placid countenance reflected nothing but cordiality. When she nodded, he said, "I am your neighbor, Lord Latteridge."

"I suspected as much. Harry Derwent has a similar cast of features."

Seldom was the earl at a loss for words, but he found himself hard-pressed now. At length he said, "I trust your aunt is better."

"Much better, thank you. In fact," she amended almost seriously, "well enough to partake of the soup and fruit you had sent. I trust you received our acknowledgment of your thoughtfulness."

"I'm sure I did." Some recollection of William laying the note on his desk returned to him but he did not think he had read it.

Marianne had used the knocker and Roberts now opened the door. "Good day, Lord Latteridge. I hope you receive no ill from your soaking." And then, irrepressibly, as the door closed after her, "But send for Dr. Thorne if you do; he's very talented."

Whether amusement, perplexity, or wonder was uppermost in his mind, the earl could not decide. He turned his

energies instead to calculating whether it would be socially
acceptable for him to call on her the next day—to inquire
as to her well-being after such a harrowing adventure. Not
that she had seemed the least discomposed by it, but
still . . .

8

Latteridge had forgotten, in his preoccupation, that he had a match scheduled with Sir Reginald Barrett the next day at the Knavesmire track. Neither gentleman chose to ride his own horse in the race, as Latteridge's weight was too great, and Sir Reginald's foppish taste recoiled at the spectacle he would present. On the other hand, neither of them was content to observe the proceedings from Carr's standhouse, since last minute instructions had to be given the jockeys. A goodly number of viewers lined the course, on foot, on horseback, as well as the ladies in carriages.

The two horses were well-matched, a chestnut and a bay, and a hundred guineas rode on the outcome. At the start, Sir Reginald's colors of purple and silver preceded the earl's scarlet and gold, but Champignon quickly gained on the showy Challenger until the two ran neck and neck for most of the course. A handkerchief fluttered onto the track, startling Champignon, who broke stride and lost just enough ground to be defeated by a neck. The earl was resigned; Sir Reginald was jubilant.

"What did I tell you, Latteridge? Fastest horse in the North, by God! And not even at his best today. I've seen him faster, you know. Outran that nag of Fotherby's without even trying." Sir Reginald minced over to his triumphant steed, but hesitated to stroke the sweaty neck, having a great admiration for his spotless pearl-gray gloves. The victory, however, put him in charity with his opponent and he allowed his tongue to wander on thoughtlessly.

"Saw you yesterday in the promenade when you dragged that sailor out of the river. Ruined your clothes, I'll be bound. And the woman was Miss Findlay, wasn't it? Can't miss that vulgar red hair of hers. She acted like some five-pound maid rescuing a prize gosling from a pond!" He leaned toward the earl, whose expression he entirely mis-read, in a confidential manner. "I think your brother has a mind to set her up. I've seen him go into her house several times. Don't say I didn't warn you about her! Next thing you know the place will become a regular bordello. Not that it's not a handy situation for your brother, but the neighborhood . . . !"

"As usual, you have imposed your own prurient thought on the situation," Latteridge informed him coldly. "Miss Findlay's aunt has been dangerously ill, and Harry has kindly visited to inquire as to her progress. You will be de-lighted to hear that the aunt is recovering now."

"Delighted be damned," Sir Reginald muttered, his face suffused with color. "I still think she doesn't belong in the neighborhood. Any number of the first families of the county have houses in Micklegate, Latteridge, and there she sits in that run-down shambles with her lodgers."

"The house looks a great deal better than I remember it. True, it is small, but the broken gutters have been replaced and the window trim painted. Actually, I think it makes both of our residences appear the more to advantage, in contrast to its moderate size."

Sir Reginald had not considered this facet of the matter, but he was undaunted. "She's not a lady, Latteridge! No gentlewoman would have gone to the assistance of some ragged sailors."

"Nor walked home with a gentleman in my miserable condition, I suppose," suggested the earl placidly, a gleam in his eye which should have warned the obtuse Sir Regi-nald, but did not.

"She should give her right arm to be seen in your com-pany, disarrayed or not! You are too easygoing, Latteridge.

Such upstarts should be put firmly in their place. The next thing you know she'll be telling her friends, you *asked* to escort her home."

"I did."

Sir Reginald's eyes bulged. "I wash my hands of you. Have you no regard for your dignity?"

"Obviously not, or I wouldn't be standing here listening to your spiteful drivel, my dear fellow."

"You're just annoyed because Challenger took the shine out of your mushroom. That's what it means, doesn't it? Champignon?"

"Yes," the earl replied with a quiet chuckle. "Your accent is deplorable."

"Bah!" Sir Reginald started to mince away to a group of friends. "One must mimic French fashions, but I can see no reason to exert oneself to learn the language. Of course, your mother is French, so it comes naturally to you."

Lord Latteridge shook his head mournfully and turned to console his jockey. "Don't blame yourself, Timothy. It was an unfortunate accident. Champignon is a bit skittish yet, but he'll settle down."

"I don't believe 'twere an accident, my lord," the little fellow grumbled, scratching his head. "'Twere one of Sir Reginald's friends lost his handkerchief."

"Don't tell anyone else, if you please. Nothing would be achieved by such a rumor." The earl smiled at his disconsolate rider. "We'll just bear it in mind for the future."

On the ride back from the race course, Latteridge was silent, and William chose not to interrupt his thoughts, which apparently were perplexing, as the dark brows were lowered over narrowed eyes. Eventually the earl shrugged and turned to him. "I finally met Miss Findlay yesterday, William."

"Did you, sir?"

"Yes, she was helping to fish some drowning sailors out of the river. With Dr. Thorne. Do you know him?"

"We've met, but for the most part I've only heard of him.

A very respected doctor in town, though he's young and hasn't been here all that long."

"Apparently he's quite devoted to his work. Is he married?"

"No, a bachelor." William unobtrusively studied his employer. "Are you not feeling well?"

"Me? No, no, I'm fine. We have no family doctor in town since Bradshawe died. Prudence dictates that we have someone to call in an emergency. You think Dr. Thorne would be a wise choice?"

"From everything I've heard. He seems to have pulled Miss Effington out of a very dangerous illness."

"Miss Effington?"

"Miss Findlay's aunt."

"Yes, of course. I'd forgotten her name. William, it is going to be deuced difficult to get to know that woman."

With a straight face, William asked, "Who, my lord? Miss Effington? She's fifty if she's a day, and she has a ferocious tongue. Are you sure you want to know her?"

"And this is the man I offered to help," Latteridge repined. "Base ingratitude. When I think of the years I have harbored a serpent in my bosom . . ."

"Don't tell me you are asking *my* help," William laughed. "When I think of the Misses Haxby, Condicote, Winscombe, and Horton, not to mention Mrs. Tremaine, hanging on every word from your lips . . ."

"You forget that Miss Findlay does not hold my family in esteem. I have learned from Harry that it has to do with Mother." He exchanged a significant look with his secretary and proceeded. "But that is not the major difficulty. At least, I trust it isn't. Sir Reginald sees every male who enters Miss Findlay's house as—shall I be blunt?—a potential patron of her favors. He has already suggested her tenants and my brother, and, though I could perhaps silence his ramblings, I feel it would hardly be fair to her to give him new pickings for his feverish brain, when I would simply welcome the opportunity to further our acquaintance."

"Did Miss Findlay give any indication that she would appreciate seeing you again?" William asked curiously.

"None, but she showed no animosity."

"What would you have me do?"

"If you would call on her this afternoon with my compliments and inquire as to her well-being after yesterday's adventure, I would be grateful. Beyond that, well, I will have to consider the matter."

William was decidedly hurt. "You don't think Sir Reginald will look askance on *my* calling?"

"My dear fellow, he is far too arrogant to notice you at all," Latteridge retorted with a grin.

"I think that fellow has his eye on you," Aunt Effie announced when Dr. Thorne was barely out the door.

"You think *every* man has his eye on me. First poor Mr. Oldham and now Dr. Thorne. Who next, my dear? Mr. Geddes?"

"Don't scoff, Marianne. The doctor took you walking yesterday, didn't he? And he's been here everyday for the last week or so."

"Well, of course he has," Marianne answered practically. "You've been sick."

"I'm not any longer, and I shall get up this very minute." A challenging determination settled over her features, and she pushed back the covers with only a slightly questioning glance at her niece.

Marianne laughed. "Very well, Aunt Effie. Let me help you with your dressing gown."

A sly light gleamed in Miss Effington's eyes. "I'll have my clothes, if you please."

"Oh, no, you won't, my dear," Marianne retorted. "Tomorrow perhaps, if you are still feeling well, but today it will test your strength enough to simply sit up in the drawing room *en déshabillé*. Come, slip into your gown."

With a disparaging sniff the old lady allowed herself to be wrapped in the flowery silk wrapper, its purple and yellow splotches making her face pale by comparison. "Where are my spectacles?"

"I'll bring them to you once we have you settled on the sofa, Aunt Effie." Marianne paid not the least heed to her aunt's grumblings, as she led her from the bedroom into the drawing room, and draped a shawl about her knees. When she returned a short time later, she had not one, but both pairs of spectacles with her, and she held them out for her aunt to make a choice.

"Those aren't mine," Aunt Effie muttered, pointing to one of the pairs with a slightly unsteady finger.

"They are, though. Mr. Geddes has fitted them with short temple pieces. I know you have never been able to tolerate turnpin temples, but you will find these quite comfortable, if you will but try them. The circles press against your head to hold the frames in place; Mr. Geddes saw some just like them in a spectacle-maker's shop in Coney Street, and he adapted yours for you. And look what he's done, Aunt Effie. This silver chain attached to the rings . . . Here, I'll show you." Marianne put the steel-framed spectacles on to demonstrate how they stayed in place, and then let them fall to hang around her neck by the silver chain. "This way you needn't be forever misplacing them, my dear. Isn't that clever?"

"Why did he do it?"

Marianne lifted the spectacles from around her neck and handed them to her aunt. "Because he wished to do something for you when you were sick."

"Humph. He wished to do something for *you*, more like. He's too young for you, Marianne; I shouldn't encourage him if I were you."

"For God's sake, Aunt Effie," Marianne said with undisguised exasperation. "I told you you'd hit on Mr. Geddes next. *No one* is interested in me, and I have no intention of tossing my cap at anyone, either."

"Now, now, don't take offense! I'm not saying you've been the least forward with any of them, and you know I should like to see you married, but you must first decide which you are to have. Mr. Geddes is too young, Mr. Old-ham is a bore, Harry Derwent is ineligible, so I think you should concentrate on Dr. Thorne."

"I cannot believe you're serious, Aunt Effie!"

Her aunt carefully adjusted the spectacles at the bridge of her long nose, noting with some surprise that they fitted exceedingly well and stayed in place as the ones without temple pieces never would, and eyed the indignant young woman with calculated impatience. "Play no airs off on me, Marianne. How do you think a woman in your position gets a husband? By sitting back and watching life pass her by? There may be those, possessed of fortune and birth and looks, who appear to do so, but let me tell you, it is *never* the case. Every successful courtship is carefully planned, if not by the woman involved, then by some other guiding hand. And we are not speaking of the Almighty! He has quite enough to do without bothering himself with the likes of you. No, my girl, matchmaking is a very temporal matter, and treating the good doctor like a brother is a wretched strategy!"

Marianne lowered herself into the chair opposite her aunt and said gently, "I thought you didn't like Dr. Thorne."

"I have no objection to him as a husband for you. If his practice of medicine is not always to my taste, still I keep an open mind." She ignored her niece's snort. "He will doubtless achieve a measure of success because he is a personable fellow and . . . and because he was not altogether clumsy in his treatment of my case."

"Oho, I see. You are so grateful to him for curing you that you thought to offer me as a reward."

"Men do not like pert, saucy women," her aunt proclaimed with a majestic wave of her hand. "If you intend to captivate him, you will have to cultivate a more pliant nature."

"I do not intend to captivate him."

Miss Effington narrowed her eyes shrewdly. "You like him, don't you?"

"Of course."

"And you respect his professional abilities, do you not?"

"Yes."

"He is not an unattractive gentleman—well-dressed and courteous, sensible with engaging manners and a quick understanding. Perhaps a little too lively for my taste, but certainly not for yours, I would have thought. In short an excellent match for you."

Marianne cast her eyes heavenward. "He has no intention of marrying me, Aunt Effie."

"To be sure, but that can be changed. What do you think we are discussing? Precisely how to alter his casual friendship into a warmer regard."

"But, my dear, I don't want to marry him."

"Nonsense! We have already established that he is a perfectly suitable *parti*. You cannot afford to be too nice in your choice, my girl. The advantages of matrimony are far too numerous and obvious to bear repeating. You are already past the age when you can expect men to consider you as a potential mate, so you must take measures to clear their vision." She allowed the spectacles to fall about her neck on the silver chain and regarded them with satisfaction. "I can slip them right under my handkerchief and no one will notice them at all. Thank heaven he made the chain long enough!"

Marianne was willing enough to have the discussion sidetracked. "I shall tell Mr. Geddes that you appreciate his thoughtfulness. Would you like me to have him fix the other pair as well?"

"Since when do I have a second pair?" Miss Effington asked sharply.

"I found it convenient to have them made some time ago, considering the frequent occurrence of their being mislaid. We should have less of that problem now, but the spare pair will come in handy if those should be broken."

"Don't ask Mr. Geddes to do it. That would only make you beholden to him. You must concentrate on Dr. Thorne. Men like women to be dependent, Marianne, though luckily Dr. Thorne is likely to see the advantages of a capable woman, he being a doctor. Still, you must flatter his intelligence and superior strength; nothing is so sure to fire his interest in you."

"How am I supposed to do that?" Marianne asked with suspicious sweetness.

"Don't be dense! Ask him about his work and let him know how impressed you are by his skill. Tell him how clever you think him. I've seen dozens of ladies do just that."

"Simpering misses, Aunt Effie?"

Her aunt eyed her placidly. "They all have husbands now."

"Unanswerable," Marianne returned with deceptive meekness, as she allowed a long, heartful sigh to escape her. "Poor Dr. Thorne."

"Bah! He *needs* a wife. It must be intolerably lowering to the spirits to spend the greater part of one's days with sick people. He will rejoice to come home to a healthy, attractive woman who admires him. You aren't getting any younger, Marianne. Another year or two and even Dr. Thorne would hesitate, knowing that you are well into your childbearing years. That aspect is important to men."

Marianne smiled mischievously. "Tell me about it, Aunt Effie."

"Graceless girl. Bring me my work box. And you should sew some new lace on your morning gown. You don't want Dr. Thorne to think you a pauper."

9

Sir Joseph Horton and his family made a stately progress from Cromwell to their town house in York, which was situated in Castlegate. Some might have been chilled by residing so close to the old castle which housed a spacious prison for forty felons, but the Hortons were of a disposition, all three, to relish the proximity of retribution on the heads of poor devils who had transgressed God's (or at least man's) laws. They felt somehow that their situation justified their own unusual beliefs and were wont, when visitors called, to point out the circumstance. Few of their visitors were impressed.

In her heart of hearts, Clare Horton acknowledged that this was the season when she must capture a title for herself. At twenty, and entering her third year on the social scene in York (her parents refused adamantly to carry her off to the iniquities of London), she was in a position where she felt she must achieve her goal before the spring came and those marvelously wealthy, titled gentlemen withdrew to London. Lord Latteridge's visit to Cromwell had encouraged her immensely, for she knew she had looked her best that day, and her best was beautiful indeed.

Clare was positive that nowhere in the wilds of Yorkshire was there another lady to compare with her loveliness, her natural graces, her sterling character. Her limited understanding she was not aware of, but had she been, she would have found it no handicap, as gentlemen notoriously shied away from intelligent women. Nor was she aware that her two previous seasons and her growing desperation had wiped away any traces of charming innocence and inexperience which might once have clung to her from the very nature of youth. But if she was lacking in any quality (which she would never have contemplated believing), she was most certainly not deficient in determination and perseverance.

Miss Horton was, as any lady of refinement must be, knocked up by the short journey from her home to York. Addressing her cousin Janet Sandburn with her accustomed roughness, she ordered, "Have my apricot silk gown ironed while I have a rest, Janet. If the servants are too busy settling in, take care of the matter yourself." When her dresser murmured that she would have the matter attended to, Clare said sharply, "You are to see that the rest of my clothes are properly put away, Perkins. It's not asking too much of Janet to see to one simple matter for me. Lord knows she's lazy enough, forever sneaking off to read a book when she could make herself useful. 'Idle hands are the devil's workshop.' Run along, Janet." Clare, distracted by the reference to hands, regarded her own long, smooth fingers with infinite pleasure as her cousin, without a word, closed the door behind herself.

Lady Horton's sister had married beneath herself, a country parson with a paltry living, not to be compared with Sir Joseph's situation. One might have thought that the Hortons would have viewed the marriage more charitably, considering the magnitude of their own religious convictions, but such was not the case. Janet Sandburn was the only child of that union, and, since her parents, being dead, could no longer feel the opprobrium as yet insufficiently vented by Sir Joseph and his lady, their daughter was the beneficiary of their continuing rancor. Of course, they would not have considered abandoning the young lady to her fate, being good Christians themselves, so they had taken her in on sufferance.

Janet had been raised in an atmosphere of loving country

hospitality, where scarce a day passed by when the parsonage was not visited by several neighbors, or the family was
not invited to dine at the local squire's or some other comfortable home. The shock of having first one, and then the
other, of her parents die of a fever raging in the village, had
not diminished before she found herself yanked from the
only home she knew, to the barren wasteland of Cromwell.
For some months, she had been too numb to realize the true
extent of her loss, and when she did, her situation seemed
hopeless. There was some money, to be sure, but it would
not come to her until she married, or came of age, and Sir
Joseph, as her guardian, had informed her that he would
apply to the executors of her father's estate for recompense
for her room and board during the period she resided with
his family. He had, in fact, insisted that until the matter was
settled, Janet was to contribute thirty of the forty pounds
she received per year from the executors to offset her main-
tenance.

During the first year, Janet had lived with this arrangement, but she had no intention of doing so for a second.
Unfortunately, Sir Joseph, as her guardian, was sent the
money and, short of resorting to legal action, Janet was unsure how she was to carry out her resolution. Another fourteen months remained until she came of age, and counting
the days was no solution, though she thanked God each
night that she had made it through another day and asked
for strength to face the next one. She spoke only when spoken to, and then, only if she was sure that she could control
her tongue. The only ray of light she had enjoyed in the entire stay at Cromwell was the Earl of Latteridge's visit. And
not the earl himself, but his secretary had provided her with
the first laugh she had experienced in over a year. The removal of the household to York held for Janet only one
benefit, and that was that she might catch a glimpse of
William Vernham in the charming old walled city.

Lost in her thoughts, Janet was startled by Perkins's
voice. "I'll take care of the dress, Miss Sandburn. There
will be several of them to touch up."

"I don't want to cause you any trouble, Perkins. Perhaps I had best see to it."

"No, miss," the girl said firmly. " 'Tain't fitting. There's plenty of time before Miss Horton will be a-needing of it."

"Thank you, Perkins. I'll be in my room; please don't hesitate to call for me if you need my help."

Janet smiled and hastened to her room, realizing that part of Clare's irritation with her stemmed from the fact that Clare's own season in York the previous year had been cut short by the death of Janet's parents. Clare was wont to point this out to her cousin on any given occasion as the reason several young gentlemen had not been given the opportunity to declare themselves. Lady Horton had insisted on their return to Cromwell in mourning, fearful that her acquaintances would consider her disrespectful if she failed to observe this tradition, but inwardly quite as annoyed as her daughter at the necessity. Sir Joseph had been indifferent; after all, he had the liberty of going shooting everyday in his own domain, instead of sitting in smoky coffee houses; and reluctantly attending the York assemblies with a daughter who was proving inordinately difficult to get off his hands.

The room assigned to Janet was on the second floor, though the family had their rooms on the first. Being set further apart from them did not have the desired effect on the girl, however, as she was pleased to escape from their vicinity whenever she was able. Hers was not a maid's room, but a secondary guest room which had not been attended to in years, overlooking the street through smallish windows. Janet was delighted with it—the faded wallpaper, the ill-hanging door, and the drafty windows—because there was a charming window seat with a battered pillow which she could sit on and watch the movement in the street below. Never having spent much time in a city, she was fascinated by the strollers and riders, the occasional street vendor or ragged dog. Janet busied herself distribut-

ing her few possessions about the room, drawn time and
again to the window at the clop of horses' hooves or the cry
of "Lavender!"

Instead of bringing the mourning dresses she had been
wearing for the last year, Janet had chosen from among the
clothing she had brought from the parsonage. Lady Horton
had frowned on her gowns these last weeks, urging her to
enliven them with lace and aprons, "For I won't have you
looking like a bereaved widow when you are in York, miss.
You have no call to depress everyone's spirits with your
drab dresses; it is time you forsook your mourning."

How Lady Horton expected Janet to enliven her mourning gowns on the dismal pittance her husband had granted
the girl, Janet did not know, but she had said nothing, carefully attending to her former apparel in readiness for the
trip. Now she removed the black bombazine, suitably alle-
viated by lace, which she had worn for the journey, and
held up the pomona green striped poplin with its quilted
petticoat. It caused her a moment's sadness, remembering
the last occasion on which she had worn it before her parents' illnesses, that lovely dinner party where they had all
laughed with their friends, unaware of the tragedy about to
strike.

Resolved to remember those happy times, to cling to
them when she had nothing else to support her, she carefully dressed herself in the walking gown, chose a round-
eared cap and set it on the scarred dressing table while she
brushed out her long black hair. It might be wise, too, to
loosen the severity of her hairstyle, she decided, as she regarded her reflection in the glass, the dark eyes thoughtful,
the full lips rueful. No need to give Clare further opportunity for snide remarks on her resemblance to a village
schoolmistress.

Before she had quite finished, there was an imperative
summons to accompany Miss Horton on her promenade.
Sufficient experience had taught Janet that it was diplomatic to answer such a call promptly, and she allowed the

hair to remain free, save for a small clip her father had given her, grabbed up the green cloak, and presented herself at Miss Horton's room, where she found her cousin as yet unready to depart.

Clare sat at the glass admiring her reflection as her dresser settled a low-crowned, wide-brimmed hat carefully on the silver-blonde tresses. The apricot gown had triple falls of lace just below her elbows, and was held wide from her body by panniers, so that Perkins had to avoid them as she came around to touch the hat into place. When she moved, Clare for the first time saw her cousin in the glass and her eyes widened. "Well, Miss Sandburn, what have we here? A new gown? Sadly out of fashion, I fear."

"No, it's not new."

For a moment, annoyance at the surprisingly attractive sight her cousin presented contorted Clare's features, but she had only to level her eyes on her own reflection to reassure herself that there was no comparison. With a spiteful laugh she said, "I suppose it is better than those black rags you've been wearing, but don't expect anyone to pay the least heed to you."

"I won't, cousin."

"Then let us be off." Clare rose and pulled on long white kid gloves. "We will take the promenade by the river. That is perhaps the best way to announce my arrival in York. And we will call on Mrs. Whittaker on our return to take tea. She can spread the word to anyone we miss."

"Won't you take a shawl?" Janet asked, as her cousin swept gracefully toward the door.

"And spoil the effect of my gown? Nonsense. It is still summer, after all."

And indeed the sun was shining brightly, so that their walk to the river was hot and dusty, but the breeze coming from the river made the promenade cooler. At first Clare did not seem to notice, as they stopped frequently to exchange a few words with acquaintances, but when they had left one group behind, she eyed Janet's green cloak enviously. "I feel quite chilled," she remarked pointedly.

"Yes, I think you would have been wise to bring a shawl. Shall we return to Castlegate?"

Clare stamped an impatient foot. "I needn't be cold if you would lend me your cloak."

Fortunately, Janet was spared the necessity of answering her when they were overtaken by Lord Latteridge, who too late realized his mistake, having been deep in thought.

"Miss Horton and Miss Sandburn! I had no idea you were in York already. When did you arrive?"

"Only today, my lord," Clare replied with a demure curtsy. "How fortuitous that we should meet so soon."

"Indeed."

"Have your mother and Lady Louisa arrived? I shall have to call on them."

"They come next week." Latteridge turned to Miss Sandburn. "Is this your first visit to York, ma'am?"

Janet nodded. "It's by far the largest city I've ever seen, and lovely with the old walls and posterns and gates. I understand the Minster is exceptional."

"Oh, it's vast but a great deal overrated," Clare interpolated. "Wouldn't you say so, Lord Latteridge?"

"Not at all. I consider it York's finest achievement." He noticed Clare's shiver and remarked, "The wind is rather biting this afternoon. May I see you ladies home?"

"Perhaps so far as Mrs. Whittaker's in Clifford Street," Clare suggested archly. "I must pay my respects to this month's Queen of the Assemblies. She will want to know that I've arrived in town."

Though Latteridge strongly doubted the truth of her assertion, he politely said nothing. In fact, he found little opportunity to say anything during their walk, as Miss Horton assumed he would be interested in her plans for the coming weeks of her stay, and he was content enough to be warned. Miss Sandburn likewise was silent, but he watched her avid interest in the people and places they passed, her dark eyes alive with curiosity. When they reached Mrs. Whittaker's imposing residence, he declined Clare's invitation to join them, protesting that he was engaged elsewhere, but before taking leave of them he turned to Janet.

"I believe Mr. Vernham has looked up that book he mentioned to you, Miss Sandburn. Shall I tell him that he may call in person with it?"

"Why, yes, that would be very kind of him, my lord," she replied without a trace of confusion, though for the life of her, she could not remember having discussed any books with the earl's secretary. As her cousin mounted the steps, she impulsively held out her hand. "Thank you, sir."

Latteridge clasped it firmly and said, "Not at all. Shall we say a book of Thomson's poetry?"

"That I am to borrow?" And she quickly followed her cousin into the house.

Latteridge's study, relieved of its excess chairs and pipe racks, but retaining the bronzes, books, and prints, had a less cluttered air, but the earl surveyed it with little satisfaction. Bringing some order to it had not relieved it of the stale aura which clung like old pipe smoke. There remained no imprint of his own. He stood with his shoulders propped against the mantelpiece, one leg crossed over the other, the gray eyes languidly thoughtful. Somehow he could not interest himself in his study.

There was a discreet tap on the door, and he bade his secretary enter. "Ah, William. I wanted to let you know that I had the . . . ah . . . pleasure of encountering Miss Horton today. They have just arrived in York. Miss Sandburn accompanies them, and I told her you would want to bring around the book of Thomson's poetry you had mentioned to her."

"Did I mention any particular volume?" William asked, fascinated.

"I don't believe so. She didn't mention it."

"Perhaps over a period of time I could take her several."

"An admirable idea," Latteridge agreed, as he drew a gold snuffbox from his pocket. "It occurs to me, William, that Miss Sandburn might welcome a friend outside Miss Horton's circle. There could be some advantage to making her known to Miss Findlay, if that were possible."

"Some advantage for whom?" William wondered, as he watched the earl absently take snuff.

"For all involved, but most especially Miss Sandburn herself. When I came upon the two ladies, Miss Horton was exhorting her cousin to lend her her cloak, having been remiss in providing herself with sufficient cover. I don't believe Miss Sandburn is accustomed to such conduct, and is in no position to protect herself from it. Perhaps Miss Findlay could provide some much-needed encouragement." Latteridge fixed his secretary with a baleful eye. "I am not only thinking of myself, or of you, my dear fellow."

William grinned. "I'm sure I never suggested such a thing, sir."

The earl's brother poked his head in at the door to say, "I'm off, Press. Shan't be back for at least a week, I dare say."

"We're expecting Mother next Tuesday, Harry."

"Shouldn't think she'd miss me if I'm not back by then," his brother retorted. "I've been angling for this invitation for days, Press. To Hall's castle, you know. Really great sport there."

"So I've heard," Latteridge said dampingly, as his brother waved a hand and disappeared.

On the first opportunity after Miss Effington's recovery from her illness, Mr. Oldham, attorney to the great and near-great (by his own acclamation), visited aunt and niece in their living room. Although Mr. Oldham had already decided that Miss Effington would not fit into their household after they were married, he was excessively polite to the old lady.

He set down his teacup and said, "Your niece and I very

nearly despaired of you, ma'am. And now here you sit in the pink of health again like the old days. Hardly to be credited in one your age, a most remarkable constitution you have. And a great deal is owing to the young doctor, of course. We gentlemen in the professions must stand by one another." His laugh, fortunately not a frequent occurrence, was a high peal, very piercing to the ear.

Aunt Effie snorted, and her niece considered setting fire to the chair on which he sat. "My aunt does not sit up late," she said, with a pointed glance at the case clock in the corner, "owing to her recent illness."

"No, no, of course not. Don't let me detain you, ma'am! I shall be content to keep your niece company." This was a very encouraging sign from Miss Findlay, and one he had not been given any reason to expect, though he now clearly saw signs of her previous indications—the manner in which she had offered the chair, the way her eyes met his, her obvious appreciation of his kindness to her aunt. These older unmarried ladies were quick to grab at their few remaining chances, he decided with a complacent smile.

There was a spluttering sound from the sofa. "My niece does not sit alone without me! When I leave, she leaves— and I am leaving now!" The old lady struggled with her shawl, which had become entangled on the carved medallion atop the sofa back, and lurched to her feet. "Come, Marianne. Mr. Oldham will excuse us."

Mr. Oldham regarded Marianne's apologetic smile as the most encouraging sign yet.

10

William Vernham was coolly received by Lady Horton and her daughter. He made it known that his visit was to Miss Sandburn and signified no reflected glory from his employer on either of the ladies of the family. Finding the Thomson volume had presented no problem, compared with delivering it. Lady Horton and her daughter were seated in the back parlor, and made no immediate attempt to have Miss Sandburn sent for. Instead, they took turns questioning him.

"Does the earl intend to spend the entire season in York?" asked Lady Horton.

"He has not indicated his intentions, ma'am."

"Well, you must know if he plans to travel outside the county," Clare insisted.

"Not necessarily. Lord Latteridge does not, of course, consult me on when and where he chooses to go."

"I have heard it said," Lady Horton mused archly, "that the earls of Latteridge are the wealthiest nobility in England. Of course there are the settlements on each of the children, and on the Dowager now, but still . . . There must be any number of families who would welcome a connection with him."

William made no comment.

"I don't believe Lord Latteridge mentioned what day his mother and sister were to arrive," Clare remarked. "I should like to call on them as soon as may be."

"I understand they will be here shortly."

Such laconic replies with their lack of sought-after information eventually discouraged Lady Horton and her daughter, so that Janet was reluctantly summoned and shortly appeared. Her simple amber sack dress may have borne little resemblance to the rich and modish gowns of the Hortons, but William was as charmed by it as by her warm welcome.

"Mr. Vernham. How kind of you to call, and to have remembered the volume we discussed. And here I had completely forgotten it." Her laughing eyes met his briefly, before she turned to Lady Horton. "Are you familiar with Mr. Thomson's work, ma'am?"

"I don't believe I am," was the cold reply.

"This one I am not acquainted with, but his *Castle of Indolence* is an allegory written in the stanza and style of Spenser." Janet belabored the technicalities of Mr. Thomson's writing until Clare fled the room and Lady Horton withdrew to her embroidery. Her eyes full of innocent distress, she turned to William and said, "I hope I am not boring you, Mr. Vernham."

"Not at all, Miss Sandburn. I should like to point out to you some differences in style between this volume and *Castle of Indolence*, before you read it, so that you may particularly notice them." He made a pretense of noting Lady Horton's wearied countenance for the first time. "But we are distracting my lady from her work. Perhaps you would care to walk with me while we talk? The weather is glorious, and we might benefit from the exercise." William turned a charming smile on Lady Horton who, for all her apparent disinterest, had heard every word. "Would that meet with your approval, Lady Horton? My walking with Miss Sandburn?"

Lady Horton was torn. It seemed unlikely she would glean any information about Latteridge from their dull discussion of poetry, and yet she was reluctant to see her niece the first of the two young ladies asked to walk out. On the other hand, it would not do to offend the earl by seeming to

object to his secretary's companionship for Janet. To deny
Mr. Vernham's request would be tantamount to impugning
his character; there was no harm in a midday stroll in York.
"Very well," she said grudgingly, "but have her back in
good time."

The two escaped the house like truant schoolchildren,
breathing an amused chuckle as the front door closed behind them. William tucked the book under his arm and
asked, "Shall we walk toward Micklegate? There is a lady
there, a Miss Findlay, whom I thought to introduce to you,
if you would care to meet her. I let her know I might bring
you, if I could spirit you away from Castlegate."

Janet was slightly disappointed that she would not have a
chance to spend the time alone with him, but agreed. "Does
she share your passion for Thomson's poetry?"

"I haven't any idea," he admitted. "She's a neighbor of
Lord Latteridge's, and a delightful woman, with a sharp-
tongued aunt and two eccentric lodgers." William regarded
her quizzingly. "Perhaps not the sort of household into
which you would wish to be introduced?"

"Quite the contrary," Janet replied. "You intrigue me."
And though this was perfectly true, she determined to
school her thoughts more closely, as they had a tendency to
bound away from her when she was with him. And that was
foolishness. He was a kind gentleman who recognized her
discomfort in the Horton household, who had taken special
care to talk with her when the earl had visited Cromwell,
and now again was thoughtfully providing her with an out-
ing to meet his friend—a lady. She must guard herself
against even the smallest expectation or hope bred out of
her misery at the Hortons. In fourteen months, she would
be free, and until then, surely she could be patient.

Unaware of her thoughts, William proceeded to draw her
out on her youth, and allowed her to question him on his
travels, pleased with her evident enjoyment of his anec-
dotes and disturbed by the contrast between her present situation and the life she had known. "This is Miss Findlay's,

and I live next door with the earl." He tapped the polished knocker and Roberts showed them directly into the drawing room, where Marianne and her aunt awaited them, a newly renovated chair providing the necessary seating. A faint odor of furniture wax clung to the air.

Janet found herself easily accepted by Miss Findlay, and keenly regarded by Miss Effington, the moment she disclosed the parish near Bury St. Edmund where her father had been rector. The old lady actually dug her spectacles from the folds of her neck handkerchief and put them on. "Your village cannot have been a dozen miles from Long Mellford where I was raised. Do you know Willow Hall?"

"Oh, yes, ma'am. The Conway family live there now, and they are great friends of our squire, Mr. Drummond. Mrs. Drummond took me there once, to go over the house and ground when the family was not in residence."

"That was my father's house," Miss Effington said, her voice unsteady. "Is it . . . Is everything in good order there?"

"Indeed it is. Mrs. Drummond and I thought it the finest house we saw, and we visited Mellford Hall and Kentwell Hall as well. The Conways take great pride in maintaining such a noble old building, and the grounds are delightful, especially in the summer." Janet dug in her memory for some special impression of the visit which might be meaningful to Miss Effington. "I remember standing in the schoolroom looking out the latticed windows at a most magnificent willow tree, all lacy in the afternoon sunlight."

Under that willow tree, Miss Effington had made her farewell to John Deighton, and there was a suspicion of moisture about her eyes as she murmured, "How lovely to think it is still there, that neither time nor tempest has brought it down. You wouldn't know any of the neighbors, of course."

"I fear not, ma'am. We met the rector at the village church, and he showed us over the rectory, but I don't believe he had been there very many years."

Marianne was watching her aunt's face, and knew that she wished to ask about her gentleman-farmer, but realized it was useless. Instead, the old lady said, "My parents are buried in the churchyard there."

Although the conversation drifted onto different topics, Marianne could see that her aunt's mind was still in Long Mellford, and she took Janet aside just before she left. "I hope you will come again, Miss Sandburn, anytime. Would it be rude of me to inquire if you correspond with your squire's wife?"

"Of course not," Janet replied, surprised. "I do, regularly."

"My aunt has lost touch with a former friend near Long Mellford, a Mr. John Deighton. I wonder . . ."

If Marianne hesitated to ask, Janet did not hesitate to offer. "I will be writing Mrs. Drummond soon, and I shall ask if she will inquire of him from Mrs. Conway. How nice if we could supply her with some news."

"Well," Marianne laughed, "she would snap my nose off if she thought I'd asked, but I know she's curious as to how he goes on. Thank you."

As William and Janet walked back to Castlegate, she said, "I thought Miss Effington a dear. Why did you say she was sharp-tongued?"

"She usually is. You disarmed her by coming from Suffolk. What did you think of Miss Findlay?"

The question was innocent enough, but Janet read significance into it and tried to answer carefully. "I liked her. She's warm and frank and very good-natured."

"Yes," William mused, "and a handsome woman, with no lack of spirit or intelligence." He grinned at Janet. "Shall I tell you what she said to Sir Reginald Barrett?"

"Please do." Although she felt disheartened at his dwelling on Miss Findlay, she could not resist laughing at the story of the gold buttons. "I don't suppose he was pleased."

"Far from it." His expression became serious. "He has

said some insinuating things about her to Lord Latteridge in his pique. They have no foundation, of course, but in his own fertile mind, and I trust he has not imparted his scurrilous tales to anyone else. I would not have taken you there if I thought there was a shred of truth in them."

"Anyone can see Miss Findlay leads a perfectly blameless life," Janet responded indignantly.

"Sir Reginald is offended that she takes lodgers. Micklegate is not, to his mind, the proper place for aught but family town houses of irreproachable dignity. When Harry Derwent, Lord Latteridge's brother, called on her during her aunt's illness, Sir Reginald put an unsavory connotation on the visits."

"I see." While she appreciated the unhappy position in which this put Miss Findlay, Janet saw clearly that it did Miss Findlay no good to have gentleman callers, and if Mr. Vernham wished to visit, it was wise for him to have a female companion. She bit her lip and said with determination, "I shall call on her frequently."

Startled, William broke his leisurely stride. "You mustn't think I told you this to incite your compassion, Miss Sandburn! Miss Findlay doesn't even know of Sir Reginald's slurs, and I doubt she would pay him any heed. But I thought you should know the situation; perhaps I should have told you before I took you."

"Nonsense. My parents were very firm about not listening to malicious gossip, Mr. Vernham. I like Miss Findlay and, when I can get away from Castlegate, I shall visit her."

"Let me be your escort," he begged, a light dancing in his eyes. "Lady Horton may not have a footman or maid to spare for accompanying you, and it would give me the greatest pleasure."

Disturbed by the smile he bestowed on her, Janet dropped her eyes from his. "Thank you. I shall look forward to seeing Miss Findlay again."

"And me?" William asked gravely.

Janet allowed herself to glance at him, and smile. "Of course, Mr. Vernham."

Marianne and her aunt were forced to suffer a visit from Mr. Oldham every evening at teatime. These visits were short, as Miss Effington could not tolerate him, and soon insisted that they were retiring, but on the evening after Miss Sandburn's call, Aunt Effie was deep in reminiscences of Willow Hall, and Mr. Oldham's droning attorney's voice soon lulled her to sleep, dreaming pleasantly of those long-gone days of her courtship. No better opportunity was likely to present itself, and Mr. Oldham prided himself on always acting at the first knock of opportunity—not waiting for the second or third pounding, which any fool could recognize. He was instantly at Marianne's side reaching for her hand.

"Sit down, Mr. Oldham," she said sharply, refusing to yield so much as a finger to his clasp.

"But we have matters of great moment to discuss, my dear Miss Findlay," he protested in an urgent whisper. Although he desisted in his attempt to gain her hand, he did not move from her side.

"I cannot imagine what they might be."

"Can you not?" He raised a coy eyebrow.

"Sit down, if you please."

Mr. Oldham had heard that women were exceptionally nervous when being offered for (he had no personal experience), and he grudgingly took his chair, balancing himself on the edge of it, so that by leaning forward, he might be as close to her as possible. "I believe you are aware of my position in York, of my industry in adding to my personal substance, of my genteel background. Perhaps you are unaware," here his features contorted into something resembling a smirk, "of my admiration of yourself, though I have, in my own humble way, attempted to indicate the depth of my emotions. You are, in every way, a suitable wife for a man such as I—attractive, well-bred, capable of running a household, aware of the value of money, as well-read as most women of your station, and, even if this house is your only dowry, I am not such a small man as to quibble at its meagerness."

Marianne regarded him with astonishment, rapidly turning to annoyance, which she attempted to hide from his fatuous gaze only out of inherent politeness. "You honor me with such a proposal, Mr. Oldham, but I . . ."

There was a hasty knock on the door, followed by Mr. Geddes's excited voice. "May I speak with you, Miss Findlay?"

The difficulties of running a lodging house had never been so apparent to Marianne. Before calling to Mr. Geddes to enter, she firmly said, "Thank you, Mr. Oldham, but I cannot marry you."

He had no chance to reply before Mr. Geddes hastened into the room.

"I've worked it all out! Down to the very last detail! I'm sure you will see in a moment what a savings of time and energy it will be, Miss Findlay." Mr. Geddes stood before them, pink with pleasure under his rumpled wig, only vaguely aware that Mr. Oldham was frowning, that Miss Effington was roused abruptly from sleep, while Marianne herself was utterly ignorant of his meaning.

"What is it that you've worked out, Mr. Geddes?" Marianne asked calmly, a steadying hand to her aunt's elbow.

"A system of bell wires! Every room can be fitted with a pull, and there will be a board with bells on it in the servants' quarters. They will know in precisely what room they are wanted, because the bells will be numbered, and a pendulum will continue to vibrate after the bell stops ringing. Imagine such efficiency! And the larger the house, the greater savings in time. Why, I dare say it will eliminate the need for several people just standing around in the truly magnificent homes."

Marianne accepted the drawing he offered showing wires and cranks and various other items which he identified with obvious enthusiasm. "It's all very well to have a bell rope, Miss Findlay, though I realize that you don't, but this system is by far more intricate and useful."

"I can see that it is, Mr. Geddes, but in order to install it, the walls would have to be opened to run the wires through, a very expensive proceeding."

"Yes, I thought of that, but I've devised a method where the openings would be minimal. And I would be willing to bear the expense, of course, if you would let me have it installed to use as a model for demonstration. Well," he asked triumphantly, "what do you think?"

His audience responded in a variety of ways. Miss Effington snorted, Mr. Oldham wrung his hands with frustration, and Marianne smiled gently. "I will have to study the plan and the rooms and give it some thought, Mr. Geddes. Understand, I think it a marvelous idea, but mine may not be the appropriate house in which to test the scheme. May I keep the drawing until tomorrow morning?"

"Certainly! There is no need to make an immediate decision. I had just figured out how to keep the pendulum vibrating, and that was essential, you see. Otherwise, if the servants were occupied and couldn't get to the board immediately, they would have no way of knowing which bell had rung. We could, of course, have bells with various tones but you know, Miss Findlay, not everyone has an ear for such things. This is by far the better method, I think."

"I'm sure you're right, Mr. Geddes." As Aunt Effie struggled to her feet, Marianne rose with her and the gentlemen were dismissed, much to the old lady's satisfaction.

"Next time," her aunt grumbled, "you might choose lodgers who only show up here to sleep." Marianne didn't even consider telling her the worst of the evening's events.

Dissatisfied with the results of his first offer, Mr. Oldham hung about the lower hall for some time in the morning, in the hopes of catching a glimpse of Miss Findlay. He could not be content with her first answer; ladies were notoriously capricious, and the disturbance Mr. Geddes had caused was enough to shatter any woman's fragile nerves. Unsure as to whether or not Miss Findlay had risen yet, he did not wish to tap at the drawing room door, so, when she did not appear, he eventually took himself off, and had the good fortune to find a chair at the corner. Marianne allowed the curtain to fall back after seeing him depart, and with a sigh went in search of Mrs. Crouch, whose shopping expedition had been delayed on her employer's unaccountable insistence. Although she meant to accompany the cook, Marianne had no intention of encountering Mr. Oldham along the way. This was to be Aunt Effie's first expedition since her illness, and Marianne refused to have it marred.

After leaving Mrs. Crouch to see to her purchase, Marianne and Aunt Effie walked slowly up Stonegate past the silk mercers and linen drapers, the glove-makers and tailors. In the windows of apothecaries and perfumeries there were displayed tincture of pearls for removing freckles, and Eau de Charm for bathing the temples (or taking internally for palsy), pulvil powder in a rosewood box, and perfumed pomatum. At the Minster end of Stonegate, was Charles Pearson's where riding habits could be ordered—or clergymen's gowns. Marianne instinctively averted her eyes from the fetching costume on display, but her aunt caught the subtle movement and halted in the narrow street. "You need a new habit, my dear. This is as good a time as any to have one ordered."

"Whatever do I need a habit for? I haven't ridden in over a year."

"Then it's time you did. Are you coming?"

"We can't afford it, Aunt Effie."

"Of course we can. We now have two lodgers who more than meet the household expenses." Her aunt covertly lifted the spectacles and quickly observed the riding costume. "In green velvet it will suit you to perfection."

As the spectacles were whisked back into the folds of her aunt's handkerchief, Marianne smiled ruefully. "There are probably any number of things we need more, but I don't deny I should love to have something so elegant." She drew herself up sharply. "If we are going to spend money on clothing, a morning dress would be far more practical."

"Ridiculous," Aunt Effie snapped. "You've worked hard for the last year and you've earned something you *want*, not something you need. And perhaps it will induce you to hire a hack and get out into the countryside now and again."

"I can't ride alone, Aunt Effie."

"We can spare Roberts to ride with you. Lord, it's only a few shillings for some hacks." The old lady's mind was made up, and she stomped to the door, pushing it open with such vigor that the little bell jangled crazily. With less reluctance than she thought she should have felt, Marianne followed.

They emerged some little while later into the sunny street, Miss Effington smug, and Marianne's eyes sparkling with pleasure. In three days, the riding habit would be delivered to Micklegate and, after being fitted for the handsome, tailored coat and long, wide skirts, Marianne no longer felt the least compunction about purchasing it. Even the high-crowned hat with its plumes suddenly seemed a necessary extravagance. She could ride again. After the dim light of the shop, she blinked in the sunlight, only to find that they were being converged on from both directions, Dr. Thorne from their right, Lord Latteridge from their left. Marianne experienced a most unusual sensation, a feeling of panic. She had not told her aunt of the encounter with Lord Latteridge; had scarcely mentioned the rescue of the sailors, and although Dr. Thorne had called since, she had managed to keep discussion away from the incident itself, and on the progress of the wounded man.

Both gentlemen were doffing their hats and bowing to her, acknowledging one another and waiting for her to speak. "Lord Latteridge, I don't believe you've met my aunt, Miss Effington. Nor have you, perhaps, been properly presented to Dr. Thorne." Marianne ignored the glint in her aunt's eyes and the mutter of "Another Derwent." With polished grace, the earl also ignored the murmur, and made a handsome leg to the old woman, since she made no move to offer her hand. Dr. Thorne was amused by the encounter, and Marianne shrugged slightly in despair.

Under cover of the earl's polite inquiries as to Miss Effington's health, Dr. Thorne waved a hand at the shop they had come from and asked, "Are you to have a new riding habit from Pearson's?"

"Yes, a great indulgence for me."

"I'm glad to hear it, for now I shall have not the least hesitation in asking you to ride with me. Will you?"

Marianne was very aware that Lord Latteridge had overheard this request and was watching her thoughtfully, but before she could answer, her aunt interposed, "Well, of course she will. Marianne has been longing for a ride for ages, Dr. Thorne, and I have only but convinced her of the ease with which she can hire a hack. There must be half a dozen posting inns in York where they are available."

"There's no need for that." The earl's calm voice broke into their discussion without the least hesitation, or the least offense, as it was accompanied by a charming smile. "Our stables here are full of horses which need exercise—my brother is out of town and my sister has yet to arrive. I pray you will avail yourself of mounts at any time you may desire them."

It was an extraordinary offer, considering he was barely known to either of the potential riders. For a moment, he held Dr. Thorne's eyes with a kindly authority which allowed no refusal, and the young man grinned and said, "You are very generous, Lord Latteridge."

"Not at all. You would do me a favor. Perhaps Miss Findlay would allow me to accompany her occasionally as well."

Again the feeling of panic gripped Marianne, though there could be no possible reason for it. His friendly gray eyes were not insistent, nor his invitation pressing. In fact, it was hardly an invitation at all. One had only to say, "Thank you," and it could be interpreted in any way one chose. Why then did she find herself unable to say anything at all?

To her surprise he spoke as though she had answered him. "Good. The day after tomorrow at ten, shall we say? That will give Dr. Thorne a chance to take you riding tomorrow."

Dr. Thorne, apparently unmoved by this management of his affairs, nodded and remarked, "I should be finished with my rounds by one tomorrow, Miss Findlay. Will that be suitable?"

Uncertain, she protested, "My new habit won't be ready for three days."

"Wear an old one," he answered cheerfully, unperturbed. "I must see Mr. Boothe now. Tomorrow at one?"

"Very well." And he was gone, marching down the street with his springing step, not once turning to look back. Marianne watched until he turned the corner, unable to look at the earl, and feeling more stupid than she ever had in her life.

Aunt Effie's reaction to the scene was indecipherable. Although she could not object to the earl riding with her niece, and did not wish to object to Dr. Thorne doing so, there were other nuances which she did not understand, and was not sure she liked. Nonetheless, her sharp profile told nothing to her niece who stood inexplicably silent.

"If we are to meet Mrs. Crouch in good time, we will have to finish our errands, Marianne," she said with a nod to the earl. "I'm sure Lord Latteridge will excuse us."

"By all means. I shall call at ten on Saturday with a mount for you, Miss Findlay."

"Thank you." This time the words meant acceptance; she felt powerless to say anything else and saw his bow and departure with an uncommon detachment. What the devil was the matter with her?

Her aunt echoed this sentiment as she propelled Marianne toward the mercer's shop. "I never thought I'd see the day you stood quaking before a Derwent, child. If you didn't want to ride with him, you should have said so, but I thought you would show more spirit. Have you forgotten that his mother made a muddle of your life? Oh, I'm not saying it wasn't your father's fault to begin with, but her part was the more insidious. We could never have expected less of Sir Edward, loose screw that he is. And I say it even though my sister was married to him. You didn't act this way with the brother. Are you so stricken with awe for an earl? Or are you alarmed that he harbors his mother's opinion of you?"

"I don't know."

Miss Effington eyed her keenly. "How did you meet him? Through the brother?"

"No, he escorted me home from the promenade when Dr. Thorne had to see to his sailor-patients."

"And you never told me!"

"What was there to tell? He didn't realize who I was until we reached the door. I had no trouble talking with him then." Marianne absently fingered a length of lace on the counter before her. "I don't think Harry Derwent knew about my contretemps with his mother at all; perhaps his lordship doesn't, either."

"If he doesn't, he'll learn. His mother is due shortly in York, according to Mr. Vernham. If he makes you nervous, why didn't you refuse to ride with him?"

"I don't know, Aunt Effie," Marianne said hopelessly, as she picked up a spool of embroidery thread. "Will this do for your seat-cover? Have you the matching thread with you?"

"You can send a message that you won't be able to ride," persisted her aunt.

"No."

And Miss Effington found that her niece had no more to say on the subject.

11

Mr. Geddes was delighted to receive permission to place one bellpull in each of the three lodging units, provided he could obtain Mr. Oldham's permission regarding his rooms (which would obviously be disrupted by the installation). Mr. Oldham thought to ingratiate himself with his landlady by agreeing, and the work was begun, but he found that Roberts had instructions to prevent his routine evening visit to Miss Findlay and her aunt, by insisting that the ladies were not receiving. At this point, he would have enjoyed rescinding his permission, but there was a hole in his wall and he could not very well call a halt to the work. So he sulked and awaited an opportunity to approach Miss Findlay for a second time.

When Dr. Thorne called to take Marianne riding, there were two men working on the installation of a pull in her drawing room under Aunt Effie's fierce eyes. He pursed his lips and regarded the old lady wryly. "Do I detect the hand of Mr. Geddes in the current upheaval?"

"Very clever of you, Doctor." If her niece refused to use the proper tactics, Miss Effington was quite willing to make up for this oversight. "Marianne would be impressed by your shrewd guess. We are to have a system of bellpulls to call the servants. A simple brass bell on the table is not good enough for Mr. Geddes. Nor would a silver one be, presumably. No, no, one has to have a System. Daily we become a more Efficient household owing to that young man's persistent inventive genius."

Her sarcasm amused the doctor, and he laughed as she waved him to a seat. "Is Miss Findlay at home?"

"She has not forgotten that you are to take her riding and will be with you in a moment. What sort of horses are they?"

"Spirited but well-trained. Does your niece require a particularly gentle mount?"

Aunt Effie regarded him as though he had lost the small ground he had made with her. "Does she appear to you the sort of girl who needs a hobby horse, Dr. Thorne?"

"Not at all," he protested, his eyes dancing. Before he could attempt to reclaim ground, Marianne entered in an old blue habit hopefully adorned with a new fall of lace at the cuffs which she had, at her aunt's insistence, just completed attaching.

"I've kept you waiting, Dr. Thorne. Forgive me."

"I've had the pleasure of a little chat with Miss Effington," he replied with a grin, "and other than your own companionship, what more could a fellow ask?"

"Obviously nothing." Marianne bent to kiss her aunt's cheek. "We shan't be long, I imagine. If you need anything, Roberts and Beth are both here."

Miss Effington nodded her satisfaction. "I told you the lace would help. Don't hurry back on my account."

Knowing that Aunt Effie believed that the longer she spent with Dr. Thorne, the more likely he was to take an interest in her, Marianne laughed. "Very well, dear, but I shall be back to dine."

Satisfied, the old lady watched them smugly as they departed, the doctor informally attired in buckskin breeches and her niece, even in the old habit, quite a lovely sight. All the doctor needed was a little encouragement, Aunt Effie decided as she settled to her embroidery, and he would see the advantages of aligning himself with such a personable girl. If need be, Miss Effington was willing to make the supreme sacrifice—she would find some other relation to live with so they could start a married life alone. Of course, she did hope that would not prove necessary, but she was, for her niece's sake, resigned to the possibility.

Her disappointment would have been grave, had she been party to their discussion on that ride. Far from showing the slightest inclination to develop their friendship into something more lasting and intimate, the two participants, out from under her eye, squabbled like brother and sister on every matter, from the direction in which they should ride, to who was the more accomplished maker of cordials.

"You must realize, my dear Miss Findlay, that as an apothecary, as well as a surgeon, I am expert in the precise mixing of various ingredients. Do you, for instance, make your Barbados water only with orange and lemon peel?"

His expression clearly indicated that he was attempting to trick her, but she merely laughed. "I do, Dr. Thorne. Do you add some spice?"

"My Barbados water," he assured her with mock haughtiness, "is an old family receipt which is *never* divulged to anyone outside the family, excepting our servants, of course, who are usually the ones to actually make it. I shall bring some for you."

"Too kind," Marianne murmured with unconvincing humility. "You do have an advantage, I daresay, with all those jars and pots of outrageous herbs and spices. I came across a receipt for a cordial that called for wormwood, calamus-aromaticus and galingale, among any number of other exotic ingredients. It sounded more like a Pectoral Julep for easing a cough."

"And did you make it?"

"Heavens, no! I made a simple shrub instead, and it served very well."

"Unadventurous woman! Have you no desire to explore the mysteries of finer cordials?"

"Not if they use up all my red poppy seeds and saffron

root," she retorted. "Shall we cut cross-country to that stream?"

"You are mighty ambitious for a lady who hasn't been on horseback for some time," he protested. "Don't you think we should keep to the road?"

For an answer, she guided the bay mare onto the harvested field with a jaunty wave of her hand, and set the horse to the gallop. With an exasperated snort, the doctor took off after her, calling, "Your aunt will skin me if any harm comes to you."

"Pooh! I was practically raised on horseback, my good fellow, and it is the outside of enough to be expected to plod along some pitted dirt lane when we can have a good run. Aren't you up to it, Doctor?"

Their good-natured teasing lasted the whole of the ride, and when Marianne dismounted at the earl's stables, her cheeks were flushed with the exercise and enjoyment. As a groom led the little bay off she remarked, "What a lovely mare. Is she Lady Louisa's?"

"Yes, ma'am, though her ladyship's only had the animal a few months."

When Marianne turned back to Dr. Thorne, she found that Lord Latteridge had entered the stable and was regarding her with interest. "We wished to thank you, sir, for providing such splendid horses."

"You enjoyed the ride?"

"Immensely."

"That's excellent. Shall I bring the same mare when I call for you tomorrow?"

This was her opportunity to cancel their ride, if she chose, but she did not choose to do so. "Yes, if you would, my lord." She covertly studied his face as he spoke with Dr. Thorne, attempting in vain to analyze why the clear gray eyes and the deep, drawling voice so intrigued her. His casual attire was similar to Dr. Thorne's, and though his height was greater, there was nothing so strikingly different about the figures they presented, that one should have such

an effect on her and the other none at all, especially when
she was so entirely at ease with Dr. Thorne and so unnerv-
ingly disturbed by his lordship. Perhaps her aunt was right,
that she was conscious of the earl's status, or fearful of his
opinion. Neither seemed a logical explanation for her reaction, since such considerations had not previously concerned her in the least. Marianne found herself shaking
hands with Lord Latteridge before she had completely dispersed these thoughts, and refused to allow the decided
twinkle in his eyes to discompose her. On the other hand,
she could not have recounted later what Dr. Thorne discussed on their walk to her house.

The earl looked up from the letter he had just finished
reading, his lips pursed thoughtfully. "I won't be needing
you this morning, William, if you have business of your
own you'd like to attend to."

"Perhaps I'll call on Miss Sandburn and bring her to
Miss Findlay's. They appeared to enjoy one another's company."

"Miss Findlay, I hope, will not be at home this morning,"
his employer remarked. "If her aunt has not convinced her
otherwise, which I cannot be sure will not be the case, I am
to take her riding."

"You've met Miss Effington then?" There was a suspicion of amusement about the secretary's deferential face.

"A redoubtable woman. When I politely enquired as to
her health, she informed me that she had never been better,
and that the whole matter had been a tempest in a teapot. I
was also informed that the variety of peaches which we
sent could not compare with those grown at her old home
in Suffolk, but that possibly the pears were a similar variety, as they were passable. And of course she thanked me
for my concern."

"Of course." William shook his head wonderingly. "All
the same, I think I shall take Miss Sandburn there this
morning if I can dislodge her from Castlegate. She's made

a vast impression on the old lady by having seen the house in which she grew up."

"I wish you luck." Latteridge tapped the letter he had just set aside. "Susan explains the whole situation, William, and it's a most regrettable and, I would think for Miss Findlay, a most unforgivable, incident. Apparently she is Sir Edward Findlay's only child, and he had his heart set on a match with her cousin Percy Petrie, so that his estates could be kept in the family. Susan describes this fellow as," he lifted the letter once more and sought the proper place, "'a foppish, impertinent, good-for-nothing.' Although she accedes to his generally being considered handsome, she herself has always found him to be 'surly, vulgar, and disagreeable.' I wonder why that description sounds so familiar."

A clear picture of Sir Reginald Barrett rose in his mind, but William said only, "I wouldn't know, sir."

"Yes, well, never mind. It is Susan's understanding that Sir Edward Findlay arranged for his nephew to abduct his daughter, since she had expressed her unwillingness to have her cousin."

"Dear God."

"Just so. Miss Findlay was put into her father's coach after an evening at Ranelagh, only to find that her Aunt Effington, her chaperone, was excluded and Mr. Petrie to accompany her. Susan has no way of knowing what happened then, except that Miss Findlay obviously was not driven home as she should have been, and her father spent the evening at various gambling halls spreading the word of how clever he had been."

"What a despicable devil. He should have been thrown in gaol."

"His part is little worse than Mother's," the earl sighed. "Susan does not know how Miss Findlay—Marianne, she calls her—accomplished it, but the very next evening she was at Lady Wandesley's ball, with her aunts Petrie and Effington as chaperones. The very fact that her abductor's mother was with her should have stilled the gossip created by her father, of course, and it was a prodigiously sensible move on her part, I dare say, but Mother . . ." He clenched a quill so tightly that it snapped, and he laid it calmly on the desk top carefully aligned with two others. "You must understand, William, that my sister was about to become betrothed to Frederick Holmes, Lord Selby, and that my mother was very desirous that the match take place."

"For any particular reason?"

"The best, William," Latteridge murmured with an edge of sarcasm. "Not only was he titled, rich, and with considerable address, but his mother, too, was French."

"I see."

"Yes. Well, it seems Miss Findlay had known Lord Selby all her life, and they were very great friends. Susan thinks Mother feared that Selby was in love with Miss Findlay; that's the only explanation she can find for Mother's actions. When Miss Findlay arrived at the ball, Selby was with Susan but he made to go to her. Everyone was aware that they knew one another, and everyone was waiting to see how he would react when she entered. Mother forbade him to go to her; swore she would not allow his marriage to Susan if he consorted with . . . Well, you can imagine what she would have said. Susan, being Miss Findlay's friend, was defiant, but very much in love with Selby, and Mother reiterated her stand that they would not marry if either of them had anything more to do with Miss Findlay. So Susan and Selby stayed with Mother . . . and Miss Findlay was ruined."

"Was there no one else to come to her aid?" William asked incredulously.

"Mother held a powerful position in London in those days. We are speaking of eight years ago, William, when my father and I were on the continent and Mother, for her own amusement, swayed society at will. I don't know whether Miss Findlay could have braved the evening, but her Aunt Petrie, whom Susan calls a 'quivering jelly,' became hysterical at the intended snub and the whole party

left, never to make another attempt to reenter society.
Susan, against Mother's express orders, sent a note to her
friend the next day, but never heard from her."

"It must have taken a supreme amount of courage for
Miss Findlay to appear at that ball."

"Only to have her worst fears realized," Latteridge
sighed. "Susan is ashamed of her own part in the matter,
and after her marriage she attempted to get in touch with
Miss Findlay again, but she and her Aunt Effington had removed from their rented house in London, and Susan was
not able to trace them."

"They haven't been in York that long."

"No, I suppose they've been somewhere else in the
meantime." Latteridge rose and walked to the windows
which looked onto the courtyard. "Susan said Selby has
heard that Sir Edward intends to disinherit his daughter and
leave everything to Mr. Petrie."

"He outdoes your mother for vindictiveness," William
murmured so low that the earl barely heard him, but it was
merely an echo of his own thoughts and he nodded.

"Little wonder Miss Findlay and her aunt are alarmed
that my mother is coming to town. Do you know how Miss
Findlay came to own her house, William?"

"Only that she inherited it."

"Hmm. Susan says her mother had been dead since she
was a child. Some other relation left it to her, I suppose.
Well, I must be off. Give my regards to Miss Sandburn."

Miss Effington's reception of her niece's caller was not
nearly as cordial as it had been the previous day for Dr.
Thorne, but on this occasion, Marianne was ready in the
drawing room, of necessity dressed in the same blue riding
habit. When Latteridge accepted the offered chair, Aunt
Effie defended the room's chaotic condition in a rather belligerent tone. "We are having a bellpull system installed. A
very simple concept, and yet I dare say even the larger
country homes are still dependent upon a table bell."

"Ah, the young man who designed the self-propelling turnspit and the ingenious walking stick," he murmured.

"Mr. Geddes," Aunt Effie said grandly, "is a superbly clever young man. He does not fritter away his time over a bottle and a pack of cards, as any number of gentlemen of my acquaintance are wont to do."

Since it was evident that she longed to lump him with this category, Latteridge assumed a suitably grave countenance and uttered the one word, "Admirable."

"Your brother was quite taken with some of Mr. Geddes's inventions," Marianne offered by way of softening her aunt's acerbity.

"Yes, we have just acquired one of the turnspits, and Harry would not dream of going anywhere without his new walking stick."

Afraid that her aunt would find some further area of contention, Marianne rose. "We shouldn't keep the horses standing, Aunt Effie."

"I hope you won't be gone long," the old lady quavered, picking up her embroidery with an observably feeble hand.

Such a fine display of acting won Marianne's amusement and the earl's admiration, but neither made any attempt to reassure her as to how soon they would return. In the street, a groom stood patiently holding the reins, and Latteridge assisted Marianne onto her horse with a minimum of fuss. There was no discussion of where they should head; the earl did not ask her preference, and she did not offer it.

When they had passed from the built-up area into a quiet country lane, Latteridge left off his comfortable social chatter to turn to her with a more serious countenance. "I had a letter from my sister Susan this morning."

"How is she?"

"Fine. They all are—Lord Selby and the children, too. I had written her because Harry and William both seemed to think there was some . . . problem between my family and yours. I didn't know of it."

"It was a very long time ago," Marianne said softly, as

she watched a hawk glide through the shimmering blue sky above.

"Susan is still distraught about it. She said she wrote to you afterward but never heard from you."

Marianne swung back to face him, a tiny frown between her eyes. "I never had her letter, but I did write to her, telling her that ... well, that I understood. It was enough, knowing that they wished to help."

"Selby considered himself honor-bound by his word to Mother; Susan, knowing her a great deal better, did not. I suppose Mother contrived to interfere with the delivery of both your letters. She has a great deal to answer for."

"Pray don't concern yourself over the matter, Lord Latteridge. I tried to make your brother realize that I feel the past best forgotten. Not that it will be particularly comfortable when Lady Latteridge arrives in York," she sighed. "Ironic, is it not, that we should so long after be such close neighbors?"

"How do you come to have the house in Micklegate?" He shrugged away the question. "That is none of my business, of course."

But Marianne chose to answer. "My Aunt Petrie died a year and a half ago and left it to me. Her son was livid, of course, but it's such a negligible property and he has such glowing prospects of my father's estates ..." A rueful smile appeared. "Aunt Petrie was my father's half-sister and *her* father had bought it as a speculation—because it was next door to the Earl of Latteridge's York house! And I must say, the prestige of such a location was a decided factor in my lodger, Mr. Oldham, choosing to live there. So you see, it *has* proved worthy of its object, if not quite in the way he expected."

"Are you in communication with your father?"

"No. That is, I write him twice a year and the letters don't come back, but I never hear from him. Don't tell Aunt Effie that I write. She wouldn't understand."

"I'm not sure that *I* do," he retorted. "You realize that he probably tears them up, if he is so lost to all feeling as to have treated you the way he did."

"Probably. That doesn't matter so much, though. Even if he doesn't read them, he knows that I've written. And although he thinks he hates me for ruining all his plans, there are those times from long ago which I can't believe he can forget so easily—trotting along beside my first pony, clinging to me when my mother died, presenting me with my first dress without leading strings." Marianne smiled sadly. "I will not perpetuate a family feud, Lord Latteridge. Not in my family *or* yours. So by all means convey my deepest affection to Lady Susan and Lord Selby, and by no means mention the matter to your mother."

He was watching her with troubled eyes and did not speak for some time. When his horse shied at a leveret dashing across the lane, he quickly brought the animal under control and reached a hand for her bridle, but the mare was unmoved by such activity and merely tossed her head. Finally, he said, "You must resent what Mother did."

"Certainly I do. Aside from my father's part in the affair, I consider her conduct the most odious I've ever encountered." But there was no heat to her words, and she made a negligent gesture with her hand. "My lord, if I allowed such things to eat away at me, I would be destroyed, consumed by anger and despair. Wherein is the usefulness of that?" A little chuckle escaped her. "Absurdities have become a special *divertissement* of mine, the abberation I have developed from the whole misadventure. Aunt Effie doesn't understand that either, not completely, but she makes a wonderful companion with her biting tongue and blunt approach to life. She may not laugh at the absurdities she sees, but she certainly remarks them."

"And your cousin Petrie doesn't bother you?"

"Why should he? He can inherit from my father without all the bother of marrying me. I think, though," she mused, "that if he were to marry someone else, my father might be given a jolt. Still, Percy has never shown any inclination to marry, and he now has his father's estate, so I doubt if that worries him."

"Is your aunt the only relation you have other than your father and cousin?"

"The only close one. I have some distant cousins in Hampshire."

Latteridge's face was unreadable when Marianne turned to smile at him, in an effort to alleviate the seriousness of their discourse. He was weighing the merits of offering her some assistance, divided by the knowledge that she would refuse it, and the certainty that his mother's actions had, as much as her father's, brought her to the pass in which she now struggled. As though she could read his thoughts, her frank eyes clouded and she turned away. With a mental shrug he dismissed the problem for the time being. "Shall we have a run, Miss Findlay? Trooper is itching to stretch his legs."

12

The cavalcade which arrived bearing Lady Latteridge and her household, included liveried outriders and postilions, two carriages in addition to that in which she rode, and mountains of luggage strapped to each. When William informed the earl that the carriages were arriving, Latteridge promptly presented himself at the front door where his sister, oblivious to her mother's scowl, rushed up to hug him, murmuring, "You will be *so* pleased with our news! Sophia Everingham was unable to accompany us, owing to having a bilious attack yesterday."

"I hope it is nothing serious," the earl pronounced solemnly, as his mother was handed down from the carriage and stiffly joined them.

"Most unfortunate," the Dowager proclaimed, allowing him to place a salute on her worn cheek. "On the other hand, it is better to know beforehand if a woman is inclined to be sickly. I don't hold with illness myself."

Her companion, Madame Lefevre, grunted, her black eyes darting contempt until they came to rest on Lady Louisa. The affection she held for the young lady never failed to compensate for her days of trial as the Dowager's companion, and was probably the only reason she remained at her post. She gave a curt nod to the earl, who acknowledged it with faint amusement, and bundled her charges into the house with a lack of ceremony nicely calculated to raise the Dowager's ire, without being exceptional enough to call for a rebuke.

Lady Latteridge looked about the hall with a critical eye, in an attempt to find something or someone out of place, but all was in order, and precisely as she had left it the last time she came to York. As luck would have it, however, a footman coming out of the dining parlor, swung the door wide to allow for his burden of a large silver epergne, and she caught a glimpse of the new wallpaper, only just completed. With an agitated finger she pointed accusingly to the room. "What have you done with the dining parlor? That is not what I had on the walls."

Her family obediently trooped behind her as she stalked to the door, flung it wide with a dramatic gesture, and glared on the improvements. "Well?" she demanded, her piercing eyes on her eldest son. "What is the meaning of this?"

Unmoved by her belligerent attitude, Latteridge surveyed the completed work with satisfaction. "Don't you like it, Mother? Due to an unfortunate accident, it was necessary to replace the wallpaper, and, though I regretted the necessity, I am perfectly content with the results."

"It was the servants!" she declared, ready to launch into a tirade.

"Not at all. A rather boisterous supper party, I'm afraid. Come, you must be tired from your journey. Let Madame Lefevre show you to your room."

"I know where my room is!" she grumbled, but permitted her companion to lead her from the room and up the stairs, where she called from the head, "Come along, Louisa."

"I'll be up in a moment, Mama." Louisa made no attempt to move from where she stood until her mother had disappeared from view, and then she linked her arm with her brother's. "She's very annoyed with Sophia for succumbing to this illness, Press. She had great plans for Miss Everingham."

Latteridge regarded his sister's twinkling eyes and said with suspect gravity, "Yes, I thought as much. Are you as eager as Mother to see me married, Louisa?"

"Not to Sophia Everingham! In fact, not at all, unless you are so inclined, my dear."

"I went to visit a number of county families once Mother put the idea in my head," he confessed as he seated her in the library. "A glass of wine?"

"Thank you, no. Who did you visit?"

"Haxby, Condicote, Winscombe, Tremaine, and Horton."

Louisa gave a gurgle of laughter. "Poor Press. Were you *aux anges* with Sarah Winscombe?"

"I'd forgotten what you told me of her fan trick," he retorted mournfully, "but it is Clare Horton you will have to contend with. She's come to town."

"Oh, Press, how could you? Well, it will do her not the least good to flutter her devout eyes in Mama's presence; Mama cannot abide her."

"You relieve me." For a long moment he was silent, his eyes abstracted, as he regarded the elegantly wrought standish on his desk. "Louisa, does the name Marianne Findlay mean anything to you?"

"Lord, yes." The girl stared at him wonderingly for a moment. "Susan was so wretched over the whole affair. I was very young at the time, but she confided the entire story to me in her distress, and over the years she has recalled the name in her letters, always saying she could not discover what had become of her friend. I'm surprised you should ask; you were abroad when it all happened."

"She lives next door."

"Here? Have you met her? Do you know what happened?"

"Yes, I wrote to Susan and had her answer a few days ago. Miss Findlay's father has obviously abandoned her and she lives with an aunt, Miss Effington. In order to make ends meet, she takes lodgers. I've been riding with her."

"Have you?" This simple statement seemed of no little interest to Louisa, and her bright eyes scanned his handsome face searching for further enlightenment. "I remember her, you know. What would I have been—ten? She was very kind to me and once brought a little doll for my collection. Will you take me to see her?"

"Certainly, but I would prefer Mother didn't know of her presence unless it's unavoidable. Our esteemed parent is unlikely to reverse her previous position, and I feel that Miss Findlay has suffered quite enough at her hands."

"Indeed yes." Louisa rose and brushed out her crumpled skirts, not meeting his eyes. "Do you like her, Press?"

"Yes, my dear, I do. Bear in mind, though, that in spite of her generous attitude toward Harry and me, she has suffered a great injustice from our family. And her aunt," he said dryly, "never forgets for a moment."

Aunt Effie had been gratified when Dr. Thorne called. The romance, she felt, was progressing well, when one considered that Dr. Thorne was a busy medical practitioner and could not call every day. Feeling that she could not, with propriety, withdraw and leave the young people alone, she nonetheless dropped out of their conversation and pointedly busied herself with the fringe she was knotting. The intrusion of Mr. Vernham and Miss Sandburn was, in her opinion, superfluous and uncomfortable; there were not enough chairs. Their guests seemed unaware of any awkwardness, and Miss Effington had at last decided that the best approach was to hurry them off as soon as possible, when the Earl of Latteridge and Lady Louisa Derwent were announced. She fixed them with glowering eyes.

Having a room full of standing guests was not Marianne's idea of a proper way to entertain, but she had sent Roberts in search of chairs from the bedrooms, and she was enchanted to see Lady Louisa grown from a child into a young woman. "How kind of you to call, Lady Louisa! I *think* I would have known you on the street, but there is a vast change in eight years."

Louisa approached with outstretched hands and clasped Marianne's warmly. "When Press told me you were living here, I could hardly believe my good fortune, Miss Findlay. I have not forgotten your goodness to me when I was but a child."

"I remember the time you stomped into the back parlor wearing Lady Susan's finest hat and announced you were the Princess of Ackton Towers, and nothing would do but for us to address you as 'Your Highness' for the whole of the afternoon," Marianne laughed. "Let me introduce you to my aunt and our friends."

Though Miss Effington was disarmed by Lady Louisa's youthful spirits and almost shy acceptance of the introduction, the old lady was ever-mindful that this was yet another Derwent of whom to be wary, and her greeting was gruff. And not even Marianne's admonitory shake of the head could make her more than civil to Lord Latteridge, who accepted her brusqueness with equanimity. As Roberts brought in more chairs, Lady Louisa was seated beside Janet, with Dr. Thorne standing at her side. Latteridge was making polite conversation with Miss Horton's cousin, and Louisa fell into a discussion with the cheerful medical man.

"How did you choose to practice in York, Dr. Thorne?" she asked, ever inquisitive as to people's motives.

"I was raised near Good. London is fascinating but overrun with the products of their medical training, who are forever scratching at one another to get ahead in their profession. York has more need of practitioners and there's not such rugged competition." His grin lit the cherub face with self-mockery. "I enjoy being prominent as well as the next man, and it is a great deal easier to do here than in London."

"When I was in London as a child I loved the continual racket—everyone ringing bells and hawking ribbons and hot pies, fresh spring water and quack medicines. I bought a charm from an old crone who promised that it would make me the most beautiful woman in the world if I wore it around my neck for five years." She giggled. "It fell apart after five days!"

"Nonetheless, it seems to have worked," he teased, meeting the gray eyes with appreciation, but instantly turning the subject. "Have you been to the theater or the Assembly Rooms?"

"Not yet; we've only just arrived. Years ago I went to see a pantomime at the theater here, but everyone took to singing 'God Save the King,' and we missed the farce entirely. I was frightfully disappointed."

Dr. Thorne grinned at her. "That's nothing. When I was in London at St. George's, we made a party to go to the Haymarket Theater one evening, being the going-away party for a young surgeon who had joined the navy, Mr. Thomas Denman. Unfortunately, we had all drunk deep at the Devil Tavern beforehand, and the tragedy was most appalling, where an uncle killed his niece in the very first act. One gentleman of our party cried stoutly for the watch, when the uncle hired a highwayman to kill the niece's gentleman friend, and in leaning over the box, my friend's wig slipped onto the stage. The audience glared on us, but the fellow merely wrapped the curtain about his head and went to sleep. Alas, when he woke he took someone's cane to fetch the wig, his head being chilly, you see, but as luck would have it, he accidentally caught the ghost's robe and it fell off. The little actress who played the ghost was dressed only in a shift and the common folk and gentry made quite a whooping."

"You're quizzing me," Louisa protested, her eyes dancing.

"Not a bit. The highwayman was furious, and crossed the stage to shake his fist at my friend, who rose to make a leg and apologize to the actress, but being foxed, he pitched right onto the stage and the highwayman caught him on the seat of his breeches and tossed him into the orchestra where he broke a cello and a fiddle. Another friend, St. Clair, haloos and jumps onto the stage to fight the highwayman, giving him such a blow that he crashed into the scenery and brought the moon down—it being only a lantern hanging from the ceiling. Then everything became confusion."

"I don't wonder," Louisa murmured.

"Blumenfield popped onto the stage to comfort the actress and she scratched him; the audience set upon us, though the gentry rose in our defense, having to do battle not only with the actors, but the carpenters and workmen of the theater. The fellow who started it all retrieved his wig and fought back with the broken cello, but we were all eventually landed in the gutter outside the theater."

Dr. Thorne finished his tale to the delight of the whole company (not least Miss Effington), who had all turned their attention to him when Lady Louisa had succumbed to giggles. "And did your friend get to the navy after all the excitement?" she inquired in an unsteady voice.

"Lord, yes. After all the gruesome sights we saw, that was but a bit of letting go."

"What sort of things did you see?"

Dr. Thorne shifted uncomfortably from one foot to the other; he could not very well tell her of the grisly amputations and the long hours of dissections. "Working in the hospitals is rather harrowing."

"Yes," Louisa said thoughtfully, "I can see that it would be." She could also see that several eyes were on her, alarmed that she would pursue her line of questioning, so she pulled the discussion back to the York Theater, determined that in the future, she would question Dr. Thorne further when she was not in a position to upset a group of people by his, hopefully frank, answers.

Meanwhile, the earl had managed to gain Miss Findlay's attention, noting that the new bellpull with its center of enameled roses, apparently was complete. "Is the system working?"

Marianne bit her lip to stifle the chuckle which bubbled in her. "Well, after a fashion, my lord. We were to test it last evening, and sure enough, when I pulled it Roberts appeared. Unfortunately, Mr. Geddes had planned to test it at just the same moment and Beth answered his call. But there was a crossover of wires to the bell board, so that it was Mr. Oldham's bell which showed, and when Beth went in response, without knocking of course, she found him . . . ah . . . quite unprepared for her entrance." Marianne's eyes danced wickedly. "I'm afraid Mr. Oldham may not stay here long."

"Very embarrassing, I'm sure," he agreed solemnly. "And such a pity, with the dual enticements of a baronet and an earl next door."

"He is sadly torn," she admitted, thinking of Mr. Oldham's blustering fury, tempered by his profuse protestations that he did not hold her to blame. Beth had stood giggling in the lower hall, whispering to Roberts that Mr. Oldham wore pads on his calves to give his spindly legs the proper appearance in his elegant clocked stockings, and Mr. Geddes, all apologies, had attempted to placate his neighbor by interesting him in one of his clever walking sticks. Aunt Effie muttered of newfangled contraptions, and Mr. Oldham through it all, attempted to maintain his dignity so that Miss Findlay would recognize what a worthy man he was, though he had the most dire suspicions that the maid would inform her employer about his calf pads. All in all, it had been a very entertaining evening.

"And is the bell system sorted out now?" Latteridge asked.

"I hope so. It's a simple system for us, only the three rooms connected to the board. I'm sure Mr. Geddes would like to try a more expansive setup, but ours is not the house in which to do it, I think." She regarded him questioningly.

A faint smile touched his lips and made his subsequent sigh not quite martyred enough. "We have his self-propelling turnspit, I suppose we might invest in a bellpull system as well. Can I meet this ingenious young man? Harry seems to feel he has a brilliant career ahead of him."

Marianne stepped to the fireplace and pulled the lever before answering him. "Roberts can tell us if he's in his rooms. I'm sure he'd be delighted to meet you. Having such a system is remarkably useful, you know. One needn't have footmen stationed all over the house listening for the tinkling of bells from obscure little rooms."

"Actually, we haven't any obscure little rooms; they are all obscure large rooms," he complained, taking a watch from his pocket. "Shall I see how quickly he answers?"

But Roberts was already entering the room, and Marianne threw the earl an "I told you so" look before addressing the footman. "Is Mr. Geddes at home?"

"Yes, ma'am."

"Would you ask if he could join us here?"

When the footman had disappeared, Latteridge pointed out his other objection. "I have already had to find other work for the skipjack; he is to be Louisa's page. What am I to do with a lot of useless footmen?"

"Oh, dear, I hadn't thought of that. We are so understaffed that the system simply makes things easier for our people. Forgive me for pressing the matter, my lord. I have no wish to see your footmen lose their employment." Despite the stab of guilt Marianne suffered, she could not resist adding just one observation. "I should think, though, that footmen who simply wait about in the halls without any other duties would be bored to death."

"We try to vary the men at their posts. Mornings polishing silver, or delivering messages, afternoons waiting in halls. That sort of thing."

"I see. Well, we needn't mention the bell system to Mr. Geddes. Perhaps you could find something kind to say about the turnspit." Her voice was questioning, and once again she felt paralyzed under his intent gray eyes.

"The cook is more than satisfied with it, and delighted not to have a mischievous little boy underfoot. I'm sure . . ."

He broke off when Roberts held the door for Mr. Geddes, his wig slightly askew as always and rather nonplussed to find so many people in the drawing room. Marianne beckoned him with a smile and presented the earl, who, to her astonishment, not only praised the turnspit, but inquired as to the possibility of Mr. Geddes devising a bellpull system for his house. The inventor waxed enthusiastic about the potential savings for such a large establishment, and the earl made no demur. There was even a hint that if the operation was successful in Micklegate, Ackton Towers might profit from a similar installation. Marianne watched bemusedly as the young man departed, intoxicated by the instant success of his scheme so that he seemed not to notice the curious glances of the other people in the room; it was unlikely that he remembered the presence of others at all.

Latteridge touched Marianne's hand to regain her attention. "Will you ride with me tomorrow?"

"But . . . but Lady Louisa is here to ride her mare."

"I'm sure we have sufficient horses to mount both of you. Will you ride with me?"

It was curiously difficult to think of any reason to refuse him. "Yes, thank you. I should like that."

13

Although the earl had left his card at the Hortons' house in Castlegate one morning while Clare and her mother were out shopping, he had not been again to call on them, and Clare was struggling with fits of jealousy because her cousin had several times been escorted on a walk by Mr. Vernham. She was also vaguely suspicious about the timing of the earl's call, as she had herself caught a glimpse of him in Coney Street while they were out, and felt he might have known that they could not possibly have been back in Castlegate by eleven o'clock when the footman, interrogated, had said he made his visit. Nonetheless, the very fact that he had left his card, gave her the opportunity, she felt, to pay a return visit, when his mother and sister were in town, of course. So she waylaid Janet on her return from her walk with Mr. Vernham, determined to find out precisely when the Dowager was to arrive.

"Why, they came to town yesterday," Janet admitted.

"Did Mr. Vernham tell you so?"

"He said they were here and then I met Lady Louisa."

"You *met* Lady Louisa?" Clare almost squeaked. "Where?"

"At Miss Findlay's home." Janet was not at all sure she wished to impart the information, but it was awkward to avoid her persistent cousin's questions.

"And just who is Miss Findlay?"

"A neighbor of Lord Latteridge's."

Clare raised a haughty brow. "*I* have never heard of her. Is she an old lady?"

"No, though she is some years older than I."

A horrid suspicion that the earl might be interested in someone else crossed Clare's mind. "Was Lord Latteridge with his sister?"

"Yes."

"And his mother?"

"No, just the two of them."

"It is high time Mama and I called on Lady Latteridge if she has been in town two days. How remiss she will think us! You should have told me sooner."

"I didn't know," Janet said softly.

It was obvious from Clare's cold stare that she did not believe her cousin, and she had a good mind to urge Lady Horton to disallow Janet's excursions with Mr. Vernham, but prudence restrained her. Lord Latteridge might take offense, and Clare wanted nothing less. Her mother, although sympathetic to her desire to visit Lady Louisa as soon as possible, protested fatigue, and promised to accompany her daughter the very next day. Janet was not invited to accompany them.

For the occasion, Clare had her hair dressed *à la Pompadour*, and wore a white satin gown with muslin puffs and muslin full-hanging sleeves, a white bead stomacher, and a white satin hat with feathers. Satisfied that she looked the picture of sophisticated innocence, she pinned a ruby-colored rose bud on her gown to add just the right touch of seductive appeal, for it was her firm conviction that although men admired freshness above all else, they liked the illusion of passion only slightly less. Lady Horton was almost as pleased with the results as Clare herself, and it was the greatest possible disappointment to both of them to find that Lord Latteridge was not at home with his mother and sister.

As Louisa had told her brother, Lady Latteridge did not like Clare Horton. That might, in fact, be a mild way to state her feelings toward the girl, whom Madame Lefevre had heard her refer to one occasion as "that prissy hypocrite," but the Dowager was conscious of the necessity of receiving at least one call from the Hortons, and felt she might as well endure it now as later. Given sufficient opportunity, she could easily wound the sensibilities of both mother and daughter so that they dared not enter her sanctum again, a plan she was considering when Clare, with a forced laugh (she had been practicing), brought the visit to a climax when it had hardly begun.

"My dear Lady Louisa, your brother has given me the most delightful report of your progress, and here I find you quite grown into a lady. I understand you met my cousin Janet yesterday at Miss Findlay's house. And she never said a word about how fashionable you have become! I remember you as the veriest hoyden." Here Clare paused to offer an arch lift of her brows before continuing her flattery, but to her horror, Lady Latteridge, ostensibly attending to Lady Horton's diatribe on the merits of close proximity to a felon's prison, interrupted her with a bark of awesome fury directed at her daughter.

"Miss Findlay? Miss Findlay? Which Miss Findlay, Louisa?"

The girl lifted her chin and fearlessly met her mother's eyes. "Susan's friend Marianne, Mama. She now resides in York."

"And you dare to tell me that you have visited her?" snapped the Dowager.

Not wishing to quibble, Louisa said simply, "Yes."

"Never! You are never to do so again! Do you hear me? I will not have you call on that loose woman!"

Clare was drinking in every syllable as though her life depended on it, but now Louisa answered coldly, "You know that is not the truth, Mother. It is owing to your twisted planning that Miss Findlay has suffered ignominy, and for absolutely no purpose at all. Press took me to see her, and I intend to call again."

"I absolutely forbid you to do so," Lady Latteridge roared.

"Discuss the matter with Press, Mama. He is my guardian and if he feels I should not call, I will not."

"He could not have taken you there knowing the situation."

"But he does. He has had a letter from Susan, explaining."

"And what did she know? She was a child at the time! Oh, she wanted her Selby, but she would not look to her own interests."

Louisa, very aware of the two Hortons listening with goggling eyes and fervent enthusiasm, put an end to the argument. "I won't discuss the matter further, Mama. You must take it up with Pressington."

Complete silence fell over the group. Clare was too immersed in the ramifications of the scene to offer a word of social chatter and her mother, having considered Lady Latteridge's uncompromising anger, felt too inhibited to do so. Madame Lefevre smiled benignly on the stunned party and made no effort to restore peace. Eventually Louisa herself attempted to breach the gap with a few questions as to race and assembly dates, but the responses she received from the Hortons were hushed and incomplete, as though they were afraid to break in on the Dowager's magnificent wrath. Shortly they excused themselves, and Louisa slipped from the room with them in order to avoid a further confrontation with her mother.

During the acrimonious dispute, Lord Latteridge was himself riding with the object of Lady Latteridge's scorn, though his mother had no inkling that this was the case. Louisa had made no objection to his taking the mare for Marianne, had in fact pressed him to do so whenever he chose. The riders made their way along the Ouse until it joined with the Foss, the aroma of late summer wafting over the water and the last of the fields being harvested. In

a farmyard to their right, a young man fed a sow and her litter, while the dairymaid sat in an improvised shade milking
the cows. Beyond, two children carried mugs of home-
brewed beer to the haymakers, as the farmer surveyed their
work from the back of a plodding nag, a puppy scurrying at
its heels. The sun glared down on the peaceful scene, only
the swish of scythes and the occasional murmur of voices
floating on the still air. Though Marianne had received her
new riding habit, she had not worn it, owing to the heat of
the day; it was almost too hot to ride comfortably.

Their way took them from the river, and after awhile they
entered the cool of a small wood. Even under the wide-
brimmed bonnet, Latteridge could see that her face was
flushed with the heat, so he suggested that they dismount
and rest for a while by the stream, sparkling where arrows
of sunlight pierced the trees and danced chaotically on the
ripples of water. The spot was enchanting, but secluded,
and Marianne studied his face for a moment before nod-
ding.

With the aid of his hand, she swung herself off the mare,
and while he tethered the horses to a tree, she walked to the
bank of the stream. Her face still prickled with the heat, so
she reached down to dip her handkerchief in the rushing
water. The wide skirts of her habit hampered her and she
felt a steadying hand on her shoulder.

"Allow me." Taking the tiny linen square from her, he
shook his head wonderingly as he dipped and wrung it out.
"It is a source of amazement to me that ladies find the least
usefulness in such a tiny bit of cloth."

When she had seated herself on a flat stone, he returned
the handkerchief and settled himself beside her, his knees
drawn up, and his hat discarded, watching the stream as she
patted at her flushed cheeks. "I'm not ordinarily so affected
by the heat," she said apologetically, slipping the damp
handkerchief up her sleeve.

"You probably don't get outdoors enough."

"Of course I do. Aunt Effie and I walk about town frequently."

"Which precludes a brisk pace, and truly fresh air. York is better than London, I grant you, but one has to get out of town altogether to enjoy smoke-free air. Think about it, Miss Findlay—butcher shops with their refuse, rotting vegetables in the market, sea coal fires on every hearth, litter from horses, cows, sheep, goats, dogs . . ."

"I don't want to think about it," Marianne protested, laughing. "I live in town and try to make the best of it."

"But you were raised in the country and are accustomed to a more congenial air."

"There are off-setting virtues to town life; its convenience, its diversions, the access to company."

"Have you many friends in York?"

Marianne withdrew the handkerchief and patted once again at her cheeks. "Not so very many, I suppose. The Whixleys—you wouldn't know them—and Dr. Thorne, and a few others. We've only been here a bit over a year, you see, and have spent most of our time getting the house in order . . . to take lodgers," she finished, almost defiantly.

"Do you go to the theater and the assemblies?"

His curious gaze disconcerted her and she traced the embroidered "M" on the handkerchief. "The theater, yes; the assemblies, no."

"Why not?"

"Why do you suppose?" she asked rather sharply, exasperated.

"I haven't the faintest idea. Tell me."

He was lounging there so comfortably that she wished to shock him out of his lazy mockery. "Because I'm a social outcast, Lord Latteridge."

Undaunted, he opened his drooping eyes wider to determine to what extent she really believed what she had said. "Are you? What constitutes a 'social outcast' in your eyes, Miss Findlay?"

"For a lady, a damaged reputation. Mine is irretrievably damaged."

"And yet you didn't seem to think so when you attended Lady Wandesley's ball."

"You know very well that was a trial. If I had been acquitted . . . But I was not."

Latteridge noted the slight tightening of her lips, nothing else. Absently, he picked up a pebble and tossed it into the stream. "That was eight years ago, and this is York, not London." His voice was almost impatient.

"Do you think I lack the courage to face them?" Her eyes flashed momentarily, then shrank before his. "Perhaps I do. There is always someone who remembers, some tenacious, sordid memory stored away, ready to be recalled. And then the clusters of whispering groups, the hostile eyes. You see, after Aunt Effie and I retired to Hampstead, I thought time might heal the damage. Four years we waited, years that seemed an eternity to me . . . but not to one old roué. We attended an assembly there and this . . . gentleman approached me for a dance. His countenance betrayed his knowledge, his *hopes*, I might even say. I refused him. Within the hour I was the object of every eye in the room and the Master of Ceremonies was approaching. I would not suffer that final disgrace, and we left. How can you think it would be different here, especially since your mother has come to town?"

"It wouldn't be different, I dare say," he murmured, "but wouldn't you like to face them all down?"

"To what purpose? Just to prove that I've developed a skin thick enough to ignore their horrified gazes?" Marianne rose and paced along the grassy bank. "I don't think you understand, my lord. What others think of me is of little concern. *I* know the truth. That is enough. Usually. I have no desire to make other people uncomfortable. My attendance at an assembly would be upsetting not to the gossips, who would find it delightful conversation for weeks, but to those who sincerely believe that my presence is a threat to the moral tone of society." She read his amusement where he still sat following her progress with his eyes and said sternly, "It is no laughing matter. If young girls entering society saw that their elders made no distinction between the virtuous and the . . . the impure, where would be the incentive to lead a moral life?"

The earl attempted valiantly to keep a straight face, but he was not successful. First his lips twitched, then his shoulders shook, and finally, the wicked man, he burst out laughing. Marianne, hands on hips, stood before him, glaring uncompromisingly on his unseemly mirth. But her outrage had no effect on him; he merely laughed the harder. When he at last gained a measure of control over his mirth, he rose to his feet and Marianne turned away from him, embarrassed by the delight still dancing in his eyes.

"My dear Miss Findlay," he said to her stiff back, "don't you see how ludicrous it is for you to take such a stand? A lady falsely accused of immorality refuses to go out in society because her supposed immorality might lead others astray?"

"It's true, nonetheless," she retorted fiercely, though she allowed him to turn her around and stood breathlessly still when he did not remove his hands from her shoulders.

"I think you have allowed your sense of humor to desert you on this point," he told her seriously, surveying the wary face before him. "Or are you only able to see the absurdities of your companions, and not yourself?"

Stung, she shrugged away his hands. "I don't consider people's enthusiasms to be absurdities, and I assure you that I don't take myself any more seriously than those around me. There is a substantial difference, however, in contemplating such little oddities as I may previously have mentioned, and the situation we are now discussing. You would not have introduced your sister Louisa into my home had you believed me to be a wanton woman, would you?"

In spite of himself, the earl could not resist grinning. He was aware of her earnest gravity, but such words as "impure" and "wanton" issuing from her lips was too much to be borne. "I had no idea there was this streak of propriety in you, Miss Findlay. Much sooner would I have supposed you wouldn't care a fig for such things as appearances."

His choice of words was not perhaps felicitous. Although his only intention had been to tease her out of her rigid if estimable stand, Marianne regarded him with owlishly disbelieving eyes. "Just what is it you *do* believe about me, Lord Latteridge?" She could not resist glancing quickly past him to where the horses stood.

"For God's sake, don't be a goose! I'm not Sir Reginald! Have I not told you that Susan wrote to me? I promise you I consider your virtue beyond question."

Marianne drew herself up to her most dignified height. "And what does Sir Reginald believe?"

"Who cares what the devil he believes?" Latteridge responded with asperity, annoyed with himself for such a careless slip.

"I care, of course. Not about what he thinks, but about what he says. Is he spreading malicious gossip about me in York?"

Latteridge shook his head uncertainly. "I really don't know. You annoyed him over the explosion, and he has twice tried to denigrate you to me. Whether he does so with others . . ."

"Well, of course he does. Have you ever met one of his kind who didn't use their meager mental powers to find fault with anyone who dared to cross him?" Marianne frowned. "How does he happen to know about what happened so long ago?"

"He doesn't. He based his suppositions on your taking lodgers."

"With Aunt Effie in the house?" she asked incredulously.

"I don't think he's met your aunt." Latteridge observed with satisfaction the delightful dimple that emerged when she chuckled.

"Ah, well, that explains it. Perhaps I should arrange for

him to make my aunt's acquaintance. That would repay him
for his scandalous conclusions."

"A very wise precaution," the earl murmured as he
straightened her disarranged bonnet. "Will you allow me to
escort you to the next assembly?"

"Thank you, no. I realize you would like to undo what
has been done, but it's not possible, my lord. I'm quite content as things are. At my age, and with my new occupation,
assemblies are a thing of the past in any case. Sometimes
we have a dance at the Whixleys, you know, and among
friends . . . Your sister is the one you will be escorting, and
nothing should stand in the way of her enjoying her introduction to society."

"She would be only too pleased to share the occasion
with you."

Marianne shook her head. "Nonsense. And even if she
were, your mother . . . Well, there is no need to say how
your mother would react."

"I am more than capable of seeing that my mother be-
haves properly," he said shortly.

"Are you? Yes, I believe you are. But my answer stands,
Lord Latteridge." She turned aside from him then and went
to the mare. "Shall we go?"

"Of course." When he had handed her onto the mare, she
asked his opinion of the shaky nature of the current government, and whether he expected to see a change of administration. He had no choice but to go along with the change
of subject.

14

Lady Louisa had intended to waylay her brother on his return to prepare him for their mother's latest storm, but she had ducked into the kitchens for a moment to satisfy her curiosity about the new turnspit, when he walked, all unsuspecting, into the house. Lady Latteridge had disposed herself in the closest room to the hall, the door open, and her workbasket untouched, so that she might concentrate her entire attention on listening for her son's footsteps. When they came, she instantly rose to her feet and stood in the doorway saying only, "Pressington."

Her ominous tone might have shattered the composure of her minions, but the earl smiled. "Mother. Would you not be more comfortable in the drawing room?"

"I will not be comfortable anywhere until I have had a word with you."

"I see. Well, let me just change out of my riding clothes and I'll join you in the drawing room."

Lady Latteridge clenched her hands in an agony of impatience. "The matter is urgent. This once you may join me in your dusty condition."

Murmuring his gratitude at such condescension, he followed her into the cheerless antechamber where she had awaited him and, although she waved him to a chair, he chose to stand by the window, his hands clasped lightly behind him and a polite air of attention about his countenance. Sure that she would launch directly into her subject, he made no attempt to speak.

"It has come to my attention that Marianne Findlay lives in York and that you have taken Louisa to visit her. I will not allow it! That my daughter should associate with a woman of the grossest of morals is not to be tolerated. You should be sunk in shame for such an action. Your own sister! Have you no sense of what is fitting?" Under his cold stare she abruptly stopped speaking.

"Have you no sense of justice at all, Mother?" he asked, his voice as cold as his eyes. "Are you not content with persecuting that poor girl eight years ago without dredging up your infamy? Do you intend to reopen a matter which sheds such a deplorable light on your own character?"

"*My* character! You are misinformed, Pressington. I'm not surprised, if you have had your information from that empty-headed sister of yours, but you will please to speak to your mother with the respect which should be shown her." Lady Latteridge sat unbending in her indignation and dignity, but her son was not to be intimidated.

"Perhaps you forget, Mother, that I am the head of the family now, and responsible for the behavior of all of us. I should like to hear your justification for the way you treated Miss Findlay." When she did not reply, he said, "Come now, Mother. What was Miss Findlay's crime?"

"She spent the night alone with her cousin."

"I see. And how do you know that?"

"*Everyone* knew it."

"In other words, common gossip. You surprise me, Mother."

But Lady Latteridge did not flinch under his disdainful tone. "Her father made no secret of the fact."

"Did he tell you personally, Mother?"

"No, of course not, but I had it on the best authority."

"Whose?"

"Your cousin Charles," she said triumphantly. In the whole course of his life, no one had ever doubted one word which sprang from Charles Hastings's lips, since he was an uncommonly pious fellow, not only a believer in Methodism, but addicted to it.

"And what did Charles tell you?"

"He was in a coffeehouse where Sir Edward Findlay proclaimed that his daughter had run off with her cousin."

Latteridge tapped the windowsill like a judge calling the court to order. "If you expect me to believe you, Mother, you had best be more precise in your wording. 'Run off with' denotes a willingness on the part of both participants."

"What does it matter?" she complained petulantly. "She spent a night, alone, with a man."

"I should think it made a great deal of difference. Did Sir Edward, or did he not, profess to have taken part in a plan to have his daughter abducted by her cousin?"

"So Charles said; he was livid."

"And so should you have been, Mother. Instead of the treatment you accorded the girl, in all humanity you should have helped her through such a trying evening. She was, after all, Susan's friend."

Lady Latteridge's nostrils flared. "You never saw Selby with her! They had a thousand little familiarities. She knew how he took his tea, what he thought of Pelham and Pitt, Halifax and Bedford, what his tutor's name was, where he'd traveled on the continent. Susan knew nothing! All she could do was watch him with big sheep's eyes and listen to him talk, enthralled. Miss Findlay was entirely at ease with him; Susan went red whenever he entered a room. Now I ask you, Pressington, which of the two was he the more likely to wish to marry—inane little Susan, or the self-possessed Miss Findlay?"

"As I understand it, Mother, he had already expressed his intention of marrying Susan."

"But it wasn't announced! And Susan would have done anything for Miss Findlay, even renounce Selby's suit."

"You are being absurd. If she were that much in love with him, no influence of Miss Findlay's would have swayed her. Miss Findlay and Selby had grown up together. If they had wanted to marry, I'm sure they would have done so." Latteridge regarded his mother with a sorrowful shake of his head. "You saw bogeymen where none existed, Mother."

"None of that is to the point," she snapped. "Miss Findlay had the nerve to attend a ball where everyone knew of her damaged reputation. What unmitigated gall! And the first thing she did when she entered the room was look to Susan to champion her. I saw it at once and put a stop to it! The daughter of an earl does not associate with a strumpet!"

"A strumpet," mused the earl, remembering the words Miss Findlay had used but a short time previously. "A poor girl abducted, possibly raped, and you call her a strumpet." For a moment he stared out the window into the sun-baked street, oblivious to the passersby. All his life he had considered his mother cantankerous: frequently rude, always haughty, often irrational, occasionally malicious. He had found extenuating circumstances; somehow in this particular case, for whatever reason, he could not. To play God in someone's life, to wantonly destroy it, was something he could not, would not, understand. "Louisa may see Miss Findlay whenever she pleases. If you attempt in any way to hinder her, I will send you back to Ackton Towers."

Lady Latteridge watched incredulously as, with a nod, he paced to the door and turned the knob. Her voice was shrill when she called, "You forget, Pressington, that once a lady's reputation is shattered, she has nowhere to turn but to a life of degradation. I have not the least doubt that during these last eight years she has been the kept mistress of any number of men."

"Haven't you, Mother?" The normally kindly eyes were filled with bitter reproach. "Is that what you would like to have seen become of Miss Findlay? I'm sorry to disappoint you. She lives next door with her Aunt Effington and takes lodgers because her father has disowned her. Do you know

Miss Effington, Mother? I think you must. She has lived with her niece since you and her father and her cousin ruined her. I doubt anyone with even the smallest intention of attempting Miss Findlay's virtue would get past Miss Effington." Instead of leaving then as he had intended, the earl leaned against the panels of the door and held his mother's eyes by sheer force of will.

"Do you know what distresses me almost as much as what you did to Miss Findlay, Mother? It was your lack of faith in Susan. She was your own daughter and you didn't believe in her merit enough to see that she had indeed won the heart of the man she loved. Under your watchful, disapproving eyes, small wonder that she appeared awkward compared to Miss Findlay. Far from being 'empty-headed,' Susan is an exquisitely accomplished, gracious, intelligent woman. Can you not see your actions for what they were? You were jealous that Miss Findlay appeared to outshine *your* daughter—surely a sin for which she could never be forgiven in your eyes. Don't play the same tricks with Louisa, Mother. She, too, has infinite charm which you may be unable to perceive, but unfortunately, I doubt she will be as harassed by your disapprobation. Susan was more compliant, I imagine, feeling it your due. Louisa has seen too much, I fear, to feel the same."

Now at last he opened the door, aware that his mother had no intention of acknowledging what he had said, but one further matter occurred to him. "Did you actually keep a letter of Susan's from going to Miss Findlay, and destroy one from Miss Findlay to her?"

His mother's eyes dropped before his, but she did not answer, and he carefully closed the door behind him, only to find Louisa wide-eyed in the hall. "Come, we'll discuss this in the library."

As though the meltingly hot day had been a last gasp of summer, the weather turned cooler, the haze of heat became the sharply clear air of autumn, and the shortening days

took on a timeless quality which made them, if not pre-
cious, at least treasured by certain of those assembled in
York for the company. Lady Latteridge's uneasiness over
her son's disgust with her, was meliorated by being nomi-
nated to succeed Mrs. Whittaker as Queen of the Assemblies, a position she regarded as fitting, and from which she
could rule polite society for the month's span, not perhaps
as powerfully as she had in the old days in London, but
quite enough to keep her own family in line, surely. She
was not the least interested in William Vernham's continued attentions to Janet Sandburn, since she considered both
of them quite beneath her notice. Nor would she have paid
the least attention to Clare Horton, had she not been aware
that the young lady managed to pass on the information she
had received about Miss Findlay to Sir Reginald and others
of her set, a circumstance which, perversely, Lady Latteridge considered as vindicating her own views.

The Dowager prided herself on her network of informa-
tion-gatherers, and she was aware each time her daughter
Louisa visited Miss Findlay's house, and it was seldom less
than three times a week. Although she realized that these
visits in themselves constituted a strengthening of re-
spectability for the woman, they were not the cause of her
greatest anxiety on that front. It also came to her ears that
the earl frequently rode out with Miss Findlay, and had
once even been persuaded to dine there with his sister.
Lady Latteridge congratulated herself, however, as each assembly came and went, that Miss Findlay did not appear,
though it would have given her even greater satisfaction to
have snubbed her once again. She was not as yet convinced
that her son would make any move against such a repetition
of her former mischief.

What the Dowager was not aware of, was the company
into which her son and daughter went when they entered
Miss Findlay's house. It had not occurred to her to inquire
as to who else called there regularly and even if it had, she
would not have drawn the least suspicion from the list of

other visitors: Janet Sandburn, William Vernham, Dr. Thorne, various members of the Whixley family, the two lodgers. Exhortations from the Hortons had not deterred Janet from her growing friendship with Miss Effington and her niece; threats of discontinuing her allowance, since it had not arrived, were useless. If the earl and his sister visited the Micklegate house, Janet told them placidly, she saw no reason why she should not, pointing out that any rumors about Miss Findlay were obviously unfounded. And since Clare had her moments of glory at each assembly, where her beauty attracted the unsuspecting to her side, she was too preoccupied with capitalizing on her advantage to pay much heed to her undistinguished cousin. After all, who but Mr. Vernham stood up with Janet? Only a few doddering clerics and uninteresting (untitled) gentlemen. Clare was intent on snaring the earl, to be sure, but she reasoned that her best plan of action was displaying how incredibly in demand she was. Had she not, at the last assembly, been engaged for every set? Even Lady Louisa could not claim such a triumph.

And it was perfectly true that Louisa had sat out two dances. Not, as Clare believed, because her hand had not been solicited for them, but because she chose to do so. Lady Latteridge, magnificently attending to her duties as Queen of the Assemblies, yet paid a great deal of attention to Louisa's dancing partners. She did not, however, bother to ascertain with whom she adjourned to the Refreshment Room for hearte cakes and orange chips. While the flute, *hautbois* and *viola da gamba* resounded in a minuet or the York Maggot, she promenaded about the Egyptian-style hall with its crimson damask seats just as though it were her own ballroom at Ackton Towers. The rooms were crowded, not with the entire four or five hundred subscribers, but still intoxicatingly full of the aristocracy and gentry of the county, and Lady Latteridge ascribed the healthy attendance to her own role as hostess.

Aware that her mother would have objected to her giving

Dr. Thorne more than one dance in such a distinguished assemblage, Louisa chose instead to honor him with her company when she wished to take refreshment. Beyond the entrance hall, black to the top of the doorway from the *flambeaux*, there was a round room on the right for hazard, *quadrille, basset, faro*, and whist. Opposite was the Refreshment Room where in addition to tea, coffee, and chocolate, one could obtain *arrack*, mountain wine, and French claret, as well as the little cakes. Louisa had developed the habit of sitting out one set at each assembly, usually with a friend, and when she was sure that her mother had seen her, she would smile at Dr. Thorne, and he and another young man would arrive to take them off for something to eat and drink. It was a small subterfuge, and the part of the evening to which she most looked forward, aside from the one prudent dance she allowed him.

At first Dr. Thorne had thought of himself as looking out for the girl's welfare. He was, after all, knowledgeable about York and its residents, and he had thought to offer his own small contribution to Louisa's guidance. Though his feelings had changed considerably over the weeks, he would not acknowledge the fact to himself. It was ludicrous for a doctor, no matter how gently born, to consider anything more than friendship for an earl's sister. And Lady Louisa, he told himself sternly, depended on his familiar face in the ever-changing pattern of new ones. They were both friends of Miss Findlay, had met there in fact on any number of occasions, and Lady Louisa depended on him to provide some substance in the nebulous world of society. Dr. Thorne watched with determined satisfaction as she danced with her peers, but he never failed to come forward when she sat out a dance. There was no harm, after all, in seeing that she had a cup of chocolate and a hearte cake to refresh her from her exercise; it was practically his medical duty!

If Lady Latteridge was not aware of this situation, the earl watched it with mounting concern. Personally, he liked

Dr. Thorne, and he would perfectly understand Louisa's friendship with him, just as he did Miss Findlay's. One could not ask for a more likeable fellow, with his elegant dress, his cheerful cherub face, his very real interest in other people, expressed not only as a doctor but as a gentleman. There was no vice in him: he didn't drink or gamble beyond that for companionship's sake. But Louisa, he thought sadly, could have no conception of where such an attachment might lead her. At eighteen, she knew only a life of pampered indulgence, despite their mother's rigorous demands. And in her position, she could expect to lead a fairly similar existence for the rest of her life. Oh, there would be the responsibilities of marriage, children, a household—hardly negligible responsibilities, but ones which would be carried out in a scene similar to that in which she had been raised, where there was sufficient, even an excess, of money, the highest of social positions, none of the cares of a struggling existence. Set against that the life of a doctor's wife . . . Latteridge belatedly began to consider how best to gently unravel the growing ties.

"You're a fool, Marianne," Aunt Effie proclaimed as she gave an exasperated tug at the knot she had just made.

Startled, Marianne pricked her finger with an embroidery needle. "No doubt, Aunt Effie, but you might elucidate."

"Can't you see what's happening before your very eyes? I told you you should make a push for Dr. Thorne. Now he's heartsick over Lady Louisa. Not that that will do him the least good, of course, but he'll be in no mood to offer for you for a long time, if ever."

Marianne had hoped, futilely as it turned out, that her aunt would not notice the couple's growing attachment. If Aunt Effie had noticed, it was unlikely that the others who came to call were any less observant. Powerless to put any barrier between Dr. Thorne and the girl, Marianne watched unhappily as the hopeless attraction developed. She was sure that Dr. Thorne realized the impossibility of the situation; she was not as sure that Lady Louisa, in the first grip of love, understood that their positions were too different to allow of a successful conclusion to their glorious meeting of souls. And that is what it appeared to be: Even the most casual observer could not fail to sense the kinship of spirit between them. After the first few meetings they understood one another as though they had been close friends all their lives, a look sufficing for unspoken words, a sharing of sentiments on any matter of substance, an accidental touch, the goal of passing a teacup or biscuit plate.

On those occasions when the couple met at Marianne's house, she had watched Dr. Thorne attempt to join in the general conversation, and be successful for a while. Then he seemed inexorably drawn to Lady Louisa, and always they would end up a little apart from the group, deep in conversation, and not even sure how the change had happened. Marianne ached for them and the inevitable separation which must occur, but she was having problems of her own which distracted her attention. Well, one problem, really. The Earl of Latteridge. The sight of him tended to play strange tricks with her emotions, and had, practically from the first time she met him. She was far too old and, had for far too many years, been in control of her social behavior to succumb to such interior chaos. With Lady Louisa's example before her, she desperately strove to appear outwardly calm and unaffected, that no one would guess her secret failing as everyone could guess that of the girl and the doctor. At least, and the thought was bracing, her aunt had not ascertained her own dilemma.

Marianne forced a rueful smile. "Well, Aunt Effie, if Dr. Thorne has deserted me, shall I set my cap at Mr. Geddes?"

"Don't talk nonsense." Her glare, coming to rest as it did on her niece's bent head, was wasted. She watched the nimble fingers set another stitch and snip the little golden thread. There was nothing amiss with the action, nothing unusual in the posture, and yet Aunt Effie felt unaccountably disturbed. Surely the girl wasn't letting her head be

turned by Lord Latteridge's visits! And yet it would be no
wonder if she were, poor thing. Despite Aunt Effie's implacable hatred of the Dowager, and her assumption that all
the Derwents must, of necessity, share their mother's guilt,
she was not immune to the charm of the earl and his brother
and sister.

On the occasion when Latteridge and Lady Louisa had
agreed to dine, Miss Effington had enjoyed herself so
much, she had literally forgotten who they were. Dr.
Thorne had dined that night, also, and unconsciously Aunt
Effie had thought what a fine couple he and Lady Louisa
made and, perhaps because she had had more claret than
usual, she had also paired her niece and the earl. But in the
morning, with a clear head, she had dismissed the ridiculous notion as a senile fancy, and had carefully scrutinized
Marianne's behavior for any sign of an ill-advised attachment. There was no more chance of a match between the
two, than there was between the doctor and the earl's sister,
of course. And it was with a great deal of relief that Miss
Effington found Marianne as outwardly possessed as ever,
with no sign of having lost her heart to the fascinatingly in-
dolent earl.

On the other hand, it was obvious that, in his own casual
way, Latteridge was fond of her niece. If Aunt Effie had not
known for certain that he was aware of Marianne's ruined
social position, she would have attached a great deal of significance to his attentions to the young lady. His calls, his
taking her riding, his dining with them—all would be interpreted in quite another light if there were a chance of his
forming a connection with her. But there was not, and Miss
Effington regarded his continued gallantries as a dangerous
effort to offset his mother's cruel behavior. Dangerous indeed, Miss Effington decided, as she studied her niece's
averted face. For the first time she was fearful that what she
had suspected after the dinner party might indeed be true—
that Marianne had grown altogether too fond of the earl.

In an effort to share her perspective with her niece, and

to offer her some sort of consolation, Aunt Effie cleared her throat and said gruffly, "You know, Marianne, I've come to have a certain regard for Lord Latteridge. That's to say, I don't hold his mother's grotesque behavior against him anymore. Just look at the effort he's made to compensate for her failings. Even now that she's in town, he honors us with his calls and brings his sister. Of course that can never make up for what you've lost, but it shows the proper sentiment, don't you think?"

Marianne's heart sank, but she managed to smile at her aunt. "I do believe I'd best send for Dr. Thorne, Aunt Effie. Surely you can't be well, to take such a forgiving attitude toward a Derwent."

"I don't think I'm an unreasonable woman," Aunt Effie said quite untruthfully. "He's done what he can, and I give credit where it's due. Unfortunately, there is nothing further to be gained by his visits, rather the opposite. He cannot have failed to observe Lady Louisa's unfortunate *tendre*. I don't suppose we'll be seeing much of him anymore."

The possibility had occurred to Marianne, but she was not sure she was ready to face it. She had come to depend on those visits and rides in a way she would not have believed possible even a few months before. Just now she had been reliving their last, and most unsettling, ride. By unspoken consent they had ridden again to the glade by the stream, not so lush now as a few weeks previously, but with the pungent smells and glowing colors of autumn. When he had handed her down from the little mare Melody, he had retained possession of her hand, as though unconsciously, while they walked to the stream, and she made no effort to release it. They stood side by side, watching the rippling water, and he told her about Ackton Towers and the lake there with a brook meandering off across the meadows and through the park. He carefully described, too, the house and outbuildings, as though he wished her to picture them and the life that went on there.

"I'd forgotten how much I loved the place until we returned last year. My father seldom spoke of it, and God knows I hadn't spent all that much time there since I was a boy—first to school, and then traveling on the continent. But this last year has been thoroughly enjoyable becoming reacquainted with the riding, hunting, shooting, farming, the neighbors, the tenants, and most especially my family." He had smiled down at her with a gleam in his eyes. "And you would be fascinated by some of the characters in the village, my dear. We've a blacksmith who reads Shakespeare, and a butcher who raises magnificent roses. The dame school is run by a woman surprisingly like your aunt, and the parson's daughter has gone off to make her fortune on the London stage under Garrick's auspices. I imagine it's much the same sort of country life you knew when you were growing up."

"My fondest memories are of the countryside. Even Hampstead wasn't the same; it's far too close to London. You don't seem to have the same knowledge of people in a city as you do in a village. There weren't many young people where I lived, but Freddy—Lord Selby—and I, roamed about pretty much at will. He was like a brother and taught me to shoot and row a boat. Papa was often away from home, but I had a dear lady for a governess until I was old enough to come out."

Although she released his hand in seating himself, Marianne found that he reclaimed it when they were comfortably disposed and she met his eyes rather timidly, but said nothing.

The earl acted as though nothing out of the ordinary were going forward. "Did the Petrie cousin live near you?"

"No, but he came on visits. Freddy and I thought him odious, forever blaming any misadventures on one of us, though he was so inept that he was invariably the one to fall into the river or snag his breeches climbing a fence. I remember a time when he teased one of the dogs so wickedly that it bit him, and then he went wailing to his father that it was a mad dog and should be shot. Freddy hid the dog until tempers had cooled down, and we were able to convince my father that there was not a grain of truth to the story."

"He sounds a wretched fellow," Latteridge commented in the most indifferent tone possible.

"I could almost feel sorry for him, he was so laughably clumsy." There was something she very much wanted to tell the earl, but found it impossible to do while he held her hand, so she very gently withdrew it. He made no effort to restrain her. "The night he abducted me, I was furious with him. Percy is too much of a marshmallow for anyone to be afraid of him, you know, so I spent my time attempting to convince him that I wouldn't marry him under any circumstances. But Percy was always rather in awe of my father, and he just sulked and stubbornly refused to take me home."

Marianne had been speaking to the bush closest to her, but now she turned to look at Latteridge, her lips twitching almost impishly. "I'm afraid I was a little hard on him. We drove for two hours without a change of horses, and when I chided him for being so thoughtless of his beasts, he called to the postboy to stop at the next town. Percy had no intention of getting out, of course, but I told him I wished to stretch my legs. In true cavalier fashion, or perhaps because he thought I intended to escape, he started to get out first . . . and I tripped him. The long and short of it was, that he broke his leg and I had the *post chaise* take us back to London."

Latteridge shook his head wonderingly, and reached for her hand, which she hesitantly replaced in his. "You could have made a wonderful story of it for the *ton*. From what Susan says, they would have believed you."

"It would have damaged his pride irreparably, and he wasn't really to blame. He let Papa goad him into it, and he was greedy for the estate."

"Better that his pride be ruined than your reputation," he said dryly. When she frowned, he pressed her hand with comfortable reassurance. "We won't speak of that. I know you take the matter seriously, much more so than you ought. I'm glad you told me, my dear, for I confess to having some rather vengeful thoughts toward your cousin, and I see he's unworthy of the effort and has already been well repaid."

"Why, of course he isn't worth your lordship's slightest thought," Marianne protested, horrified.

"If you say so, Miss Findlay, I shall certainly take your word for it," he murmured with perfect agreeableness. "I must admit that I had rather not think of him. My mind is fully occupied at present."

His eyes rested gently on her face and she flushed, but in a moment, when she realized that he might well be talking of something quite different, such as his sister's predicament, she hastened in confusion to her feet. "I think we had best be getting back, Lord Latteridge."

Marianne had turned the conversation over and over in her mind, inspecting it from every possible angle, but there was nothing to be gained from such an exercise. As her aunt had just said, it could as easily be interpreted as showing the earl's concern for the whole situation his mother had exacerbated. Aunt Effie was forcing her to be realistic, to see Latteridge's attentions through her own detached, though compassionate, eyes. Marianne set aside her embroidery with an aching heart. "I would miss them if they didn't call anymore. Shall we walk to Micklegate Bar, Aunt Effie?"

15

As if having the concern over Louisa were not enough, Latteridge was growing increasingly concerned about the fact that his brother Harry did not return from his sojourn at the castle. Although Lady Latteridge had desultorily inquired after her younger son, she evidenced no chagrin that he had deserted York for other pleasures. Her time was fully occupied with her role in society, both at the assemblies and in the house in Micklegate, where she entertained lavishly when the mood took her. Her dinner parties and musical evenings served the dual purpose of exhibiting her social prominence and displaying her daughter to the eligible bachelors who might be interested in making an advantageous match. The earl was aware that his mother invited most of the young men who chose to dance with Louisa at the assemblies, always provided they met her superior standards. Surely it had never crossed her mind to include Dr. Thorne.

No word had come from Harry, except for a brief note after the first week of his absence informing his brother that he planned to stay on for a while. Latteridge had actually begun to pen a note to his brother when the young man himself knocked and entered. There was a ghastly pallor to his face and he walked unsteadily, gripping his stick until the knuckles on his hand turned white.

"Good God!" Latteridge was instantly on his feet and lowering the young man onto a sofa. "Have you had a fall?" As he drew out his handkerchief to wipe the perspira-

tion from Harry's forehead, he gave a violent twist to the
new bellpull. "Just rest a moment and get your breath." He
tugged off the dusty boots, loosened the crumpled cravat,
and made to push back the coat and waistcoat, but his
brother stayed his hand.

"Let it be a minute, Press. I need a doctor." His voice
was no more than a whisper.

William came in response to the violent summons and
took in the situation at a glance. "Shall I go for Dr.
Thorne?"

"Please. Hurry!"

The secretary gave a brief nod and disappeared, the
sound of his hurrying footsteps dying away after a moment.
Latteridge turned back to his brother, whose eyes were
closed now, but one of his hands pressed feebly against his
waist. Frowning, the earl gently pried away his fingers and
opened the coat and waistcoat to find the shirt stained with
blood, and beneath was a makeshift bandage, also soaked.

Harry's eyes opened to meet his brother's, a sickly attempt to smile contorting his lips. "I've made a mess of it,
Press. I'm deeply in debt and I've fought a duel."

There was a gasp from behind them and Latteridge
swung about to find Louisa staring horror-stricken at
Harry's bandage. He was about to comfort her and send her
away when she stepped closer and took hold of one of
Harry's hands. "I saw William hurrying away, and a footman said Harry had come. Have you sent for Doctor
Thorne?"

"Yes, love," Latteridge said gently. "Why don't you find
Mother and tell her, but don't bring her here. I'll come to
her when the doctor has seen Harry."

Louisa didn't move. "She's not at home right now, Press,
and I don't expect her back for several hours. I'll stay here
with you and do what I can. Would you like some wine,
Harry?"

"Brandy, if you please, Louisa. I'm sorry."

She pressed his hand and smiled. "Don't be silly. I'll be right back."

Left alone, Harry attempted to speak, but the earl placed a finger against his lips. "You can tell me later. Save your strength."

Harry shook his head with fretful determination. "I want to tell you now in case . . . in case I can't tell you later. Everything was fine for a while. We had races and went shooting and fishing, and in the evenings we sang and gambled. Had a frightfully jolly time, in fact, but there was always burgundy and claret, port and punch, and my head was seldom clear. Not that anyone else's was either. Or so I thought. I went through everything I had with me, and then I started to write notes, mostly to Harper. I'm not sure how much I lost, but it has to be several hundred pounds."

"I'll take care of it."

Harry grimaced. "Not the notes to Harper, Press. The other day I remembered what you said, about gambling when your mind wasn't clear. I'd forgotten. But I was losing so badly each night that I became rather desperate, you see. I wanted to leave but I kept hoping I could win the money back. What a fool I am!"

Louisa had returned with the brandy which she brought herself on a tray with several glasses. She set it down on the monk's table and poured a glass, then held it while her brother took several small sips and motioned it away. Unwilling to interrupt Harry's urgent tale, and fearful that the earl would send her from the room, she slipped into a chair some distance away and sat quietly listening.

The brandy seemed to restore Harry somewhat, and he continued his story in a slightly stronger voice. "We had been out shooting one day and I bagged three brace of partridges with eight shots, so naturally I thought that luck was running with me. You know how it is, Press."

"Yes, I know," the earl said sadly.

"I decided not to drink that night. Not because of what you'd said," he confessed, "but because something at din-

ner didn't agree with me and the liquor made my stomach
curdle. Everyone else was as foxed as usual, and after some
raucous singing we sat down to the tables in earnest. It's
funny, you know, but I didn't want to seem different than
anyone else, so I was acting as though I was as bosky as the
rest of them. I hadn't the least idea how a roomful of disguised gentlemen must look to an outsider. The jests
seemed coarse instead of amusing, the clumsiness totally
foreign to the usually elegant graces they displayed. Someone would overturn a wine glass and the others would
laugh. The cards were sticky and there were wet glass rings
on all the green baize covers. It was disgusting, Press."

"Yes."

Harry sighed. "Anyhow, we were playing deep at basset,
and the long and short of it is, that I saw Harper cheat. At
first I didn't credit my own eyes, but I watched him circum-
spectly for some time and there was no doubt of it. What do
you do in a situation like that, Press?"

"There's no good solution, Harry. I myself leave the
game and hint at my knowledge to the cheater another time.
One doesn't want one's friends to be taken, and yet calling
a man a cheat is a very serious matter."

"Can I have another sip of the brandy?" When the earl
held the glass, Harry again took a few small swallows.
"Well, I tried to just leave the game. But Harper already
had several of my markers and I was angry, too. When he
twitted me about being a poor loser, I said I liked to play
where I had a fair chance."

The earl groaned and Louisa's eyes widened but neither
said anything.

"Of course, that put the fat in the fire; he couldn't very
well let the matter alone. He jumped to his feet, overturning
the table in the process, and demanded if I was calling him
a cheater. I couldn't back down then, Press. I said I had
been watching him cheat for more than an hour." Harry
gave a helpless shrug which caused him to wince. "Harper
immediately took the tack that I was trying to welsh on the

notes I'd written him, and they were very substantial losses. I could see that some of them believed him, so I told the whole group precisely what I had seen him do. Of course, he challenged me."

"Poor Harry," Louisa murmured.

"I didn't mind so much. I'd never been out before, but I'm pretty good with a small sword. Well, yes, I did mind, really. Harper has been my friend for some time, and I felt disillusioned, and all I really wanted to do was never see him again. The others were so drunk that they thought it all a lark, our meeting. Half of them stayed up drinking the rest of the night, so there was a pretty rowdy company to witness the duel. All I wanted to do was pink him, Press." His voice broke on something suspiciously like a sob. "I found myself fighting for my life. He must have known that I was thrusting only for a touch, but he wasn't. It was awful. Finally I got him in the arm and I was withdrawing satisfied. Before the seconds could step in to push up the swords he skewered me. I'm not sure what happened then. The next thing I knew I was being bandaged by one of the fellows at the house party. I was sick over the whole thing; I didn't want to stay there. So Hall agreed to put me in a post chaise and send me here. I think he was relieved to be rid of me."

Latteridge's lips were pressed tightly together but he said only, "Well, I'm glad you're here now so we can have you taken care of, but it was not wise to travel such a distance in your condition. Please rest, Harry. William should be back with the doctor soon."

Harry obediently closed his eyes, satisfied that if he should die, the earl would know exactly what had happened. He did not know whether or not he was fatally wounded, but he thought not, despite the loss of blood and the pain of the wound. If something vital had been pierced he felt sure he would already be dead, rather hollow comfort in his weakened state, but sufficient to temporarily ease his mind. Despite his disillusionment and the wretchedness of feeling a fool, Harry did not want to die.

The room was silent for a few minutes, the earl studying his brother's pale face and Louisa silently praying for Harry's recovery, but soon there were footsteps in the hall and William held the door for Dr. Thorne. The doctor went directly to the injured man without a glance about the room. As he laid aside the bandage, he let out an involuntary whistle.

"A sword wound?" he asked, puzzled.

"Yes. He had a duel this morning," Latteridge informed him softly, "and he's been on the road in a carriage for several hours."

Terrified lest she faint, Louisa was yet too concerned to resist coming forward to see what caused the drawn expressions of the three men standing over Harry. Rather than a simple stab wound, there was a long gash, as though the sword had been drawn upward on being removed, and although the two edges of the cut had been drawn together and held there haphazardly with sticking plaster, the wound still oozed blood sluggishly.

Dr. Thorne had flung open his bag and withdrawn the necessary items to stitch up the wound, muttering angrily, "Damn fools. Why didn't they have a doctor to him immediately? Bring me some water and clean cloths. Get the rest of the brandy down him."

While William executed his first order, the earl complied with his second, and still Louisa watched, ready to do what she could, confident as only one in love could be, that Dr. Thorne could mend her poor broken brother, if anyone could. He cast one critical glance at her, determined that she was not going to collapse under the strain, and said, "Thread the needle; my fingers are too sticky," before turning back to gently explore the wound with his fingers. In order to deserve the faith reposed in her, Louisa, without a tremor, threaded the needle with silk thread and held it ready for him. He reached for it with a brief smile. "Good girl.

"This will hurt him, Lord Latteridge. Better hold down his shoulders, and Lady Louisa can hold his hand."

The operation was painful to watch, even more so to undergo, but Harry clenched his teeth and clasped Louisa's hand until she thought he would crush her bones to splinters. Even in his sympathy for Harry, the earl was struck with admiration for Louisa's calm efficiency. While Dr. Thorne worked quickly to seal the wound, perspiration stood out on his forehead and Louisa withdrew his own handkerchief from his pocket with her free hand and mopped his brow. He never glanced at her, but there was that unspoken message which passed between them, and Latteridge felt again the despair which each new example of their devotion inspired in him. Obviously, it was far too late to keep Louisa from being hurt, and he had no one but himself to blame. If he had not been drawn to Miss Findlay's house, and taken his sister with him, there would not have been an opportunity for their affection to develop.

With the cloths and water William brought, the doctor cleaned the wound and its surrounds, giving Harry's shoulder a gentle pat. "You'll do, young man. You're a very fortunate fellow. Quite incredible, really, that nothing vital has been badly damaged, but for all the length of the wound, the penetration was not great." As he spoke, the earl assisted him to remove Harry's coat, waistcoat, and shirt, and the doctor sprinkled powder on the wound and neatly bandaged it. "Once they've gotten you to your bed, you're to stay totally immobile; I want no strain to reopen the wound. I'll come around in the morning to check on you." He beamed his contagious smile on Harry who whispered, "Thank you, sir," picked up his bag and motioned that he would like a word with Latteridge in the hall. Before he walked from the room, his eyes met Louisa's, and he accepted his handkerchief, but instead of congratulating her on her courage, a matter unnecessary for him to put in words, he said, "My microscope arrived this morning."

"How wonderful! I hope I shall have an opportunity to see it one day."

A momentary flicker of doubt passed over his face. "I hope so, too."

In the hall he set his bag on a small table and accepted the earl's grateful hand. "I don't think there's anything to fear except fever, my lord. But he's a healthy young man and I feel reasonably sure we'll see him through this. I'll send around some Peruvian bark."

"We'll do everything in our power to see he follows your instructions. Thank you for coming so promptly, Dr. Thorne." Latteridge met the younger man's eyes gravely. "I suppose Louisa will wish to sit with him often until he's recovered."

The doctor did not flinch from the penetrating gaze. He had known that the time must come when the earl would hint him away from Lady Louisa, that he could not continue forever to meet her as they had been. "She'll make an excellent nurse for him, but don't let her tire herself. Miss Findlay was almost in worse shape than her aunt by the time Miss Effington recovered."

"I'll see that she takes plenty of exercise and eats regularly," the earl promised.

"Good." Dr. Thorne's melancholy face belied his hearty tone. "I'll be off. Just send a message if you need me."

"We will." To soften the unspoken but clear rejection of Dr. Thorne's attentions to his sister, Latteridge urged, "I hope you'll make more use of the stables. You have only to send word around that you'd like some mounts."

"Thank you." The young man picked up his bag, nodded a farewell and, when the footman had opened the door for him, strolled out into the street. Henceforth he would have to avoid Lady Louisa, even though he would be making frequent calls to her house. What madness had possessed him to ignore their relative stations and lose control of his emotions? It didn't matter so much for himself; he could learn to live with the wrenching disappointment because he would have to and he had his work in which to immerse himself. But the girl. No conceit existed in Dr. Thorne; to him it was a simple fact that Lady Louisa was in the same case as he. He should never have allowed such a thing to happen, and yet even now it seemed inevitable, unavoidable. For a moment he stood numbly in the street, then advanced to Miss Findlay's door and wielded the brass knocker.

Although several gentlemen had been so kind as to call, and some of them had brought flowers, Clare Horton was only vaguely pleased. Her mother had begun, in a very broad way, to give hints that she expected Clare to attach *someone* this autumn, whether it be the earl or another of exalted rank made little difference to her. Lady Horton found the Dowager Countess of Latteridge unnerving and her son, although possessed of every worldly consideration, little more to her liking. If there was no fault of air, or grace, or address, there lurked always that suspicious twinkle which Lady Horton could not altogether appreciate. She had the most uncomfortable feeling that he was amused by her, a lowering thought.

Clare, on the other hand, was determined that she would have the earl, and she was beginning to feel that her waiting game was not perhaps sufficient to draw his eye. Oh, he stood up with her once at each assembly, as he did a dozen other young ladies, but he had not called or sent flowers, had not invited her for a drive, or included her in any entertainment at the house in Micklegate, though she had been at pains to learn that these last festivities were inaugurated by his mother and did not bear witness to his own desires. It was hard on her, who had spent such trying efforts to cultivate a tinkling laugh, to have so little opportunity to exhibit her new skill to advantage.

When Clare began to practice on the spinet, Lady Horton

hastily gathered her workbox and retired, for there was nothing she liked less than Clare's precise, mechanical performance on that instrument. Clare did not even notice the desertion, her thoughts directed not on the music, but on a scheme to win the earl's attention. It would behoove her, she decided, to find a husband for Lady Louisa. After all, Latteridge was acting as escort to his sister and took his duties seriously. If she were to shift that burden to some worthy gentleman, not only would he have more time to consider his own unfortunate wifeless state, but he would doubtless be eternally grateful to her for her care and selfless attention to the interests of his family. And it was obvious that Lady Louisa was making no progress on her own. It might prove worthwhile for Clare to give her a few hints on how to handle gentlemen; the girl's approach was almost matronly! Far from turning out to be the flirtatious, unruly lady Clare had expected, she found Lady Louisa almost casual in her dealings with gentlemen, and nothing could be more fatal! Yes, decidedly she would point her in the right direction.

But there was still the matter of which gentleman to aim toward Lady Louisa. He should, of course, come from the same stable of admirers which she herself would consider, and she found herself strangely loath to willingly allow even one to escape, just on the odd chance that the earl could not be brought to the sticking point. There were, however, she admitted to herself, several gentlemen with whom she had had a singular lack of success in her two previous seasons in York. Surely they were the ones on whom to draw. She had just pushed back the spinet stool preparatory to making a list when her cousin entered the room.

"Back from your excursion so soon, cousin? Are you tiring of the notorious Miss Findlay's company these days?"

Used to Clare's biting tongue, Janet ignored the sarcasm and calmly retrieved a book she had left on the *marquetry* table before answering. "Everyone was a little low today.

Dr. Thorne called and informed us that Harry Derwent has suffered a severe accident. It must be very upsetting to his family."

"So Lord Latteridge and his sister were not there?" Clare asked eagerly.

"No, I don't expect they'll be out and about much for a while. Dr. Thorne seemed to think it would be several weeks before his brother was out of bed."

"Surely they'll still attend evening functions! They can be of no use to the poor fellow when he's asleep."

"Perhaps. Dr. Thorne is optimistic in his prognosis." When William had not called as arranged, Janet had gone alone to Miss Findlay's, quietly confident that he would not have failed to call without reason. And hearing Dr. Thorne's tale had explained, as had the note she found awaiting her on her return, the urgency of his remaining at the earl's home. "If you will excuse me, I should just like to write a little note to Lady Louisa."

"There's no need for you to do so," Clare informed her grandly. "*I* shall send a note to Lady Latteridge expressing our deep shock and sympathy, and offering any assistance we may be able to provide."

"I'm sure she'll appreciate that." With a quiet smile, Janet left the room and went directly to her writing table to send Lady Louisa a short, encouraging note of her own.

Clare allowed herself some time to consider this new development. At first she had been pleased simply because Latteridge was not at Miss Findlay's, but if the accident was going to keep him out of society, she was very annoyed about it. It would ruin her new plan to find Louisa a husband, and it would give her no opportunity to exhibit her virtues to the earl. What a nuisance! She was personally unacquainted with Harry Derwent, but she meditated on the possibilities of appearing as a ministering angel to him all the same. Unlikely role as it was, it would surely set her up in Latteridge's eyes. Clare could envision herself in her charming white dress with her cool hand on the young

man's forehead; unfortunately she could not imagine anyone in the Micklegate house allowing her to get so far as
the sick room in the first place. There were quite enough
family members and servants to see to Derwent, and she
could not claim any special connection which would advance her cause. No, she must simply hope that he would
recover quickly, with the aid of the broth, possets, and fruit
she would have sent around immediately.

Content that this was the best plan, she made a list of
those items she wished sent, then composed a morbid epis-
tle to Lady Latteridge, and at last set herself once again to
the task of finding Louisa a beau. Since she had herself relegated Sir Reginald to the realms of "rich, but not nobility,"
she reluctantly decided that Lady Louisa would not want
him either. Unfortunate, because he would doubtless want
her. No, the list must be exclusive in the extreme, as exclusive as the company in York allowed. Probably they intended taking Louisa to London in the spring, where the
choice would be wider, but Clare was determined to see her
engaged, through her own efforts, before Christmas, New
Year at the very latest. Lord Twickenham was well-heeled
but at fifty-odd years, perhaps a little old for the girl. Rock-
hampton would come into a title if his older brother died, of
course, but one could not depend on that; certainly there
was not the least chance that his brother would *marry*. With
a frown, Clare considered Lords Sedbury and Whitfield,
both engaged, but rackety fellows who would not necessarily make it to the altar. One or the other of them might be
induced to take an interest in the girl, but Lady Louisa was
likely to be aware of their previous entanglements. The
company in York began to appear meager to Clare, as she
swiftly discarded Lords Draycott and Lovell, since they
were currently in her own train.

Discouraged, Clare was about to abandon her project
when she hit on Lord Bowland. True, Lady Horton had told
her in no uncertain terms that she was not to allow him to
dangle after her since he hadn't two pennies to rub together.

Apparently, though, it was not common knowledge, since Clare had observed no other chaperone shun his advances to her charge. If the Bowland lack of fortune was a closely-guarded secret, which Sir Joseph or Lady Horton had nosed out on their own, the young man might prove the perfect match for Lady Louisa. *She* would come well-dowered enough for the both of them, Bowland's mortgaged estates notwithstanding. Now Lord Bowland might not be handsome, but he had a pleasing countenance and fine eyes, was good-natured and amiable, and overall, a very lively fellow. If he was looking for a fortune, he gave no evidence of it, distributing his time and attentions equally among the rich and moderately-rich, and Clare knew that he had stood up with Lady Louisa at the very last assembly.

Latteridge might object to his lack of fortune, but if his sister set her heart on him, Clare thought the earl too attached to his sister to deny her marrying him. Not once did it occur to her that the earl might not look on her with favor for advancing such a match. In Clare's mind, attaining the matrimonial state was all-important in itself, and she intended to play no small part in Louisa's approaching nuptials.

Congratulating herself for having worked out so thorny a problem, Clare stood before the mirror for some time. Beauty, virtue, *and* intelligence were a combination even the Earl of Latteridge could not resist, she decided, molding her lips into a beguiling smile, and forcing a painfully abrasive laugh, which she thought altogether charming.

16

Marianne adjusted the green velvet hat on her hair and inserted several pins to hold it in place. The flaring coat over the voluminous folds of the skirt, together with the crisp bow of her neckerchief made the habit strikingly attractive, and feminine, despite its tailored cut. The outfit was no longer new; she had worn it on several occasions riding with Lord Latteridge, which perhaps was the reason she now felt edgy donning it to ride with Dr. Thorne. It was almost two weeks since she had last ridden with the earl, and in between only a note to thank her for her concern over Harry's health. Nor had Latteridge and his sister come to call as they had been in the habit of doing. William and Janet came, and Dr. Thorne came, though not as often, but the brother and sister stayed away. Under the circumstances, it was understandable, and yet it gave substance to Aunt Effie's view . . .

The sound of the knocker drifted distinctly to her room and Marianne rapidly finished her toilette. It was unlike her to linger over dressing, and she gave herself an impatient shake before she walked to the drawing room. Poor Dr. Thorne looked in no better mood for a merry ride than she felt. His usually beaming face was spiritless, his eyes lackluster, but he approached her with a fond smile. "You look charming, Miss Findlay. Is this the habit you ordered the morning we met in Stonegate? Had I known, I would not have been so backward in suggesting a second ride."

"Tsk, tsk. He's becoming quite the gallant, isn't he, Aunt Effie?" Marianne asked with mock surprise.

Her aunt frowned on such teasing. To her mind it was a good sign if the doctor's eyes were clear enough to see another woman properly. "Just as he ought," she sniffed.

"Which is only to say I've been remiss in the past," he whispered, taking her arm. "I've left the horses right outside with the most impish-looking urchin. You won't mind if we leave directly, will you?"

Marianne found the little mare, Melody, awaiting her, and she raised her brows questioningly at her escort.

"Latteridge insists I use his horses, and I thought you'd prefer the mare to some hired hack. They said at the stables that Lady Louisa wouldn't be using her today." His face was expressionless as he assisted her to mount.

"How is Lady Louisa?"

"I haven't seen her since the day of Derwent's accident."

Watching him swing himself onto his horse she protested, "But surely you call there everyday to check on him."

"Yes, but I always make it my first call, very early. I've seen his lordship several times, and the Dowager once, but usually it is Mr. Vernham who lets me in and takes me up to Derwent."

"I see. And how is he doing?"

"Very well. The wound suppurated nicely and is tightly closed now. He didn't have much fever, and now he's beginning to walk about for short periods to build up his strength. A nice lad; I like him."

"Yes, they're a charming family." With the exception of their mother, Marianne mentally amended.

Dr. Thorne regarded her closely, but said nothing. The day was cool and hazy with a light wind blowing which ruffled the horses' manes and lifted Marianne's auburn hair as they trotted along. She expressed no wish with regard to their direction, so they rode along Blossom Street toward

Knavesmire. The races were long since over, but the view
from the mount was a pleasant prospect, and after a canter
they broke their silence.

"Do you go to the assembly this evening, Dr. Thorne?"

"I think not. Did I tell you I've received the microscope I
ordered? I'm eager to make some preparations to view
through it. I remember one particular lecture from Mr.
Kelly on the structure of the vegetable. Does that amuse
you, Miss Findlay?" he asked with a stern eye on her grinning face.

"Forgive me. I immediately pictured an apricot or a cu-
cumber waving up at you while it displayed its 'structure,'
and you, some medical *voyeur* jotting down notes on its
various attractions." Her suppressed laughter gurgled
faintly in her throat, but she studiously controlled her
twitching lips.

"There are those," he retorted with haughty dignity, "who
do not find the microscope a source of amusement. Some,
even, who consider it to be an invention which will lead
those of a scientific turn of mind to ever more enlightening
discoveries which will be of infinite usefulness to
mankind."

"I'm sure I hope it shall. Where I grew up there was a
surgeon-apothecary with an enormous sign on his office:
B.C.B. Smythe. Freddy and I used to call him Blister,
Clyster, and Bleed Smythe. They were his only remedies
for an illness, save the purple powder from one of his enormous jars which he replenished with alarming frequency.
When we watched him mix it, through the window we
would go through a litany of 'First the red jar, then the
blue, next the yellow for a glorious brew; A pinch of myrrh
old Smythe will add; if that can't cure you, you're done for,
my lad.'"

"Positively sacrilegious," he grunted, his eyes twinkling,
"and the meter is wretched."

"Well, we were very young. When we got older Smythe

died. Freddy always said it was from doctoring himself with the purple brew."

"And no respecter of the dead, either, I see. Poor Smythe. A man of science treated as though he were the merest quack. Weren't you ashamed of yourself, Miss Findlay?"

"Not the least. Mr. Smythe was a cranky old bachelor who thought children were a pestilence upon the earth, and he treated us accordingly. It is no easier for a child to separate the profession from the man, than it is for an adult to separate the man from his profession. He was a mean man, therefore doctors were mean. Fortunately his successor was a great favorite of ours, a recently married man whose wife was expecting, and he carried comfits in his pockets when he made calls. We were thus taught that there were nice doctors and mean doctors, as men, and that their medical skills were a thing apart. Now adults see the situation quite the other way around. First a man is a doctor, or an attorney, or a shopkeeper. That's what he *is*. By definition he is not a complete gentleman, no matter how gently born, since the definition of a gentleman is leisure. You know, Dr. Thorne, I consider that attitude as absurd as our childish belief that doctors were mean just because Mr. Smythe was."

They had drawn in their horses and sat ostensibly regarding the scenery. "There is a certain amount of wisdom behind it," he said cautiously. "Not in being blind to the person behind the profession, but in realizing the demands that such a life puts on a man. In the first place, he enters a profession or a trade out of necessity, to earn a living. Oh, there are those who dabble out of interest, and those who would do so even if they were well-off, but they are a small minority, and recognized as such. So having a career in itself indicates two things: a man will be frequently occupied with his work and he has little money other than what he earns at his trade."

"And do you believe, Dr. Thorne, that a man's most eminent virtue is how much money he possesses?"

"You know I don't. But it *is* important, vastly important. It determines the way in which he lives, how large a house he resides in, how many amenities he can allow himself, how much leisure time he has for amusements. And you must admit that those things *are* important. You take a young lady who has all her life enjoyed every luxury; you do not suddenly allow her to exist in humble circumstances." He was, of course, referring to Lady Louisa, but he turned to face his companion. "I may be wrong, but I think that is what has happened to you, Marianne, and it's not pleasant, is it?"

"No," she admitted, "but it's not entirely disagreeable either."

"Well, you can't expect someone who has the welfare of a young lady at heart to choose a situation that is 'not entirely disagreeable,' can you? Or one who is sincerely attached to her to wish to lower her to an ignominious financial and social position? There is a substantial difference between objecting to a mésalliance, and promoting a worldly and advantageous match. I am perfectly in accord with the theory of equals marrying. There are difficulties enough without adding to them."

"And is no consideration to be given to the wishes of the young ladies involved?" she asked gently.

"You know that's unfair, Marianne." Purposely he used her name again because he needed the closeness and familiarity it symbolized, needed a friend to understand the realities of his position. "As often as not, young ladies do not comprehend the extent of the deprivations they would suffer. One's emotions are flexible, even chaotic, when young. My sister fell in love half a dozen times between the ages of sixteen and twenty. She didn't regret later that no one had encouraged her in her passion for the footman! It is not cruelty, but kindness, to lead such a one away from a mistaken object. Time heals such wounds, especially for the young."

"Not always," Marianne retorted, remembering her aunt's story.

"Usually." He met her eyes with a sad smile. "You know it does."

"Yes." But not, I think, in this case, she wanted to add, but refrained. It would do no good to cast doubt on his good intentions. Nor would it prove of the slightest efficacy to point out that he was no more likely than Lady Louisa to find himself heart-whole in time, for this was no simple physical attraction to be superseded by someone newer and more appealing. "I'm very sorry . . . Stephen."

"Thank you." He smiled and reached across to press her hand. "I don't feel any anger in the matter, you know. I could scarcely have been treated with greater kindness and tact by his lordship. My resolution was not strong enough, being perpetually in her company, until he helped me firm it. I am greatly to blame for permitting such a hobble. And I have never felt any blindness to my personal self on his part, either. His vision is remarkably clear and he would, I think, always value the person behind the profession. You cannot have failed to remark his easy association with his secretary. His authority comes from his principles, not from his position, and there's no lack of humanity in him. He's quite as distressed for my feelings as you are, my dear." Dr. Thorne looked away from her, out over the harvested fields, and said, "I'm sorry all this, and his brother's accident, have kept him from visiting you."

Marianne flushed. Were her emotions so clear to the doctor? "He has been very accommodating to us. I only wish there were more we could have done for Derwent in his illness."

Accepting this as her decision not to confide in him, Dr. Thorne said cheerfully, "Oh, I wouldn't worry myself over that. Each time I enter the sick room I find more books, games, packs of cards, drawing materials, and the like. He's no longer in much pain, and his time is fully occupied with one of the members of the household reading to him or playing at *piquet*. Shall we head back? I would hate to incur Miss Effington's wrath at having you late to dinner."

"Will you dine with us? Aunt Effie specially ordered a roast leg of lamb and a bread pudding, in hopes that I might convince you."

"I'd enjoy nothing better." As they set their horses in motion, he pursued his previous intention and proclaimed, "*Now* I shall tell you more about my microscope. I don't think you have the right idea of it at all."

Louisa tapped hesitantly on the door, and to her surprise Harry opened it himself. He was fully clothed in buff breeches and a brown coat, his walking stick clutched firmly in his hand, looking very much as though he intended to go visiting. The determined light in his eyes did nothing to diminish this impression.

"Are you . . . going out?" she asked, attempting to keep the concern from her voice.

"I am. God, Louisa, I'm sick to death of sitting around this room. Not that I don't appreciate everyone's efforts to entertain me! But if I don't get out, I think I'll lose my mind."

"Yes, I can see that and your color is very good today. What did Dr. Thorne say?"

"He told me it would not be necessary for him to come again as I'm perfectly healed and only want strength to be right up to snuff. So you see, it's practically the doctor's orders."

"Harry, may I go with you?" she asked with unwonted eagerness. "I've been out riding with Press while you've been ill, of course, but I haven't had much opportunity to simply walk about."

Since he had intended adjourning to his favorite coffee-house, this was not the most welcome suggestion, but Harry realized that he was under no small obligation to his sister for the time she had spent with him. "Why not? Run along and get a bonnet and shawl; I'll wait for you in the hall. Is Press about?" he asked somewhat diffidently.

"No, he's taken Mother to visit Lady Ayford. I excused myself."

"No wonder."

When the two had let themselves out into Micklegate, Louisa turned to the right but Harry frowned. "I thought we might walk toward Coney Street."

"Dear Harry, are you intent on exhausting yourself? You must build up your strength gradually. I had thought we might walk toward Micklegate Bar, and then call on Miss Findlay on our return." Louisa held her breath while he considered the wisdom of her suggestion.

"Oh, very well. But tomorrow I intend to go to Coney Street, alone," he muttered with a touch of bravado.

She released her breath with a smile. "Thank you, Harry."

No one had said anything to her about Dr. Thorne, not in so many words. Her mother, she felt sure, had no idea of her attachment to him, nor of course did Harry. But Press knew, and his actions were clear enough. First, he had no longer suggested that they visit Miss Findlay, and when she had broached the subject herself, he had, with a sympathetic smile, said, "You are spending too much time sitting with Harry, Louisa, and what you need is a ride, rather than sitting about Miss Findlay's drawing room." She had considered arguing with him; after a few days she had felt like pleading with him. But she had done neither, because there was also the fact that she never saw Dr. Thorne when he paid his visits to his patient. And when Harry had insisted that they should not miss the assembly on his account, they had gone—and Dr. Thorne was not there.

Louisa was not blind and she had no lack of understanding; she knew precisely what had happened. During those hours when she was not reading to Harry, or riding with

Pressington, her mind was constantly occupied with considering how best to deal with the situation. It was no use faulting her brother's concern for her, or Dr. Thorne's selfless gallantry. There was nothing to be gained by ranting or sulking, little use even in reasoned argument: they held all the trump cards. Louisa even forced herself to study the possibility that they were right, though it made her heart ache so badly she had to bite her lip to keep the tears at bay. In marrying Dr. Thorne she would lose the privileged social position she had enjoyed all her life, and she knew that it didn't matter in the least to her, but she saw that it would sorely grieve her family, and even Dr. Thorne himself. And there was the problem of money. Dr. Thorne's practice was flourishing, but his income could not compare with the earl's. Louisa had been past his house in Coppergate, a handsome brick building which housed him and also provided space for consulting rooms. He had no country house, kept only an unfashionable gig for transport, and lived simply.

Acknowledging that she had no real concept of how it was to live on such a modest scale, Louisa could yet realistically argue that her own tastes were not extravagant. Certainly she dressed fashionably, and that was an expense; she also had her mare, and the feed and care of such an animal was not small; her delight was in her books and drawing materials, again an expense, but not so very great. No, financially she was sure she could manage.

Were they concerned, too, about her delicacy? Did they worry that she would be exposed to sick and injured people and find it trying, or worse? Louisa had, over the weeks, induced Dr. Thorne to tell her his experiences as a student and as a practitioner. Under her inquisitive questioning he had, at first reluctantly, and then with relief, as he saw she had no squeamishness, related the fascinating and the gruesome alike. Once, before Harry's accident, she had attempted a small test. Knowing that Mrs. Stillingfleet was a major subscriber to the York hospital, she had arranged to accompany her on a tour of the wards. The sights had been distressing, but her empathy had not overcome her practical outlook, and her sensible questions had much elevated her in Mrs. Stillingfleet's eyes. On her own she had become a subscriber, without mentioning the matter to anyone; her allowance was hers to do with as she wished.

Surely she had exhibited her ability to be usefully detached when Dr. Thorne had treated Harry. And the thought of being of assistance to Dr. Thorne, no matter how little, was important to her. Watching him work, knowing his concern for his patients, had made her aware of the essentially unrewarding life she led, the life everyone was so intent that she continue to lead. Louisa felt a need for some balancing influence, some purposeful object in her existence. Her mother's life, she felt, was totally without merit; her sister Susan had her husband and her family; her brother Press had the management of his estates; her brother Harry seemed to her to be unconsciously searching for something to do with himself in a restless exploration of all sorts of amusements which failed to entertain. Louisa thought perhaps Press would understand at least this facet of her situation, though he might, like most men, see her role as being fulfilled by marriage and motherhood.

The same considerations plagued her every waking hour because she could see no solution which would satisfy everyone, and no one, not even Dr. Thorne, would believe that her decision was irrevocable and based on a knowledge of herself which no one else could possibly possess. She dismissed the idea of sharing her troubles with Harry, who was agonizingly burdened by his own just now. As she walked with him she maintained, as she had for some days now, the composed exterior which was more alarming to Latteridge than any signs of distress might have been. Her disappointment at not finding Dr. Thorne at Miss Findlay's, however, very nearly cracked her hard-won facade.

"Have we come at an awkward time, Miss Findlay?" Louisa inquired, noting that not even Miss Effington was with her niece.

"Not at all. I'm delighted to see you both. Aunt Effie has gone a-shopping with her friend Mrs. Whixley, and they hope to procure us a box for the benefit at the theater tomorrow. Please sit down. You look splendid, sir. I hadn't expected to see you out so soon."

Harry's color was better than it had been since the duel, mostly on account of his exercise, but he was more tired than he cared to admit. "I'm right as rain again. Louisa thinks to pamper me but there's not the least need."

As he seated himself, Marianne pretended not to see his grimace of pain, but she shared a rueful glance with Louisa. Not until that moment had it occurred to the girl that here was someone in whom she might confide, someone who might understand and help her to sort out her confusion. When Harry in his exhaustion suggested that they should be going, she smiled and said, "If you don't mind, Harry, I shall stay a moment longer with Miss Findlay."

Too tired to object, he took his leave and Louisa found Marianne's kindly eyes on her, waiting for her to speak. The girl made an apologetic gesture with one fine, long hand and said simply, "I need to talk with someone."

"Please feel free, my dear. I'm honored by your confidence."

"You know how things stand . . . with Dr. Thorne and me?"

"Yes. I ache for you both."

"I don't know what to do. I don't know if there's anything I *can* or *should* do. Please believe that I've considered all possible arguments against such a match, and I can understand Pressington's concern. My social position, my financial position, even the distresses of being a doctor's wife, all are valid objections, but they don't really apply to *me*. They are concerns of my brother and Dr. Thorne for a girl *of my birth*. But I have led a rather retired life, Miss Findlay, and really have no taste for the social whirl. My father and older brother were on the continent for years, with only occasional visits home. Harry was at school and Mama, after seeing Susan married, was content to return to Ackton Towers, where she hasn't many social exchanges. And then Papa died, and we stayed at the Towers doing little for a year."

"Didn't you look forward to coming to York?"

"Oh, certainly. But mostly I was determined to find a husband to get out of my mother's . . . I suppose I shouldn't say that. It's true, nonetheless. And I envisioned meeting some man of my station and falling in love with him and marrying, just as Susan did. It wasn't for the assemblies and card parties and morning calls that I looked forward to coming here. They're well enough, I suppose, but they become terribly repetitious."

"And the young men of your station whom you've met?"

Louisa smiled. "They're repetitious, too. Elegant clothes, elegant manners, and concerned only with trivialities."

"Surely not all of them," Marianne protested.

"Most of them. Do you know Clare Horton?"

"I've never met her, only her cousin."

"Well, the beautiful Miss Horton is determined to have Pressington and she thinks to provide me with a partner as sort of a prenuptial gift to him, I think. Rid him of one of his concerns, as it were. How she lighted on Lord Bowland, only someone acquainted with her tortuous brain could say. I certainly couldn't. Do you know him?"

"No."

"You are very fortunate. A polished fellow, as lively as can be, with a penchant for courting anyone known to have a sizeable dowry. He is all talk of every expensive pursuit—traveling, hunting, lavish entertaining—but one seldom sees him actually spend so much as a guinea. He's hanging out for a wife who will provide him with all the elegancies of life. And Clare Horton has pointed him in my direction." Louisa frowned. "That's neither here nor there. Even if he were the most decent fellow in the world, I couldn't see him for Dr. Thorne."

"You don't think," Marianne asked gently, "that in time you could be fond of some gentleman of whom your family would approve? That if he doesn't exist here in York, you might find him in London?"

"I suppose there are some gentlemen of Pressington's caliber to be found," Louisa admitted, frowning thoughtfully at her kid boots, "and I suppose I might even develop a fondness for one, after awhile, but it would not be the same. You see, aside from himself, I *like* Dr. Thorne being a doctor. I can respect a man for reading Latin and Greek, for taking an interest in his tenants, for being generous in his dealings with his family and those unrelated to him, but Dr. Thorne is all that and more. He's *immersed* in his work. It's more than a facet of his personality, it's a part of his being. I can't explain it very well."

In spite of herself, Marianne was impressed by the quiet strength of the girl's conviction. "And you want to be a part of that sort of dedication."

Louisa turned shining eyes to her. "You *do* understand. Am I wrong to want it? To depend on someone else to belong to that realm? I don't think I'm a fanatic; certainly I've never had the least desire to marry old Dr. Miller or his young assistant at Ackton." Louisa giggled, but immediately turned serious. "And I think I wouldn't now if I didn't feel so . . . close to Dr. Thorne. Sometimes I feel as though he were a part of me, a part that's been missing all my life and has now completed me. Miss Findlay, I wouldn't feel whole anymore if I weren't with him."

"So it would do you no good to try to fall in with your family's wishes." Marianne smiled a little wistfully. "You are a most unusual young lady, my dear. Do you think you could explain this to your brother, Lord Latteridge?"

"He has a great deal of sensibility for a man, and I feel sure that in the end I could convince him of my sincerity, but he is not the major problem, is he? Dr. Thorne himself poses the major obstacle. I mean, he hasn't asked me to marry him, after all, and there is really no chance that he will. He's an honorable man, Miss Findlay, and in his eyes it would be wrong for him to do so, for any number of reasons—because he cannot offer me the position I am accustomed to, because my family would disapprove, because he feels he has captured my affections when I am young and vulnerable, because he thinks it possible that in time I will find a worthier match with which I can be happy."

"You will have to talk to him."

"How can I? He's doing his best to avoid any place where he may run into me. I had hoped, I confess, that I might find him here, accidentally, as it were. I would never ask you to arrange a clandestine meeting for me." She lifted her firm little chin, and gray eyes, so like Latteridge's, uncompromising. "My mother has made a great deal of trouble for you and I will not be the cause of further distress. But if . . . if Pressington were to ask your opinion of the affair, I would be grateful for your support."

"He is not likely to do so."

Startled, Louisa regarded her with puzzled eyes. "Why not? I can think of no one he is more apt to consult."

"I'm afraid you've misread the situation, Lady Louisa. Lord Latteridge had not known about the contretemps in London, and when he found out he wished to do what he could to rectify any damage. A noble sentiment, of course, but wholly unnecessary. I think I have convinced him that we manage very well."

Louisa regarded her incredulously but said nothing.

"Did I tell you that I heard from your sister a few days ago? Her letter was ten pages long, catching up on all those years, and Lord Selby added another two pages. And she has sent me the most beautiful shawl. May I show it to you?"

Though Louisa nodded, it was obvious that she barely heeded the rich Indian design when it was shown her and she soon excused herself, saying, "Thank you for hearing me out, Miss Findlay. It means a great deal to me, knowing that you understand." And she placed a salute on Marianne's cheek before hastening from the room.

17

Harry had been home for some time when Louisa returned, but he had long since made his way to his room, though not without being confronted by his brother. Latteridge was mildly surprised to find Harry returning from a walk, but he made no comment, especially when Harry informed him that Louisa had accompanied him.

"Did she not return with you?"

"No. We stopped in at Miss Findlay's and she stayed there. I suppose she'll be back directly."

"Were there other guests at Miss Findlay's?"

"Not a soul; even the aunt was out."

"I see. Well, I'm pleased you're feeling so well, Harry. I've put a novel in your room. If it's something you've already read, I wouldn't mind having a crack at it myself."

The door of his library was left open while he studied some accounts, and on hearing the sounds of arrival, he went to stand in the doorway. "Might I see you a minute, Louisa?"

Her eyes, sparkling with anger, met his across the hall. "You certainly may!" With decided impatience she allowed the footman to take her shawl, but she did not wait to dispose of her bonnet, which she untied as she stomped into the library and tossed uncaringly (though it was one of her favorites) on a pillow-strewn sofa. "Really, Pressington, you astonish me!"

"Do I?" he asked almost uncertainly, as he firmly closed the door. This was a complete about-face from her dutiful acceptance of her restricted intercourse with Dr. Thorne, and he was not at all sure what to make of it. Learning of her visit to Miss Findlay, he could only assume that she had hoped to meet the doctor there and been disappointed. Perhaps he should have spoken with her previously, but he thought that she understood and was attempting to deal with her unhappiness alone. Her obvious anger was the last thing he had expected. "Do sit down, Louisa."

"Thank you, no. I am entirely too agitated to sit still." And to prove the truth of her statement, she paced briskly to the window and back before speaking, all the while drawing her gloves again and again through her fingers. "Do you have any idea what you've done, Pressington?"

It boded ill for any member of his family, save his mother, to call him Pressington, and he eyed her cautiously. "I've been meaning to speak with you, for fear you should think I've been high-handed in this matter. I . . ."

"High-handed? Well, that's a very mild epithet, I should say," she stormed. "I myself would more likely term your behavior reprehensible. Have you no conception of the impression you've given?"

"I have tried to be as tactful and kind as possible."

"Tactful? Kind? Nonsense! Such a show of attention, nay, even of *in*tention . . . Every mark of affection and regard . . . What the devil can you be thinking of?"

"Now, Louisa," he offered placatingly, not at all sure of his ground, "you know there is not the least objection *personally*."

"I should hope not! A more refined, sensible, delightful person one could not hope to meet. Which is all the more reason I fail to understand your attitude."

"The truth is, my dear, that I should never have allowed the situation to progress so far."

"Is that all the excuse you mean to offer?" she demanded, irate.

"I'm afraid I was rather preoccupied," he admitted ruefully.

"With what, I should like to know? If anyone can claim to know the proper conduct, it is you. No, Pressington, it won't fadge."

"Not every situation is covered by social rules." He was thinking that there were no guidelines which could keep a young lady from gravitating to an attractive man when there was no possible objection to their having an acquaintance.

Louisa's eyes became enormous and her hand flew to her mouth in a gesture of horror. "Dear God! Surely you never considered an *illicit* relationship!"

Now thoroughly out of his depth, the earl dropped onto a chair, unable to take his eyes from his sister's shocked face. "Louisa, are you sure you feel perfectly well? I realize you are laboring under a severe emotional trial, and I was at fault not to talk with you sooner, but I am only trying to do things for the best. A lost social position is almost impossible to regain, and there is the matter of financial security."

"You *are* considering a *carte blanche!* I would not have believed it of you. How can you possibly think she would accept? Have you no idea of how insulted she will be?" Louisa in her turn dropped onto the sofa, unfortunately on top of her bonnet, and sunk her head in her hands.

"She? Who the hell are we discussing, Louisa?"

His sister lifted incredulous eyes. "Surely you are not contemplating more than one mistress at a time!"

"I don't think you need concern yourself with mistresses, my dear, mine or . . . anyone else's."

"Well, I think I do." In a voice laden with sarcasm she asked, "Do you then subscribe to Mama's view of the situation, Pressington?"

"I'm sure Mother knows nothing of this affair, Louisa. Pray don't alarm yourself on that account."

"Oh, Mama would be delighted." There was an impotent despair to her voice. "Wasn't Susan's letter enough to convince you otherwise? Or did you simply wish to believe the worst for your own unsavory purposes?"

"Susan's letter?" It was the only clue Latteridge could draw from the irate, almost incoherent speech, since Louisa's voice came trembling through her fingers. He had had a letter that day, a relieved note from his sister after his own assuring her that Harry was recovering nicely. But he was sure Louisa had not seen it, and in any case, he had not confided the situation regarding Dr. Thorne to Susan. Besides, they seemed to have drifted from the original subject to his own affairs, a matter highly improper for him to discuss with his sister. There was certainly something he was missing, but he thought to calm his sister before attempting to ascertain precisely what it was. "I promise you I have never so much as considered the possibility of your having an illicit affair with *anyone*, Louisa."

He was totally unprepared for her response to this delicately worded attempt to pacify her. One moment she was seated in the greatest dejection on the sofa as though she would never move again; the next she was before him delivering a stinging blow to his cheek, and he barely had time to catch her hands before she could swing again. "My poor love, I had no idea you were so distraught! I wish you had come to me. Did you think I had pursued this separation from Dr. Thorne because I wanted to hurt you? I can hardly bear to see you suffer so. But I can only believe that, given both of your circumstances, it is for the best. You are very young, Louisa."

"We were not discussing Dr. Thorne," she said stiffly, her attempt to release her hands unsuccessful.

"Weren't we?"

"Of course not! We were discussing Miss Findlay."

The earl did a hasty mental recapitulation of the conversation and groaned. "Why didn't you say so, Louisa?"

"Well, I did," she replied indignantly.

Cautiously he released her hands. "No, my love, you came in furious and started to berate me. I *thought* you were annoyed with me for my intervention in your attachment."

"Oh. But you said . . ."

"Please, Louisa, spare me. Nothing I have said in the course of our discussion has had the slightest thing to do with Miss Findlay. Bear that most firmly in mind, I beg you."

"Well," she muttered mutinously, "that does not excuse you for the way you've behaved."

Latteridge was all patience. "This time I would appreciate your lifting our discussion from the realms of obscurity. In what way have I behaved toward Miss Findlay that you object to?"

"I did tell you before, but I will be happy to repeat myself. You have given her every indication of affection and respect. You have called on her and taken her riding and even dined with them. Perhaps you thought me too preoccupied to notice, or perhaps you thought your actions did not speak so loudly because you did not have her here in return. But you have given *me* every reason to believe that you intend to marry her!"

"I do."

Louisa's face, which had been crumpled with hurt and distress, instantly became a picture of hopeful wonder. "But . . . but she said . . ."

Her brother raised a questioning brow. "What did she say, my dear?"

"When I gave some intimation of what I suspected, she said I had misread the situation, that you were only trying to rectify the damage Mama had caused, but that she had convinced you that she could manage. You haven't spoken with her, have you?"

"No. I've written to her father. Though I imagine I won't have a reply, it seemed the proper way to act. She doesn't need his consent, of course. And what with Harry's illness and . . ." He hesitated.

"And trying to keep me away from Dr. Thorne," she finished for him, "you have not called on her in ages. How terribly unfair to her."

"I am trying to be fair to *you*, Louisa. Miss Findlay would understand that."

Louisa sighed and walked to the sofa where she retrieved the crushed bonnet and stood unhappily regarding it. "She might, if you explained it to her. What she *does* understand is my attachment to Dr. Thorne because I have just confided in her. I'm sorry, Press."

Shaken, the earl watched helplessly as his sister fled the room.

Janet Sandburn had just received an offer from William Vernham and she was trying very hard to force words from a throat painfully tight with joyous emotion.

"I have spoken with your uncle, and although the idea obviously did not send him into transports, he has agreed that I may address you." William smiled on her radiant face. "Lord Latteridge will propose me to stand for the next election where he has any influence; in the meantime we could take a small house in York and I would continue to be his secretary. Will you make me the happiest of men, my love, and agree to be my bride?"

They were sitting alone in Lady Horton's drawing room, where Sir Joseph had told his inquisitive wife, in no uncertain terms, that they were to be left undisturbed. Actually, despite his coldness to William, he was more than pleased with the match. A parson's daughter could not do better than an earl's secretary, and he had found Janet stubbornly unbending when he had attempted to appropriate the majority of her annual allowance as he had the year before. The thirty pounds which he considered his due were, she informed him patiently, the equivalent of a curate's yearly income, and she did not believe that her upkeep could cost him so much. She had suggested again that he apply to her father's executors for such a sum, but Sir Joseph had no intention of showing his parsimonious streak to the men who thought he housed his wife's niece out of the goodness of his heart. He would be delighted to see Mr. Vernham take her off his hands. Who would have thought the chit had any spirit in her?

While Lady Horton fumed with impatience to hear the result of the interview, Janet sat smiling on her beau. "There is nothing I should like more than to marry you, William. How generous of his lordship to offer to assist you in finding a parliamentary seat."

William grinned. "He said I deserved it after putting up with him all these years. Shall you mind living in London? If I have a seat, it will be necessary."

"I think I shall like London . . . with you."

William was about to take her in his arms, something he had longed to do for weeks, when there was a discreet knock at the door. With a sigh, Janet called, "Come."

The footman who appeared knew, as did all the servants in the house, precisely what was going forward in the drawing room, but when a caller had come asking for Miss Sandburn, Clare, passing by at the time and in a fury that her cousin should receive an offer before she did herself, insisted that he inform her immediately. Thus his demeanor was rather apologetic when he announced Mr. Deighton.

"Mr. Deighton?" There was a slightly familiar ring to the name, but for a moment Janet could not place it, being far too preoccupied at the time to recall a name briefly heard and quickly acted upon.

Years of training gave William the advantage. "Miss Effington's friend from Suffolk, wasn't it? You were going to inquire of him."

"And he's here? Dear me." She glanced questioningly at her fiancé, and he nodded with only the slightest hint of amused exasperation. "Please have Mr. Deighton come here to me."

Miss Effington had returned and was sitting alone with her niece when William Vernham was announced. The older woman was in the habit of leaving her spectacles in place during such visits, so she wouldn't miss any facial expression of importance, and it was entirely owing to this circumstance that she immediately recognized the older man who accompanied William. Her hands began to tremble so badly that she had to clutch them together and press them against her palpitating bosom.

Alarmed at her aunt's distressing appearance, Marianne thought to go to her, but before she could act, the robust stranger had, in three long strides, reached the stunned woman and taken hold of her hands. "I'm not a ghost, Aurelia. Forgive me for arriving unannounced; I only thought to surprise you."

Miss Effington rallied to grumble in a weak imitation of her usual manner, "You might have let a body know, John. How do you come to be in York?"

"I came to find you," he explained succinctly.

Marianne felt a slightly more lengthy explanation might be necessary. "I had Miss Sandburn inquire after Mr. Deighton of her friends in Suffolk, Aunt Effie; she had had no reply."

Mr. Deighton looked momentarily taken aback and regarded Miss Effington with steady eyes. "Then you didn't inquire for me yourself?"

"The girl didn't know anyone in Long Mellford, John. There was no use asking her." She touched a tentative finger to his cheek. "I've tried to picture you growing old, but you've hardly aged. I would have recognized you anywhere."

"Setting aside the spectacles, you've not done so poorly yourself," he rejoined.

Aunt Effie's hand went automatically to remove them but he gave a "tsk" of disapproval and it fell to her lap. She forced herself to ask, "How is Lavinia, John?"

"She died four years ago, dear soul. The children are all grown and off to their own pursuits, except Jack. He and his wife live with me now, helping with the estate."

"The *estate*?" There was a quaver in her voice.

"I've prospered, Aurelia." It sounded more like a confession than a boast. "Over the years we acquired a number of small farms and eventually built a house as large as Willow Hall. Never so fine, of course, but one has to do the proper thing, and there were seven children, though two died young. I never could bear to have the farmhouse torn down. That's where I want to take you, not to the big house. Jack has it filled with charming brats and a lovely wife. We'd do much better in the farmhouse, alone. I love them all dearly but the noise is colossal, and the farmhouse is a great deal more elegant than it used to be."

Marianne, stunned by the turn the reunion was taking, allowed William to draw her from the room. The last thing she heard was Mr. Deighton, his voice husky and reverted to country dialect, asking, "Wilt tha ha' me *now*, Aurelia?"

Unaware that the two young people had left (since she had barely recalled their presence before they did), Miss Effington glanced about and then met his questioning eyes. "I . . . I'm not the same person I was, John. I've become a cross old woman, difficult to live with, and I was even sick a few weeks back. You don't want to burden yourself with someone who will make your declining years a torture."

He rubbed a hand thoughtfully over his chin and said with great seriousness, "No, I wouldn't like that at all. You would have to make an effort, Aurelia, for me. Have you no spark left of that affection we shared?"

"It has never died," she declared almost fiercely. "Through the years my memory has kept it fanned to a warming glow. I've remembered those times we spent together and so longed to sit and talk with you again."

"And now you shall, for the rest of your life. Almost everything is settled on the children, but I'll make arrangements for your comfort, should I die before you. The children will be surprised and perhaps not altogether pleased, for their mother was a good woman, Aurelia, and they won't understand the necessity of my marrying again, but they're a good lot when all is said and done." A hearty grin appeared on his weathered face. "And I still hold some sway in my own family, as you'll find if you accept my offer."

Miss Effington placed her hand in the large one he held out to her. "It should be too late, John, but it's all I've ever wanted from life, and I won't refuse, now that it's offered to me. I will have to make arrangements for Marianne, though, someone to live with her."

"Do you want her to come with us?"

"No, I don't think she would agree to that. I'll have to discuss it with her." Her eyes came to rest on his beloved face after a swift survey of the underfurnished room. "We've come down in the world. But long before that, I knew what a wretched mistake I had made. How I envied Lavinia, making a life with you, sharing your joys and sorrows, receiving your warmth and your . . . love. You must have made her very happy."

"I hope so. No man ever had a finer, dearer wife. I have been far more fortunate that I ever deserved or expected to be."

Miss Effington nodded, though her heart ached, and it was impossible not to regret all those years when he had cherished another woman. Knowing him as she did, she had to accept that he had grown to love Lavinia, that she herself had become a transient memory, perhaps forgotten for years on end, while the children came and the estate expanded, and they went through those thousand intimacies of daily life. And it had been a rich, fulfilling life, one of years to set against the paltry hours she had shared with him so painfully long ago. While his life had been filled with new and more deserving loved ones, hers had stretched barren with only the past to offer a glow and, more recently, her niece to offer companionship. There was no telling why he had come to her now, and she would never ask him. One did not question miracles. It was enough that he had come. For that alone she would have

uffered all those wasted years. In an unusually tender
oice she said, "I will try to make you happy, John."

He lifted her hand to his lips and kissed it. "And I you,
ny dear."

18

After Louisa's abrupt exit, Latteridge sat at his desk and considered what she had said. From his own experience of Miss Findlay he had felt certain that she would be much in accord with his own feelings on the problems of a *mésalliance* between his sister and the doctor. There was always the possibility that Louisa was interpreting Miss Findlay's sympathy as support, but Latteridge suddenly felt that he must know precisely where matters stood. In his attempts to keep Louisa from meeting Dr. Thorne there, he had necessarily not called himself, feeling that it would not be fair to Louisa. Instead he had taken his sister riding, long restoring gallops across country where she recovered the color in her cheeks, but never once spoke of the thoughts uppermost in her mind. The earl continued to feel a nagging doubt as to the wisdom of his proceedings. There was that special quality to his sister's love, that almost unnerving bond between her and Dr. Thorne, with which it somehow seemed impudent to tamper. If he could discuss the matter with Miss Findlay . . .

Even as he rose, there was a tap at the door. Recognizing it as his secretary's, he bade him enter. "Ah, William. You look large with news. Was this the day you chose to put your suit to the touch?"

The young man grinned. "It was, and congratulations are in order. Miss Sandburn has agreed to accept me, and even her uncle proved no obstacle. Janet thought it especially kind of you to offer me assistance in getting a seat in Parliament."

"I'm delighted for you, though when the time comes for you to leave, I will sorely miss your invaluable assistance. Could you and Miss Sandburn dine with us tomorrow and join us at the benefit? I've taken a large box, and Mr. Baker promises me the performance will be excellent."

"Thank you. I think Janet would like that."

"Good." The earl shook William's hand and said, "I hope you'll excuse me for rushing off when you have such famous news, but I would like very much to have a word with Miss Findlay before the dinner hour."

"I fear this would not be an especially appropriate time."

"Oh?"

"I've just come from there."

"Spreading the word, are you?"

"Not exactly. It's rather complicated to explain concisely, but let me try."

His tale was indeed a little difficult to follow, but after the fiasco with his sister, Latteridge made a determined effort. "So the man was actually proposing to her when you left?"

"Yes, and Miss Effington gave every indication of being totally bemused. I understand from Miss Findlay that Mr. Deighton was an old beau of her aunt's."

"Dear God. There must be something particularly intoxicating in the air here this year."

"Yes," William agreed with a mischievous smile, "I believe there must be."

So Latteridge did not call on Miss Findlay that afternoon, and when he called the next day, she was not at home. He asked if he might leave her a note and Roberts promptly brought standish and quill, but he was undecided as to how much he wished to say. In the end he wrote:

Miss Findlay,

There are several matters of importance which I would

appreciate discussing with you. If it is convenient, I shall call tomorrow at twelve. Latteridge

No message came during the day to defer his proposed visit, and he sat down to William's engagement dinner feeling at charity with the world. Louisa appeared in better spirits than usual, though he had to admit she had never sulked, and Harry was eager for his first evening's entertainment since his duel. Lady Latteridge was graciously condescending to William and his prospective bride, and Madame Lefevre derived entertainment from watching the Dowager make (in Madame Lefevre's eyes) a fool of herself. The trout and roast mutton of the first course were followed by brandied chickens, partridge, and a variety of puddings, while those assembled talked, ate, and drank in a properly festive mood.

Louisa's more cheerful outlook was occasioned by her having hit on a scheme for talking with Dr. Thorne, and in her quiet satisfaction that this might prove of consequence, she entirely forgot that Miss Findlay had told her that she, too, intended to be at the benefit performance that evening. If she had remembered, she would most certainly have told Latteridge, for a confrontation between the Dowager and Miss Findlay was to be avoided at any cost. Louisa had blushed for her mother more than once, but there was a great deal more at stake here than the ordinary social snub at which Lady Latteridge excelled. There was the earl's future to be considered, and for all Louisa was desperately unhappy at his decision with regard to Dr. Thorne, not for the world would she have done anything to jeopardize his own peace of mind.

Lady Latteridge was carried to the performance in the earl's black leather sedan chair with its gilt mounts and coronet. The entrance to the theater was through a passageway opposite Blake Street, a location which she deplored almost as much as she did the theater itself. Inside, the building was square with oak pillars supporting two galleries, with rows of boxes on either side of the stage. Brass chandeliers were suspended from the ceiling, and the candlelight which glowed from them was not sufficient, so she said, to illuminate the truly disgraceful condition of the chair coverings. Her grumblings were familiar to the members of her household and the only sign they occasioned was a shared grimace which passed between Harry and his sister.

If it had not been necessary for the Dowager to stop several times in her stately progress to bestow her gracious, though frosty smile, on several of her more deserving acquaintances, she would probably not have arrived at her box at precisely the same moment Miss Findlay and her party reached their adjoining seats. Latteridge had been bringing up the rear, and the first he knew of the unfortunate encounter was his mother's voice announcing in ringing accents, "Since when are they allowing the riffraff into this theater?"

Harry looked as though he wished to vanish, and Louisa said sharply, "That's enough, Mama!" but the Dowager paid no heed to either of them. "*Nothing* will induce me to sit in a box next to THAT WOMAN'S!"

Before dealing with his mother, Latteridge bowed politely to Marianne and Miss Effington and said with a smile, "Good evening, ladies. I hope my mother's rudeness has not disturbed you. She occasionally suffers from an emotional imbalance. You have my most abject apologies." Then, still not turning to his mother who stood mortified before him, he said to his brother, "Please take charge of our party, Harry. I shall return when I have seen Mother home."

"I'm not going home," she snapped.

"Yes, you are," he said evenly, taking her arm, "unless you wish to apologize to Miss Findlay." When she made no move to do so, he guided her firmly through the staring groups of people and out into the chill autumn night, where he was able to secure a chair immediately and walked beside it in silence. Despite the cold she let down the window and grated, "You cannot do this."

"Ah, but I can. I warned you, Mother. Your obsession with Miss Findlay is truly unbecoming, aside from being petty, dishonorable, and vulgar. I shall expect you to write a note of apology tomorrow morning, which I will deliver myself."

"Never!"

"You have a choice. You write the note or tomorrow afternoon you return to Ackton Towers. Think about it, Mother."

The window was snapped shut, and even when they arrived in Micklegate, Lady Latteridge said no word to him. He bid her good evening and in her hearing told the butler to summon the housekeeper, as his mother was not feeling well. With one last inflexible glance, he left.

By the time he returned to the theater, the intermission was in progress and he had only an opportunity to speak briefly with Miss Findlay, again offering his apologies, and declaring his intention of calling the next day.

"Do you think that wise, sir?" Marianne asked uneasily, her eyes locked on the flow of lace at his collar.

"Eminently." His eyes were tender when she briefly met them, and quickly looked away. "Will you introduce me to your aunt's friend?"

Because she wanted him to come, Marianne allowed the subject to drop, but her turmoil during the rest of the evening was almost more than she could conceal. Conceivably she could have misunderstood that warm light in his eyes. And there could be any number of important matters he wished to discuss with her—notably Lady Louisa's attachment to Dr. Thorne. Certainly that. Probably Mr. Vernham had told him of Mr. Deighton's declaration; he might find that of interest. But if he *were* to speak of marriage, if the impossible were to happen, what was she to say? She had admitted her feelings to herself some time ago but they changed the situation not one whit. His mother detested her, she was anathema to society, there was no dowry to speak of; surely it would be a worse mésalliance than the one his sister contemplated!

And her aunt. Dear Aunt Effie was firmly clinging to the incredible good fortune which had brought her only love back to her in her declining years. It was touching to watch her accept that her shining dream of the youthful John had to be revised to the sturdy, comfortable, dear old man whose life had for so long not included her. That false pride which had prevented the young Aurelia Effington from accepting her rough country gentleman, and which had sustained her through years of unwanted independence was abandoned without a murmur. What would Aunt Effie think of a match between her and Lord Latteridge? Though the old lady had been perfectly willing to see her marry Dr. Thorne, would she not balk at Latteridge, especially after his mother's exhibition this evening?

And Louisa and Harry. How would they feel? There was a very great difference between accepting someone as a friend, and as a potential sister-in-law. Of course, Louisa had hinted that she expected something of the sort, but Louisa was so completely beset by her own torn emotions that she could not really have considered the matter carefully.

Marianne shifted in her bed, unable to sleep, trying to face the hardest question of them all. If you loved a man, did you let him do something which would inevitably destroy the easy pattern of his life, the calm of his mind, and the unsmirched character of his name?

In addition to making calls on bedridden patients, Dr. Thorne kept office hours in his home for several hours in the morning. Those he treated ranged from the laborer to the aristocrat, and it was his invariable policy to accord each the same courtesy and attention to his ailments. He was an astonishingly good diagnostician and had enough experience of the inefficacy of some standard treatments to cautiously experiment with new possibilities. Consequently, he was often the last hope of a large number of his patients, and he tended to see a disproportionate number of the incurably ill. The morning after the play, which he had not attended, was an especially discouraging one for him, having to tell two men that there was nothing further he could do for them.

The last patient awaiting him was a boy dressed in the Earl of Latteridge's livery, who looked to Dr. Thorne, when he came out to call him, to be in blooming health. But as he motioned to the lad, the page disappeared out the door. Dr. Thorne found the incident amusing, for he knew he would see the boy again when his courage was restored. Relieved to have a break, he was turning to enter the living quarters of his house when the door opened again and Lady Louisa stood there nervously blinking at him.

"I have to talk with you, Dr. Thorne."

"My dear girl, you can't come here alone," he protested, the color rising in his face.

"I'm not alone." Louisa reached behind her and tugged on the page's coat. "Sit over there, Tom, if you please."

The boy obediently perched on a chair in the corner of the room and regarded them steadfastly where they stood by the door. Dr. Thorne shook his head mournfully. "It won't do, Lady Louisa."

"It must," she retorted with determination as she seated herself, deliberately drawing off her gloves.

"Your brother would not approve."

"Oh, pish. Tom is a perfectly adequate chaperone. Just see how he watches us."

Laughter danced in his eyes, but he said gently, "It's not just the lack of proper chaperonage, my dear. I should not see you at all."

"And how are we to settle matters if we have no opportunity to talk?"

"I'm afraid matters are already settled."

Louisa lifted her chin and said haughtily, "Not to my satisfaction."

His heart contracted within him, a phenomenon he absently noted as a medical man and suffered mutely as a man in love. Abruptly he went to the door into the hall and called for his housekeeper. When she appeared, he said, "Please bring us some coffee and biscuits, Mrs. Thomas." He left the door open when he returned, and seated himself beside her, with a glance toward the little page, who had found one of the copies of Newberry's books which he kept on the table and was deeply absorbed with it.

"I think you must understand the position your brother and I are taking, Louisa. We think of nothing but your own good and future happiness. Nothing is more important to me, I promise you."

"And I must tell you, sir, that I am convinced that I should have a say in my own fate. I am, after all, deeply concerned, as you will admit," Louisa lowered her eyes to her hands. She had planned very carefully how she would conduct this interview and she could not take a chance that the expressions which appeared on his face would influence her. This was her only opportunity and she had no intention of spoiling it with useless scruples. "Dr. Thorne, do you admit that you have, practically since the moment we met, encouraged me to an affection for you?"

"For God's sake, Louisa!"

"Do you, Doctor?"

"Yes." He rubbed a distressed hand over his brow. "God help me, I never meant to make such a muddle of this. I . . ."

"Please Dr. Thorne, if you will be so good as to allow me to continue . . . Do you also admit that by the way you treated me, you led me to believe that you had a sincere and abiding affection for me?"

He groaned, but she waited patiently for an answer. At length he said, "I did. I do."

"Thank you, sir. Now I should like to point out to you

that as an impressionable young lady, these continued marks of regard led me to the conclusion that you had an honorable course of action in mind. I think any young lady might have thought so," she said, as if considering the matter, and continuing to study her nervously twining fingers. "I have been raised among those who consider honor a most compelling virtue. There is never any need for a document to be drawn up to bind them to their word, expressed or implied. I had assumed that you, as a gentleman, subscribed to this same code. Do you?"

Dr. Thorne was becoming very uncomfortable and, had she witnessed his countenance, she would not perhaps have continued, but she did not lift her eyes. "Of course."

"And yet you did not propose any honorable action to me."

"I did not propose any dishonorable action," he muttered, disgruntled.

"Surely you know that is not the same thing. I was very . . . disappointed to have you fail me."

"Oh, Lord, Louisa, you know I could not!"

"You led me to believe that you could," she said inexorably. "There is surely no legal impediment. I have come to give you an opportunity to do so now."

The housekeeper's arrival interrupted his shocked protest. When the coffee and biscuits had been set out and Mrs. Thomas had curiously surveyed the girl and the little page in the corner, she withdrew. Louisa poured the cups of coffee and asked, "Do you wish cream and sugar as usual?"

"Please."

There was silence for some time as Louisa forced herself to sip at the hot beverage and nibble on the shortbread. Dr. Thorne made no such attempt, but kept his eyes trained on her in hopes that she would crack under the strain and look at him. If she did, she would not be able to press her advantage. But Louisa refused to meet his eyes.

In desperation he said, "There *is* a legal impediment. You are not of age."

"That does not materially affect your honoring your implied word. The end result could be affected, certainly, but it is no excuse."

"Louisa, why are you doing this to me?"

His agonized question caused her hand to tremble and she set down her coffee cup, but she did not respond. The page was studying them again and she beckoned to him and offered the plate of biscuits. After he had helped himself, he returned to his seat and retrieved the book.

"Please, Louisa, don't you see it would do no good?"

Her voice was no more than a whisper. "Am I to live my life then never knowing if you cared enough to even ask? Such a simple satisfaction to be denied, and so very unfair. I think . . . I cannot help but wonder if it is that you lack the courage to fight for something you want, and that would horridly disillusion me. To me you have always appeared as the most dedicated of men. You would keep better faith with one of your patients."

There was a crash as the coffee cup he held dropped from his senseless fingers. Ignoring the broken shards on the floor he grasped her hands and exclaimed, "You wretched girl! Very well, if we must sink, we will do it together. I should have known better than to take the whole burden on myself. Will you marry me, Louisa?"

"Yes, thank you. Stephen, if . . . if I cannot get Press's permission, will you wait for me, until I am old enough?"

"You know I will." Mrs. Thomas appeared at the hall door with every intention of sweeping away the broken coffee cup, but he waved her away. "When shall I talk to him?"

"This evening. I will speak with him in the meantime. You . . . you really do want to marry me, don't you? Nothing would be more repugnant to me than to force you. You have only to say."

He regarded the vulnerable little face with a despairing

shake of his head. "Where was this compliant miss when I needed her? Ah, my love, I want to marry you more than anything in the world."

"That's all right then," she replied with a shaky smile. "I really must go. Mama thinks I'm shopping."

"I think we should seal our bargain," he protested, but Louisa pointed to the patient page, grinned and said, "Later."

19

Lady Latteridge was in a quandary, not being able to decide which was the greater of two evils and not sure, either, that her son would carry out his threat. Since he had brought her home the previous evening against her protest, she supposed that he would, but she was placing some dependence on his not having considered the chaperonage of Louisa. Surely he would not wish to be burdened with the girl, and only by her remaining could he have any freedom. The Dowager wished to stay in York, but she would find it almost impossible to write the suggested letter of apology.

A few minutes before he was due at Miss Findlay's, the earl tracked his mother down to the back parlor where he found her idly staring out the window at the small garden. "Good morning, Mother. I trust you are feeling well. Have you decided which it is to be?"

Her face was a cold mask. "I intend to stay in York and I have no intention of apologizing for my behavior."

Latteridge languidly seated himself in a chair opposite her, pressing his hands together meditatively. "My responsibilities as head of the family are a matter I do not take lightly. I think, even aside from my own involvement in the matter, I would find your treatment of Miss Findlay disgraceful. But let me clarify something for you, Mother. I am going now to ask her to marry me." Two bright spots of angry color appeared on his mother's cheeks but she said nothing. "You have put Miss Findlay in a position where she may not accept my offer. Her scruples are a great deal finer than they ought to be, I fear. But if she will have me, there is no question that we will marry, and that, I have no need to tell you, will put you in a very awkward position."

"You're mad! I wouldn't live in the same house with her for thirty seconds."

"I wouldn't let you, Mother. I doubt even the dower house is far enough removed to protect her from your scorching hatred. The estate in Dorset would seem a natural choice for your comfort, or even a town house in London. I regret the necessity, but you leave me very little choice."

"What about Louisa? I am just beginning to bring her to Lord Bowland's notice."

"Oh, I think there was no need for you and Miss Horton to work so hard at that. He would have heard the size of her dowry in time."

"Are you saying the man is a fortune hunter?"

"Certainly. One has only to watch his nose quiver when he's in the vicinity of an heiress."

"Well, what are you going to do about Louisa?"

"I really don't know. It will depend on what Miss Findlay has to say, and what Louisa wishes. I'm perfectly happy to see to her care."

"So I am to be driven out of my home and deprived of my daughter so that you can marry a ruined woman! Is that how you see your responsibility as head of the family?" Her voice rose to a pitch of fury matched by the hammering of her fist on the chair arm.

"Mother, you know perfectly well that you would have to move to the dower house, no matter who I took as a wife. And as for Louisa, there is no reason you should not see as much of her as she wishes." A long, exasperated sigh escaped him. "Why must you persist in this fruitless persecution of Miss Findlay? Is it so very difficult to acknowledge that you were wrong?"

"I am never wrong."

Latteridge rose and sadly regarded her implacable countenance. "Very well, Mother. When I return, I will escort you to Ackton Towers, where you can wallow in self-right-eousness from morning to night without causing the innocent any grief."

"I am not leaving York."

"Then you had best look for lodgings. You are not staying in my house, and I think your acquaintances here would find that very strange."

"Perhaps I shall go to France," she said defiantly.

"We are at war with France, Mother."

The proudly erect head bowed and Latteridge went to put his arm about her shoulders. "Poor Mother. Do you know that we all love you, that my father loved you? You don't have to be perfect for your family to be attached to you. We can accept your mistakes, if you are willing to own them. Lord knows we all have enough we have to forgive ourselves. You have been the solid foundation of our family, the permanent fixture we could all rely on to be there when Father was away. But you have never admitted that it was your Jacobite sympathies which drove him into exile, and you will not confess that you treated Miss Findlay most shamefully."

"She could never forgive me now."

"Perhaps not, but that is not to say you should not offer an apology. Strangely enough, Mother, it becomes simpler after the first."

"I haven't so many errors to confess."

"Haven't you?" He grinned and pressed her hand. "Do you feel you could write a note to Miss Findlay?"

"I suppose so," she grumbled. "Will you want to read it?"

Latteridge pursed his lips. "No, I shall depend on you not to disgrace me."

As the minutes ticked away and it became a quarter past twelve, Marianne began to have doubts as to his coming after all. He was invariably prompt, not a minute late for any of their scheduled rides. Perhaps it was for the best, though she would have liked to speak with him about Louisa, at least. Mr. Deighton was detailing for Aunt Effie the characters and locations of his dispersed children, but Marianne could not seem to pay any attention to the conversation which so absorbed her aunt.

The knocker sounded at precisely twelve-thirty, when Marianne had long since given up hope, and it occurred to her that it might not be the earl at all, but one of their other friends. When the tall, handsome figure strolled into the room and his gray eyes met hers, she swallowed painfully and stepped forward without thinking to offer her hand.

"Forgive me for being late, Miss Findlay. I was delayed at the last moment, but hopefully to good purpose." He lifted her hand to his lips and kissed it, something he had never done before. After a few words of greeting to Miss Effington and Mr. Deighton, he said, "I should like to speak alone with you, if I might. Shall we take a walk?"

Marianne was not at all sure that her legs would support her through such an interview and, to her aunt's astonishment, suggested that they talk in the dining parlor. If Aunt Effie had intended to protest, one glance at Mr. Deighton determined her otherwise, "Oh, very well. We'll be right here."

The sun was streaming through the windows onto the polished mahogany table, and the last of the autumn flowers made colorful patches in the garden beyond. It was the only one of their rooms which was completely furnished, with a full set of matching chairs, newly covered, a sideboard flanked by two pedestals, a knife box, and a wine waiter. Marianne motioned him to the chair at the head of the table.

"I would prefer the window seat, if you don't mind."

"Of course, if you wish." Glancing skeptically at the minimal seat, she thought for both of them to sit there it would be almost impossible not to be touching. She found that is *was* impossible.

"As I said in my note, there are several matters I would

like to discuss with you. Are you uncomfortable?" he asked as she tried vainly to squeeze further away.

"Not at all."

"Good. Let's dispose of the simpler matter first. Louisa intimated that you supported her wish to marry Dr. Thorne. She said she had confided in you. I had hoped she would give me an opportunity to explain my reasons for separating them, but I suppose she could very well imagine them, as I am sure you do. Do you indeed think it would be wise for her to marry him?"

"Perhaps not from your point of view, but, yes, I think it would. You see, Lady Louisa explained to me not only how she feels about him as a man, but as a doctor. She's not like most girls her age, looking for a comfortable position, financially and socially. I think that would not be quite enough for her. Of course one can never fully comprehend the sacrifices involved until one has experienced them, but Lady Louisa is fired with an enthusiasm to be a part of Dr. Thorne's dedication to his work." Marianne made a futile gesture. "I'm no better at explaining it than she was, I'm afraid. She feels that Dr. Thorne is a missing part of her, necessary to make her whole, and she finds his work a benefit rather than a drawback. I don't think that particular attitude will change as she grows older and sees more of society. She is only likely to become more confirmed in it as she witnesses the trivialities of a social life."

Latteridge sat very still listening to her earnest attempt to explain Louisa's motivations, the sunlight catching only the highlights of her features as she sat turned slightly toward him. He was tempted to trace the line of her jaw with his finger, the skin looked so smooth and clear. "She's never been frivolous, though she has a delightful sense of humor. Don't you think, though, that she might find some worthy peer, who took a special interest in politics or agriculture or the like who could appeal to her?"

"I suggested as much, and all I can say is that she convinced me that it would never be the same again. You've

seen them together. They have a sort of magical understanding of one another, and I truly believe that she isn't the
least concerned with the things that you or I or Dr. Thorne
think *should* alarm her. It's not as though they will be
poverty-stricken or entirely abandoned by the *ton*. Lady
Louisa is a charmer, and she is likely to be in demand
whether she marries a professional man or not. There is, of
course, the possibility that she will not stand up well to the
more gruesome aspects of his calling."

He shook his head mournfully. "No such luck, I fear. You
should have seen how cool she was when he treated Harry's
sword wound."

"Sword wound?"

"Harry's 'accident' was a duel. The poor devil caught
one of his friends cheating at cards and was so shocked that
he let it be known. Lord, how trying it is to be young! So
you think it is useless to hope Louisa will recover suffi-
ciently from this attachment to find someone who suits her
as well?"

"Yes. I'm sorry if it grieves you," Marianne said gently.

"Oh, it doesn't really grieve me, though Mother will take
a great deal more convincing, I fear. I suppose I have
known all along that it had gone too far, which was partially my own fault. Just the other day I was thinking that it
seemed almost impudent to interfere, they are so perfectly
in accord. And the devil of it is, I like Thorne tremen-
dously." His fingers tapped absently on his leg in a motion
she had seen before when he was deep in thought. "Well, I
shall give them my blessing."

"Lady Louisa is concerned that she hasn't actually been
asked."

Latteridge laughed. "She's a determined little puss; I
don't doubt she'll find a way to get him to propose, but if
not, I'll speak with him."

They were silent for a while, Latteridge watching her
face and Marianne steadfastly staring at the carved wooden

knife box. He observed, "William seemed to think that Mr. Deighton wished to carry your aunt off with him."

"Yes, she's agreed. He's an old beau, you know."

There was an awkward pause, since he really had no intention of asking her if she planned to go with them, or what she *did* intend to do. He stood and walked to the table, straightened a chair and returned to stand in front of her. "I don't know why this should be so difficult, except that I have the feeling you're prepared to refuse me. I can see it in those gloriously expressive eyes. Do you know they were what first attracted me to you? On the way home from the river that day your smile seemed to dance back and forth between them and your lips. Not that your lips are any less appealing, you know."

"Really, Lord Latteridge," she said, flushing, "I must protest."

"It is perfectly all right to quibble on the small matters, if you will only allow me my way on the most important. If you have not surmised my errand, I am come to induce you to marry me. Please," he hastened to add, holding up an admonitory hand, "don't say anything just yet. You must allow me to present my case before you say anything rash. I can think of any number of reasons for you to turn me down, and I intend to dispose of them one by one. Will that do?"

His eyes were suspiciously merry but Marianne was too tightly drawn to respond in kind. "I'm afraid you couldn't, sir. Don't think I'm not honored. I . . ."

"Please. A few minutes should suffice. Won't you spare me such a small segment of your time? I've allowed you as much in Louisa's defense."

"I . . . For your own sake . . ."

"Good. Now, where shall I start? With your reputation, I think, since it seems to most upset you. I am not in the least concerned with it, my dear. As my wife you would find that any rumblings ceased. There is nothing quite so respectable as marrying a title, you know, and I think I do not delude myself that I am more than a match for any of the gossips. In fact, I would be very put out if you refused me on the grounds of your reputation being a handicap to me; that would indicate you have insufficient faith in my social prowess."

"Heaven forbid I should so slight you," she murmured.

"Precisely. Now we should consider my brother and sisters. All three, I know, would be delighted with the match. Louisa already knows my intention; Susan was *aux anges* with my . . . ah . . . carefully worded impression of you. Harry is already your devoted servant. He, by the by, has decided to keep himself out of trouble by forming a partnership of sorts with your Mr. Geddes for the promotion of the various inventions. That leaves only Mother."

"Only . . ."

Latteridge thrust his hand in a pocket and withdrew a sealed sheet. "This, I hope, will make some amends for her treatment of you. Of course, there is the chance that she has not kept her word, but I have placed my trust in her. Her trouble is an inability to admit fault, not an uncommon failing, but unfortunately carried to an extreme. And an almost definitive sense of pride. Still, she has many excellent qualities, which very few people have observed, I know, but they are there all the same."

Unable to force her shaking hand to reach for the sheet, Marianne allowed him to break the seal and hold it for her, so that she could read it but he could not. It was not a particularly long message but it caused her throat to ache and her eyes to shine with unshed tears.

"Is it . . . adequate?" he asked, alarmed by her emotion.

Marianne took the sheet, folded it and slipped it in the bosom of her gown. "More than adequate."

Relieved, he reseated himself beside her and could not resist asking, "I think we are making excellent progress, don't you?"

"I don't know what to say."

"There is no need to say anything as yet, my dear. I had

intended, before Mr. Deighton arrived, to suggest that your aunt live with us, but obviously that is out of the question now. Though you will miss her, I cannot but believe you are pleased for her. Do you think she would object to your marrying me? Perhaps my mother's note will provide some solace to her."

"She wouldn't object, anymore."

"Then there are, as I see it, only two objections which can possibly remain. I have written to your father to advise him of my desire to address you. Of course, there was no reason to expect him to reply and you are under no legal or moral obligation to have his permission, considering his treatment of you. And I cannot say that I wrote him out of anything more than courtesy, which is hardly owing him. However . . ." He paused at her bleak expression and took her hand. "However, this morning I had a letter from him."

Her startled eyes flew to his. "Is he well?"

"Apparently he is suffering from the gout at present, but it sounds a temporary ailment, though periodic for him. His permission is granted for the match, which he expects you will not be so foolish as to reject," he told her ruefully, holding fast to her hand when she attempted to withdraw it. "Also, he promises to settle the estate on you and your children and to grant the dowry which he had proposed if you had married your cousin. You might like to read his letter to me, but most assuredly you will wish to read that addressed to you."

He dug again in his pocket and handed her the slim, sealed missive before rising and walking to the other end of the room where he stayed some time with his back to her. When he heard the rustle of her skirts he turned to find her approaching him, a smile on her lips. "And is your father's letter . . . adequate?"

"Yes."

"And you are satisfied with the arrangements he would make for a dowry?"

"Yes."

"They aren't necessary, you know, but I'm glad they ease your mind. Now, Marianne, to my way of thinking there can be but one remaining objection."

"And what is that?"

"That you do not, and feel you never could, love me. Before I met you I was intrigued by the things I heard about you. When I met you I was beguiled by your resourcefulness, your sense, and your unusual feeling for the absurd. As I have come to know you . . . well, I could list the virtues which I cherish, but that wouldn't really explain why I feel as I do, would it? I can only tell you that I love you, have loved you practically from the moment we met, and I want to share the rest of my life with you."

"I couldn't possibly object to that," Marianne confessed, her eyes sparkling.

"Couldn't you? Excellent! Then I hope you won't object to this," he retorted, drawing her into his arms.